EL DORADO COUNTY LIBRARY
3 1738 00906 2447
P9-EDU-130

Donated by the
Friends of the Library

Living with
Jackie Chan

Living with Jackie Chan

JO KNOWLES

CANDLEWICK PRESS

This is a work of fiction. Names, characters, places, and incidents are either products of the author's imagination or, if real, are used fictitiously.

First edition 2013

Library of Congress Catalog Card Number 2012955157
ISBN 978-0-7636-6280-6

13 14 15 16 17 18 BVG 10 9 8 7 6 5 4 3 2 1

Printed in Berryville, VA, U.S.A.

This book was typeset in Minion.

Candlewick Press
99 Dover Street
Somerville, Massachusetts 02144

visit us at www.candlewick.com

For Peter and Eli,
true karate men through and through.
I love you.

PART ONE

SEPTEMBER

A true karate man

is one with a godlike capacity

to think and feel for others;

irrespective of their rank or position.

—Gichin Funakoshi (1868–1957)

Chapter 1

When Caleb, Dave, and I pull up to my uncle's apartment building, a wave of sickness rolls up my throat and threatens to spew across Caleb's dashboard. I will it back down. Breathe. The car idles at the curb, waiting for me to get out. Caleb leans forward and peers up at the building as if it's the first time he's seen one taller than four stories.

"Which floor does he live on?" he finally asks.

"Second," I say.

We're quiet for a while, but I imagine what we're each thinking.

Caleb: *You're making a big mistake, man. You can't run away from your problems. They always know where you are.*

Dave: *This sucks. Who am I going to party with now? Damn, I'm hungry.*

Me: *What if Caleb's right*?

"Guess I better get this over with, huh?" I finally say.

Dave reaches forward from the backseat and squeezes my shoulder. "It's not too late to turn around," he says. "You can come back with us."

"Just say the word," Caleb agrees.

I shake my head before they can start trying to change my mind and tell me how things wouldn't be that bad if I stayed home. How our school is so big, it's easy to avoid people you don't want to see.

I can't really tell them that I don't want to see anyone. As bad as it sounds, I don't even want to see them, even though they are my best friends.

Everyone reminds me of me. Of who I was—*am*. Don't want to be.

"This sucks," Dave says. He is a master of the obvious. "We were supposed to graduate together, man."

Caleb turns around to give him a look, like, *Shut up, you idiot*. But Dave's right. We were supposed to leave our sorry excuse of a town together. No one was supposed to bail early.

Only, that was before.

When I start to open the door, one end of the armrest on the passenger door slips down. It's duct-taped together from when I broke it last winter. The day my life changed forever.

"Sorry I never got around to fixing that," I tell Caleb. "If you bring the car to my dad's shop, he'll take care of it."

"No worries," Caleb says.

We all sit there for a few more seconds.

"I'm serious, dude. You don't have to do this," Dave says.

But I do.

"OK, boys, it's been real," I say, opening the door. They both get out, and we pull my stuff from the back. We stand behind the car in our usual circle. Caleb holds out his hand to shake. As I reach for it, Dave puts his arms around the two of us and pulls us toward him into an awkward group hug. Despite my embarrassment, my throat hurts from trying not to cry like a wuss. I swallow the lump down and give Dave a punch in the arm, for old time's sake. Goofy as Dave is, and as annoyingly perfect as Caleb can be, I know I'm going to miss these bozos. A lot.

They get back in the car and pull onto the street. Dave hangs out the passenger window, waving. I give them a salute, like we used to do when we were kids. As they turn the corner, Caleb honks the horn a few times. Then they make the turn and disappear.

Chapter 2

My uncle's apartment building towers over me. I stand here, looking at it. At my new life. No more people staring at me when I walk down the hall. No more whispers behind my back. No one knows me here. No one knows what happened. What I did. I just have to get through the year, get into college someplace far away, and leave for good.

Before I go in, I think about calling my parents to let them know I got here OK, like I promised. But I can't bring myself to pull out my phone.

My dad volunteered to take me and my stuff here in his van. But I was like, "What stuff?" Because honestly, I don't own much. So he suggested taking me out for our last meal at least. But going out with my dad means going to the pub on the corner, sitting at the bar, and staring at the TV while I eat and he gets wasted, which is the same as being at home, so why bother?

My mom said she wanted to take me but she couldn't get the time off from work, which seems like a pretty lame excuse.

So we said good-bye at home. But it's not worth describing. Saying good-bye to them was like saying good-bye to some people who used to know me when I was a little kid. Like saying good-bye to zombies. Good-bye to a memory. Good-bye to dust. The real good-bye happened a long, long time ago.

Instead of calling them, I hike my duffel bag over my shoulder and open the door.

In the entryway, it's hot and airless. I scan the list of names on the panel and find number twelve and my last name. Someone's put a Hello Kitty sticker next to it. I hold my finger down on the buzzer and wait to get clicked in.

"You're here!" Larry's voice on the intercom amplifies the tiny entryway. The inner door clicks, and I push it open. When I step inside, I'm overwhelmed by the smell of carpet cleaner. I start for the stairs just as a door clicks open and a familiar voice calls, "Sammy?"

A head peers over the railing above.

My uncle grins down at me. He doesn't have a shirt on. "Sam, my man!" he yells.

Really?

I look up and give him a smile.

"Get up here!" He actually jumps up and down.

When I reach the second-floor landing, he bounds over to me and gives me a huge bear hug. His hair is wet and he stinks of recently applied deodorant, which he probably just rubbed all over me. I step away from him, and he checks me out from top to bottom.

"Samurai Sam! I didn't expect you to be taller than me."

"Guess it's been a while," I say. *And please tell me you're not going to call me that all the time.*

Larry has called me Sam since I was eight and spent the summer with him while my parents went on my dad's last "tour" with his band. Larry didn't really know what the hell to do with me, so we played this online ninja game called Samurai Sam practically the whole time. I was so good at it, Larry decided to change my name.

"You're so *big,*" he says, shaking his head like I'm some kind of miracle. "When did you get so big?"

How is someone supposed to answer a question like that?

"How long's it been, anyway? Two years? Jeez. How did that happen?"

I don't tell him what he already knows. That my parents are in a non-marriage and would never survive the four-hour drive to his place, being stuck in the same car together that long. And I don't remind him that he probably hasn't visited us because the last time he came my dad got drunk and passed out, and my mom "got a call" saying she had to go in to work because of an emergency, which we all knew was a lie, and Larry and I ended up spending the whole miserable time walking around the neighborhood in the cold, pretending my family wasn't completely screwed up.

I just shrug. And he sighs. And I see in his eyes that he remembers. It seems our reunions only occur during desperate or last-resort circumstances.

"Where are your parents? Didn't they bring you?" he asks.

"Nah, my friends dropped me off."

"Aw, that's nice. You should have invited them up!"

"They had to get back," I say. *And thank God, because if they'd heard you call me Samurai Sam, I would never live it down.*

"They must be pretty good friends to drive you all this way and then just turn around and drive back."

"Yeah," I say. They are. The best. "They love road trips. They jump on any excuse to get out of town."

Larry carries my bag to his apartment, and I follow

him inside. There's a stick of incense burning on the coffee table in the living room. A huge, furry gray cat walks over to us and rubs against my leg.

"Wow," Larry says. "There's something you don't see every day."

"What?"

"Clover doesn't like other people. She usually hides."

The cat looks up at me.

"Hey," I say. "How's it goin'?"

"Clover, meet the infamous Samurai Sam," Larry says. "He's your new—uh—cousin."

She rubs against my leg again.

"Come on, we'll put your stuff in your room."

I follow him down a short hallway to a tiny room with a foldout couch. I loved staying here when I was little. It was a huge treat because Larry was only, like, twenty-one, fresh out of college, and had no clue about taking care of kids. We'd stay up late watching movies and eating so many Fudgsicles I'd throw up. Then Larry would fold out the couch and let me crash in my clothes. Back then he had this little dog named George who liked to sleep next to me. I loved that dog, even though he had that pukey smell only small dogs have. There was something about how he leaned against you that made you feel—I don't know—important.

Clover jumps up on the bed.

"Are you hungry?" Larry asks. "Want me to make you something? I already ate, cuz I've got a hot date. Sorry to leave you on your first night and all, but my girl-friend got tickets to this concert way before we knew you were coming and —"

"No worries," I say. To be honest, it's kind of a relief.

He punches my arm. "This is gonna be great. It really is."

"Yeah," I say. "Thanks for letting me stay with you."

"Of course! You're my nephew!" He ruffles my hair as if I'm still the little kid he remembers.

"OK, I gotta go finish getting ready. You make yourself at home. Tomorrow we'll spend the whole day together."

"Cool," I say. He drops my duffel bag on the floor and leaves.

Clover mews at me, so I scratch her head. Above the foldout couch, there's a giant Jackie Chan poster. The bookcase is filled with martial arts movies, including what must be every Jackie Chan movie ever made, and a bunch of karate trophies Larry got when he competed in high school and college. Larry's always been obsessed with Jackie Chan, even though Jackie does kung fu, not karate. Larry says it's because when he was a kid and starting to get into karate, there were never any kick-ass karate actors to get obsessed about. I guess there still aren't.

I sit down, and Clover rubs against my arm. The bathroom is just down the hall, and I can hear Larry singing "I Gotta Feelin'."

I lean back and stare at the ceiling. It's covered with the glow-in-the-dark stars he put up there for me that summer I stayed here. I remember the first night, I was scared and wanted to go home. Larry lay down next to me and we stared at the stars until they started to dim. He didn't say a thing. He just stayed there next to me, his huge muscled arm pressing against my scrawny one, letting me know he was still there.

"You OK, bud?" Larry stands in the doorway. He's wearing a white button-up shirt and black jeans. His aftershave wafts in and catches in the back of my throat. The cat sneezes and dashes out of the room.

I sit up. "Yeah, I'm fine."

He gives me a look, like he knows I'm not. But then he shakes it off. "Well, how do I look?" He turns around for me, kind of dancing. The gold chain around his neck sparkles.

"I dunno about the chain," I say.

He fingers it. "No?"

I shake my head.

"All right. I'll ditch it. So, don't wait up for me. And uh . . . If my door's closed in the morning, lie low if you can. That'll be, you know, my sign. That I have company."

"Should I hide in here till she leaves?"

"No, no. No hiding. It's just . . . I didn't want you to come knocking on the door or anything. You know. If you need something."

"I can take care of myself."

"Right. OK! Well, thanks for being cool about me going out your first night here. But wait'll you meet this girl. She's really special. You'll totally understand why I didn't want anyone else taking my ticket."

"No worries," I say. "Have fun!" He gives me a thumbs-up and sort of bounces down the hall.

I fall back on the bed again and stare up at Jackie Chan, who looks way too happy. Kinda like Larry.

My phone buzzes, but I ignore it. I know it's probably my mom making sure I got here safely. But it's too late for that. It's too late for checking in and making sure I'm OK. She should have been checking in a long time ago. But she didn't. No one did.

Chapter 3

When I wake up, the apartment is quiet. It's 2:06 a.m. I roll over and hear a high-pitched grunting noise at the end of the bed. It's Clover. I see her in the TV light, stretching out her surprisingly long furry legs. I reach for the remote and turn off the TV. I must have fallen asleep watching *Dragons Forever,* Larry's favorite Jackie Chan movie.

Up above, the floor creaks as if someone's in a rocking chair. The stars on the ceiling have all faded out, but I stare up and listen. *Creak-creak, creak-creak.* Slowly. In a definite rhythm. The creaking stops and footsteps cross the ceiling. Then it's quiet.

Clover grunts again and starts to purr. I wish I could be that happy when I sleep. But I never sleep well. Not since . . . not for a while now.

I reach over and turn on the light and wait a minute, then shut it off again. The stars on the ceiling are back. I remember Larry had tried to make actual constellations, but he got frustrated and ended up making his own shapes. Instead of the big dipper, he made a smiley face. I smile, remembering.

And then I hear it.

A faint crying above me. Like a kitten, almost. But then it gets louder. And I know what it is.

A baby.

My heart starts to thump against my chest as the cries get louder.

Then footsteps hurry across the ceiling again. A muffled voice, soothing. More footsteps. Then, *creak-creak, creak-creak*. The crying gets less frantic.

But my heart is still punching the inside of my chest.

I put my pillow over my head to shut out the sounds.

But I can still hear them in my mind.

And I can see him. My baby. Wrapped tightly in a yellow blanket, a little blue cap on his head.

And me, walking away.

Chapter 4

In the morning, I get up and get dressed before I leave my room, just in case Larry got lucky. I step into the hall and peer down to see if his door is closed, which it is. I try to imagine what a woman who's into Larry would be like, but can't.

It's only nine o'clock, so I figure I have time to make a quick breakfast before I disappear for a while and give him and his girlfriend some privacy.

I leave a bit of milk from my cereal bowl for the cat and go outside. As I walk down the sidewalk, I try to remember the neighborhood, but nothing seems familiar. At the corner, there's a Dunkin' Donuts, so I go in and buy some coffee and head back to the apartment building and sit on the stoop. It's Sunday, and the neighborhood seems to be mostly asleep. I take a sip and lean my head back on the cement wall along the steps.

Down the sidewalk, I see a woman pushing a baby carriage toward me. My heart automatically skips a beat. I start to get up to go back inside, but I realize Larry didn't give me a key yet.

I'm locked out.

Crap.

I lean my head back and close my eyes again. I quietly hum the first song that comes to mind to block out any baby sounds.

"Black Eyed Peas?" a voice asks.

I sit up. The woman, who turns out to be about my age, is standing at the base of the steps, her hands squeezed around the bar of the carriage.

"Yeah. Dumb song stuck in my head," I say. I try to act calm. But all I can think is that here's this girl, my age, with a baby. And it's too much.

"Think you could help me with this thing? This is my building."

No, I think. *No, I cannot help you.*

But instead, I say, "Sure," and purposefully head to the other end of the carriage. Together, we lift it up the steps and into the foyer. Then she unlocks the interior door.

"Thanks," she says. She waits for me to do something else. Like leave the building.

"So, um, this is my building, too," I say. "But I forgot my key."

She gives me a *Yeah, right* look.

"No, really. I'm staying with my uncle, Larry.

"Larry? The Karate Man?" The way she says it, it's more like she's saying, "The crazy guy?"

"Yeah. I just moved here."

"To live with Larry?"

"Just for the school year."

She nods. "So you'll be going to Roosevelt Tech, then?"

"Yeah."

"What year are you?"

"Senior. You?" As soon as I ask, I realize that if she has a kid, maybe she doesn't go to school anymore. Way to be sensitive.

"Same."

The baby makes a noise.

"Uh-oh, I better take him to his parents before he wakes up."

"Oh," I say. "You're just babysitting."

She laughs. "You thought he was *mine*? No, thank God. Can you imagine?"

I fake a laugh. *Yes.*

"No. I'm just the babysitter," she says. "Sometimes I take him on Sunday mornings so his parents can catch up on some sleep. He keeps them up a lot. Um, are you all right?"

"Huh? Yeah. Fine." I take another sip of my coffee to hide my face.

The baby starts crying.

"Shoot," she says. "Here he goes. He's a howler when he's hungry."

"Yeah, I know."

She gives me that creepy look again. "You do? How?"

"I could hear him last night, I think. He must be in the apartment above mine. Either that or there's another baby in the building."

She nods. "No, just him. Well, see you around, I guess."

"Yeah."

"Look. I don't mean to be all paranoid or anything, but do you mind if I buzz you in once I get to my apartment? We have strict rules about letting in strangers."

Do I really look like a serial killer?

"No worries," I say.

She pushes the carriage through the door and it closes behind her.

I lean back against the wall and wait, wondering if

she'll really buzz me in. Standing in the stuffy entryway, I feel trapped. And hot. And like I don't belong here. Not outside. Not inside. Not anywhere.

But after a minute the buzzer goes off and the door clicks, so I quickly push it open.

I was smart or dumb enough not to lock the apartment door, at least, so I go in quietly and head back to my room. Finally, about an hour later, I hear Larry singing at the top of his lungs. I don't hear anyone else, so I poke my head out the door.

"Coast clear?"

"What? Oh. Yeah. Um, I forgot about our signal and shut my door out of habit. Sorry."

I shake my head.

"Did you get breakfast?" Larry saunters into the kitchen. "What a night. I think I'm in love, Sam Man. I really do."

"Wow." *And please, for the love of God, don't call me that ever again.*

"Yeah. She's awesome. You know why she didn't want to stay over?"

"Tell me."

"She said you and I should spend time together. In fact, she almost called off our date last night, she felt so bad about me leaving you alone on your first night here."

"Oh. Sorry."

"No, no. Don't you get it? That's what makes her so cool. She's so unselfish. You've gotta meet her. I'm telling you. She could be the one." He opens the fridge and pulls out a tub of plain yogurt and a carton of eggs.

"How long have you been dating?" I ask.

"Only a few months. But, Sam, it's like I've known her all my life."

"Wait. Is me being here going to screw things up? I mean, don't you, like, want some privacy?"

He wiggles his eyebrows at me. "We can always go to her place for that. Don't worry about it. I'm psyched you're here! Are you kidding? Samurai Sammy!" He does a bunch of karate moves around the kitchen, then circles over to me and smacks my back.

As I watch him, I wonder how on earth this guy can be related to my dad.

"If you're sure," I say. I sit at the kitchen table and watch him make his breakfast.

"You gonna want some of this? It's a protein thing I make."

"Um. No, thanks. I'm good."

He starts dumping stuff into a blender. "I've been making this concoction for, like, a month, and I'm feeling great! You should try it sometime. No steroids. Just all organic stuff. It's amazing." He squeezes what looks like a half a jar of honey into the blender, then turns it on until the concoction becomes smooth and a nasty-looking brown color.

"Looks appetizing," I say.

He pours himself a giant glass and sits across from me. "Bottoms up!" His Adam's apple bobs up and down as he chugs half the glass.

"So," he says, wiping his mouth with the back of his hand. "We've got one week together before school starts. How should we entertain ourselves?"

"Don't you need to work?"

"Funny you should ask." He sits up straighter in his chair, all excited. "OK, so check this out. You know I still teach karate at the local YMCA, right?"

I nod.

"Well, they asked me to do karate camp this week. This is a great chance for me to recruit some students for the rest of the year. Because you know with my charm, one class and they'll be hooked, right? And I was thinking how you used to do karate, and you could help me out. Wouldn't that be fun? We could be partners!"

"But . . . I took karate from you that summer when I was eight," I say.

He waves his hand. "Yeah, but you were a natural."

"No, I was eight. I just waved my arms around and kicked the air."

"Don't be so modest."

"Um —"

"It'll be fun! Plus, I'll pay you."

"Really?"

"Yes. Look, come with me the first day, and if you hate it, you don't have to come back."

"What age group are the kids?"

"It's all ages, not just kids. That's what's so cool about it." He takes another bunch of swigs from his drink.

"Camp for all ages?"

"Yeah! Even adults! I've got, like, a seventy-year-old black belt coming in. He said he wanted to brush up!" He is glowing. "Whaddaya say? It'll be great! And it means we'll be able to spend time together. You know. Get reacquainted."

He looks so hopeful, I know I can't say no. "All right," I say. "I'll try it."

"Great!" He drains his glass and drops it in the sink. "OK. Well, I've gotta get over there for a couple hours to deal with some paperwork for the registrations, and then I'll come back and we'll have lunch. Sound good?"

"Yeah, sure." So much for spending the whole day together. Not that I'm complaining.

"Did you sleep all right? The couch comfortable enough?"

"Yeah, it was fine."

"Cool." He stands up. "So I'll see you later, then!"

When he's gone, I go back to my new room and make the bed. I check my phone for texts.

Caleb: u ok?

My mom: miss u

Dave: [About twenty lame jokes that I won't bother to repeat.]

My dad still doesn't know how to text, but I'm sure he wouldn't bother even if he could. He's more likely to call and act all awkward. He loves me. I know that. But it seems like it's physically painful for him to talk to me about anything besides football, the latest engine work he's had to do to keep his van running, his most recent "gig" with his pathetic excuse for a band, and how much longer our old dog, Rosie, will survive.

Clover wanders into the room and jumps up on the bed, then does that thing cats do with their paws, like she's trying to make the mattress softer. I give her a pat, then get up to unpack my clothes and put them in the tiny closet Larry said he emptied for me. There's a new-looking wire organizer with drawers for socks and underwear and stuff in the closet. I think Larry must have bought it for me, which was nice. When I'm all done, I step back and look at the closet and my noticeable lack of stuff. After eighteen years, this is all I have to show for myself. No family photos. No friend photos. Just a few pairs of jeans, some T-shirts, and a pile of socks and underwear.

Everything else, I left behind.

Chapter 5

As soon as Larry gets back from the Y he tells me he's taking me out to lunch. We walk a few blocks to a deli where he claims they have the best sandwiches ever. We order takeout and cross the street to a park where we sit on the grass. Larry doesn't eat meat, so he ordered a TLT (tofu, lettuce, and tomato sandwich). Before I could order for myself, he'd ordered one for me, too, and promised I would love it. I thought tofu would be disgusting, but it's fried with soy sauce and basically that's all it tastes like. I wouldn't say this is the best sandwich ever, but it's not too bad.

"I'm so going to give you a makeover, man," he says, looking at me as if I weigh four hundred pounds. "This is just the beginning."

"I didn't know I needed one," I say.

"You're at that age where if you don't start eating right and getting regular exercise now, you'll be doomed to a beer gut and a bad heart."

"Thanks for the warning."

"I'm not messing with you. Good habits last a lifetime."

"So I've heard," I say. "That's, like, a kids' health campaign on TV."

"Nah, I made it up."

"OK."

"I'm just saying. America is fat." He takes a huge bite of his sandwich. Juice from the tomato dribbles out the corner of his mouth.

"I played soccer all last year," I tell him. "I get plenty of exercise."

"And now karate," Larry adds.

"Right."

We finish our sandwiches in silence. Then we lean back in the grass and squint at the clouds.

Larry takes a deep breath in and slowly lets it out. "Sometimes I come here to meditate," he says.

I close my eyes and feel the sun warm my face. I imagine Larry sitting here, cross-legged with his hands resting on his knees, saying "Ommmm" to the park. I really hope he doesn't start meditating right now.

"Sometimes I come here to think," he adds.

I still don't answer.

"But I'm happy to talk, too. You know. If you need to talk. I'm here for you, Josh."

Josh.

I'm glad he remembered my actual name. I was honestly beginning to wonder. I open my eyes and tilt my head toward him. His own eyes are closed and his face is tipped toward the sun. Maybe if he looked at me, I would somehow know what to say. But with his eyes closed like that, it doesn't exactly feel like he really wants to talk. And honestly, I don't really want to, either. What would be the point? There's no way he could know how or what I feel. And there is no way he could make me feel better. No one could.

"I don't need to talk," I say, closing my eyes again.

I can practically feel the relief ooze out of him.

"Well, then, we can just think," he says. "It's a good place for that, too. Ya know?"

"Sure," I say. Whatever.

We're both quiet. Thinking.

Larry's probably daydreaming about the love of his life. Me, I don't really want to think. I mean, that's why I came here. To get away from every daily friggin' reminder of what I did. What happened.

I wish Larry could just act like I'm only here to go

to school. But no. My parents had to tell him everything so — what? He could treat me differently? Like I'm some fragile freak who might crack at any minute? Yeah, that's helpful.

After a while, Larry's breathing gets all steady and I realize he's asleep. At least he's not snoring.

I prop myself up on my elbows and look around the park. It's grassy, and there are lots of people walking around: dogs on leashes, kids racing ahead of their parents, then running back to them. It's a little like the park I went to growing up, only nicer. I never went with my parents. It was always Caleb, Dave, and me. The three amigos. Pretending we didn't care that our dads weren't around to teach us how to catch a football. Acting like we were too cool for all that crap. Whatever.

I lean back and shut my eyes again. I listen to the sounds and try to fade out, like Larry.

"Hi, there!"

We both spring up.

The girl from earlier is standing above us, rocking the baby carriage back and forth.

"Hey!" Larry says. "Stella, right? How's it hangin'?"

Please tell me he did not just say that.

Stella blushes. "Hi," she says. "Yeah. Stella. From the fourth floor."

"You signed up for karate camp, right?" Larry asks.

"Yeah," she says. "My mom thinks karate is like self-defense or something. She wants me to learn before I go to college." She rolls her eyes.

"You'll love it," Larry says confidently. "So, who've you got there? Gil and Jean's baby?"

"Yup, this is Ben." She peers into the carriage. "Poor thing's teething or something. As soon as I stop walking, he starts to fuss." She stops moving the carriage and a tiny cry of protest comes from under the bonnet. "See?"

"Bummer," Larry says.

Even though Stella starts rocking the carriage again, the baby starts to wail. "Oh, shoot," she says.

"Let me take him." Larry gets up. "Hey, little munchkin, it's your uncle Larry," he says, reaching into the carriage. "Come here, sweet pea."

My heart starts beating hard again, aching against my chest. I look around and grab the bags from our sandwiches. "I'll be right back," I say. "Just gonna throw these out."

I get up and get the hell away as fast as I can. I walk quite a ways before I find a trash can. I drop the stuff in and put both hands on the metal rim. I touch something wet and slimy on the rim and almost puke my tofu.

I know it's crazy, how seeing the baby makes me feel. But I can't help it. I squeeze the rim of the trash barrel again and close my eyes. But when I do, I see what I always see when I think of him. The hospital corridor. A nursery. A baby with no name. A baby that could be mine.

I take a deep breath and gag on the smell of rotten trash. Crap. I turn around and walk in circles.

Don't think about it. Don't think about it, I keep telling myself. *You came here to get away from all that. There was nothing you could do.*

But maybe there was. Oh, God. Maybe there was.

Finally, I get hold of myself and start to head toward them as slowly as possible. When I get closer, I see Larry putting the baby back in the carriage. I wait until Stella walks away before I go over to him.

Larry looks at me suspiciously. "You OK, Sammy?" he asks.

"Yeah. What?"

"You bolted."

"Huh? No, I didn't."

"OK." He puts his hand on my shoulder. "Ready to go home?"

Home? Is that what this is now?

We walk back a new way, through a quiet neighborhood lined with trees. "This is where I wanna live someday," Larry says. "It's so peaceful here. And clean. Me, Arielle — that's 'the one's' name, by the way — and maybe a dog. Maybe even a ba—" He stops himself. "Yeah, a dog."

"Clover may not be too crazy about that idea," I say, pretending I didn't hear what he almost said.

"Eh, Clover's tough. She can handle it." He does some sort of karate move with his hands.

"Clover knows karate?" I ask.

"I'm sure she's soaked up some of my moves."

God, Larry, you are such a freak.

As we walk through the neighborhood, I try to imagine Larry living here. Larry in his crazy-looking workout pants and no shirt, with his mystery woman and a ba—

A baby.

Why can't he just say it?

But I know. He can. Just not around me.

Chapter 6

That night, we order pizza in, and Larry and I eat and watch *Rumble in the Bronx* in the living room. Larry keeps jumping up and trying to imitate Jackie Chan's moves but finally stops when I make it as obvious as possible that he's annoying the crap out of me.

"Just trying to get you psyched about tomorrow," he tells me.

"But he's doing kung fu," I point out.

Larry jumps up again and kicks at the air, then punches it with his fist.

"Call it martial arts," he tells me. "Besides. Name one famous karate movie without the word *Kid* in the title."

Point made.

Clover reaches up from the other side of the coffee table and snags a cheese blob left in the pizza box with her paw.

"Bad kitty!" Larry says. But he doesn't try to take away the cheese.

"I'm not sure about tomorrow," I tell him. "I mean, I have no memory of this stuff."

"You're a yellow belt. Remember? You know a lot. The katas will come back to you. Don't worry about it."

I try to remember what the hell a kata is. I think something to do with the different moves you have to memorize, but I'm not sure.

Larry goes to the kitchen and brings back two pints of ice cream. One is chocolate pudding flavor, and one is cookie dough.

"Is this one of your good habits that lasts a lifetime?" I ask.

Instead of answering, he hands me a spoon and a pint and we eat our entire cartons while watching *Rush Hour,* by the end of which I feel ill and head to bed.

I wake up at 2:08 a.m. Clover makes her funny snoring sound as I roll over. Above me, I hear that *creak-creak, creak-creak,* and maybe singing, though it's hard to tell. The rhythmic sound almost puts me back to sleep, but then the creaks stop and footsteps move across the ceiling. A few minutes go by, and then the crying starts again. Sad, and longing.

Stop.

I squeeze my eyes shut as my heartbeat starts to speed up. But the crying gets louder.

Please, just stop.

I put the pillow over my head. But I still hear him.

And then I see him.

His small, angry face.

Tiny, clenched hands.

Stop.

I see my hand against the glass that separated us.

And I see me leaving him there.

I hate the words everyone uses, but they're true.

I gave him up.

I never tried to meet him.

I never tried to hold him.

I never did anything but try to see him.

Just once.

Just once to say good-bye.

Chapter 7

I wake up in the morning to the sound of Larry rapping on my door. "Rise and shine! We gotta jet!"

"Huh?" I ask.

"Camp starts at nine a.m.!" He flings the door open, throws something made of cloth at me, and disappears. The cloth is white and kind of stiff.

"That's my old gi!" Larry hollers from the kitchen. "I figured it would fit you. Plus, it's full of good vibes."

I unfold it and think vibes aren't the only thing it's full of. The armpits are stained yellow. There's also some rusty-colored spots that look like blood. There's no way in hell I'm putting this thing on. I rifle through my stuff for some sweats and a clean T-shirt and find Larry in the kitchen.

"Where's the gi?" he asks. He's wearing a new-looking one with a multicolored belt to show which degree black belt he is.

"Um, too big. Sorry."

"Really? I thought for sure it would be just right for you. Too bad. That thing has seen it all."

I bet.

"Ah, well. No time to shower, but you're just gonna get all sweaty anyway." He downs his brown smoothie. "Here, I made you some toast. And eat this banana."

I scarf down the food, and we head out.

The YMCA is only a few blocks from Larry's building, and I pray the entire way that no one will see us. Especially when Larry starts "warming up" by doing his crazy-looking karate moves as he walks down the sidewalk. When we get there, he introduces me as his assistant and we go to our assigned room.

Larry pulls a clipboard and piece of paper out of his enormous duffel bag and starts making notes. Pretty soon, people are walking in and saying hi to Larry. An old guy comes over and shakes my hand. He must be the one Larry was talking about before. "You're Larry's nephew," he informs me.

"Uh, yeah. Hi."

"Jacob, that's Samurai Sam!" Larry yells over to us.

Must he?

"Sam," Jacob says, holding out his hand. "Nice to meet you!" His gi droops off his bony shoulders.

A little kid with long hair — I mean really long hair, past his shoulders — comes running over to me and bows. What?

"I'm Drake," he says.

"Hey," I say.

"You're supposed to bow back."

"Oh." I bow to him awkwardly. This is going to be a long week.

Once everyone arrives, Larry lines us up according to rank. Jacob stands at the front, facing us, since the black belts get special treatment. In the front row, two guys who look about in their twenties have brown belts. Next row, a woman, maybe in her thirties, with a purple belt. Next row, two girls who look like high-school age have green belts. Next row, Drake and some other young kids with blue belts. Then me. Larry insists I earned my yellow belt, but I honestly don't even remember. He runs over to his bag and pulls out a faded and ratty-looking belt. "A loan," he says, handing it to me. "Remember how to tie it?"

"Not exactly," I say. And then, in front of everyone, he steps behind me and wraps his arms around my waist and freakin' ties the belt on me, talking me through the steps as he goes. Then, since this isn't humiliating enough, the door opens and in walks Stella in a crisp white gi with a white belt cinched around her waist.

Perfect.

She smiles at me. "Hi, Sam," she says. She looks me up and down and bites her lip as if she's stifling a laugh. Yeah. I look like a moron. I have some awesome bedhead, and I have a yellow belt tied around the waist of my sweatpants.

Shoot. Me. Now.

I'm about to tell her my name isn't actually Sam, but Larry bounds over to her in his puppy-dog style.

"Stellaaaaaa!" he cries, like he's dying. I can tell he's imitating his favorite scene from *Rocky,* one of the only non–Jackie Chan movies Larry has ever forced me to watch. Of course, Rocky is a professional boxer, so there's still plenty of fighting involved. I'm pretty sure Rocky cries *Adriannnnn* in the movie, though, not *Stella.* But that's Larry for you.

"I'm so glad you came," he says excitedly. "This is gonna be great!"

He sets her up in the row behind me with two little kids and one old lady in the back. I am officially the biggest loser on the planet.

Larry gives a welcome speech and has us all do about a million stretches. Finally, he tells us to kneel in our places with our hands flat on our thighs, feet tucked under us.

"Kara," he says to one of the green belts. "What is a true karate man?"

Kara clears her throat. "What is a true karate man?" she asks. The rest of the class repeats the question. "A true karate man is one with a godlike capacity to think and feel for others, irrespective of their rank or position."

She pauses every few words and waits for us to repeat her. She goes on about what a karate man does and what makes him true. I vaguely remember this part because I remember thinking, as a little kid, that I wanted to be a true karate man. Like Larry. When Kara says a phrase about how a true karate man lifts those who have fallen, I remember thinking it sounded like Superman. Only real. I remember thinking *I* could be Superman.

"Excellent," Larry says when she finishes. "Now, since so many of you are new to my class today, I wanted to go over what Kara said a bit more. 'A true karate man is one with a godlike capacity to think and feel for others, irrespective of their rank or position.' Anyone want to tell me what this means?"

Drake raises his hand. "It means a true karate man always acts good no matter what. Even if someone acts like a jerk or something, a true karate man still does the right thing instead of beating him up."

"Good," says Larry. He goes on to give some examples. As he talks in his calm, confident way, I realize he kind of does seem a little godlike, with everyone listening to him, smiling like he is giving them the greatest wisdom they've ever heard.

"The other thing you all need to learn are the basic precepts of karate." Larry walks over to his duffel bag and hands out a list to all the white belts. And me. "Most of you know these, but for the new people, you should read these over and think about how you can apply them to your daily lives."

I read the first entry and feel totally lost. "*Karate-do* begins with courtesy and ends with *rei.*" I have no idea what *do* is. Or *rei.* Those of us with papers put them on the floor against the wall, then find our places again.

"OK. Now we're going to start at the beginning and review the first kata to make sure everyone has a clear understanding of the moves and sequence. Then we'll break into groups to practice. Jacob, why don't you demonstrate."

Jacob steps forward and bows to Larry. He moves so slowly, I'm afraid he's going to keel over and die right here. But then he begins to move in this amazingly fluid motion. I can't believe it. The guy just hobbled forward like the senior citizen he is, and suddenly he's punching air like he's Jackie Chan.

Larry looks all serious as he watches. "Excellent!" he says. "Who's next?" He goes row by row and has everyone demonstrate the first kata. As he gets closer to my row, I can feel myself breaking out in a sweat. I can't remember any of this.

"Sam the man? You're up!"

Why? Why does he have to call me that?

"I don't really remember this stuff," I say.

"Let's start with the first step. Remember Precept Five when you're learning the katas: 'Spirit first, technique second.'" He stands next to me and has me imitate his stance. Then, move by move, we go through the positions, and it slowly comes back to me. I remember this feeling as I pivot on my feet and thrust my fist out. Pretty soon, I'm getting it.

"Great job!" Larry says. "I told you you'd remember. He ruffles my hair. God. "OK, let's match up with partners so you can start practicing."

Larry matches me with Stella, naturally. He winks in this obvious way, like, *I'm so going to fix you up.* I roll my eyes, grateful Stella didn't see him.

Since I'm still mostly clueless, Larry tells Drake to join us, too.

"'Sam the man'?" Stella asks, smirking, while Larry continues grouping people.

I shake my head. "Larry," I say. "He can't help it."

She laughs. "But he means well."

Right.

Drake takes us through each step. Slowly, I begin to remember the rhythm of the movements. Every time I punch the air, my arms feel a little stronger. I remember the power I felt when I first learned how to strike out. Like I could go home and beat up anyone who tried to mess with me. I realize that did not make me a true karate man. Or Superman. But I didn't really care. I was a mad kid.

"See?" Larry says in my ear. "You're a natural."

"Kee-yai!" Stella shouts as she finishes the kata. I remember that, too. I remember how good it felt to shout it. But I can't bring myself to go there. Yet.

We spend the rest of the day practicing the first kata over and over again. When we break for lunch, Larry tosses a paper bag at me. I didn't even realize he'd made me lunch. I sit alone in one corner and watch the rest of the campers chat together. Stella and Kara are busy huddled in conversation. I overhear Kara tell Stella she goes to Union, the other high school in the city. Larry is too busy walking from group to group to chat to notice I'm by myself, which is good, because he's the kind of guy who would pull me up and drag me over to some other poor loser sitting alone and make me eat with him.

* * *

After practice, people crowd around Larry to ask him questions. Everyone seems hyped about class. Larry drags a big cardboard box to the middle of the room, and I help him hand out gis to all the newbies. When we're done, there's one left, and he says it's for me.

"You're gonna be a great partner," he tells me. He is glowing. He actually looks like he might cry.

Please. No.

"Thanks," I say, and rush out to the hallway to wait for him to finish up.

The hall smells like a swimming pool and sweat. I lean against the wall and let my arms hang down. They feel like rubber and ache like hell. I guess Larry was right. I'm totally out of shape.

"Hey, Sam."

It's Stella. She comes over and leans against the wall next to me. I can smell her deodorant, but it's not nasty like Larry's. Obviously.

"Hey."

"You were pretty good in there." She smiles at me. When she smiles, it's not just her mouth, it's her whole face. Her brown eyes sparkle and — no. No. I'm not going there.

"You, too," I tell her, and force myself to look away.

"Thanks. I think this is going to be fun after all."

Yeah.

"So, what's it like living with Larry, anyway?" she asks. "It must be — interesting."

"Entertaining," I say.

She nods. "Are you staying with him for any special reason?"

I shrug. "I'm interested in architecture, and Roosevelt has a great tech program. I thought coming here might help improve my chances of getting into a college program."

"Wow, that's dedication. I would hate to leave all my friends senior year."

Yeah. It sucks.

"I guess," I say. "So, no babysitting today?" I ask to change the subject.

"No, thank God. That baby wears me out."

"He does cry a lot."

"I can't imagine having a kid. They're cute and all, but, holy crap, they're demanding."

"Yeah," I say quietly.

She gives me a funny look. "I mean, I love him — don't get me wrong."

"No worries."

"You're a strange guy, aren't you, Sam?"

"Um, about that." I'm about to try again to tell her my name isn't actually Sam, but she looks at her watch and swears.

"I gotta bolt. My boyfriend's picking me up outside, and he gets cranky when I'm late."

"Oh." I know I should feel relieved that she's seeing someone. I'm the last person who should be starting a relationship. So why do I suddenly feel so . . . disappointed?

"See you tomorrow!" she yells over her shoulder as she runs down the hall.

"See ya," I call after her.

I lean my head back on the cool cinder-block wall and close my eyes, concentrating on the pain in my arms. I think about the lies I've already let Stella believe. I think about how it will be like this with everyone I meet. About how I'm not the same person I was back at home. I'm Sam. The new guy. The stranger. I can be whoever I want, really.

The problem is, I have no idea who it is I want to be.

Chapter 8

"That was great, wasn't it?" Larry asks when he finally comes out to the hall to get me. "Man, I love watching all these people discover karate. It changed my life, and I know it'll change theirs, too. Isn't that awesome?"

I wonder if Larry ever gets sad or pissed off. He seems so goddamned *happy* all the time.

"Awesome," I say.

"Hey, I have a great idea. Let's go home and shower and invite Arielle over for dinner. We'll get her favorite takeout! She's dying to meet you."

As he starts jumping around in his puppy-dog way, I realize who Larry reminds me of: my friend Dave back home. His excited panting is equally annoying.

"OK," I say. Because, like Dave, if you don't at least act like you agree to do whatever it is he's excited about, he gets this pathetic, sad-dog look. And that's even worse.

Thinking about Dave makes me realize how much I miss him and Caleb. For as long as I can remember, I've seen or talked to those two every day. Even though we act like we drive each other nuts, we're best friends. And not having them around to drive me crazy is a lot harder than I thought it would be.

At home, I take a long shower, then check my phone for messages.

Caleb: where r u? call!

Dave: [More stupid jokes not worth mentioning.]

My mom: we miss u. pls call 2 tell us urok.

She wants me to tell them I rock? Nice texting, Mom. I know she means she wants to know if I'm OK. But I'm pretty sure the fact that I'm here means she knows I'm not. Whatever.

I call her cell and get her voice mail. Figures. She's really dying to hear from me. I hang up without leaving a message.

I send Caleb a quick text to tell him I've been busy, then Dave a quick "LOL" so he thinks I actually read his jokes. Then I join Larry in the living room, where he's setting the coffee table for dinner. He doesn't have a dining-room table, and he says it's unromantic to eat dinner in the kitchen. I point out that it's also unromantic to invite me to a dinner that's supposed to be romantic, but he just laughs.

"Are you kidding me? Taking you in has earned me major points. She thinks I'm the most sensitive guy in the world now." He fake-punches my shoulder.

So funny.

"That's not why I took you in, of course. You know that, right? It's just a perk. A bonus. I'd do anything for you, Sammy. You know that, right?"

Calm down, Larry. God.

"Right?" he asks again. He seems dangerously close to getting the sad-puppy look, so I humor him.

"Yeah," I say. "Of course. Thanks, Lar."

He steps back to admire the coffee table. He's put cloth place mats under the plates and everything. They don't match, but they still look nice.

When the buzzer from downstairs rings, Larry races over to the button on the wall and presses it. "Hey, beautiful, come on up!"

Larry is all class.

For some reason, my hands feel sweaty. I quickly wipe them on my jeans in case I have to shake hands with Arielle or something.

Larry runs out to the hall to greet her. When they

come back in, they're holding hands. Arielle is taller than Larry. Larry looks at me and kind of nods his head in her direction, like, *Told you she was hot.* And yes. She is. Extremely. But he really needs to stop doing that before she notices.

"Hey, Josh," she says, holding out her hand. Thank God I wiped mine off. We shake. Her hand is strong and bony. She's also incredibly tan.

"It's so great to meet you. Larry has been talking about you all summer. He's been dying to have you come stay with him."

Well, I'd say that's probably laying it on kind of thick, but who cares?

Larry beams.

Arielle checks out the coffee table. "Nice spread, Larry! You did this for me?"

He smiles. "What would you like to drink? White? Red? Beer?"

"I'd love a glass of red."

"Pinot OK?"

"Perfect."

"Just like you."

Oh. My. God. Could he possibly be more embarrassing?

"I'll take a beer," I say.

Larry laughs.

"What?" I ask.

"This isn't Chez My Big Brother, little man. I know your dad gives you drinks, but I'm not your dad."

Wait. Did he really just call me "little man"? He did. If Caleb and Dave were here, they would be rolling on the floor dying of laughter.

Larry heads to the kitchen, and Arielle goes over to the stereo to check out Larry's CD collection.

"So, what kind of music are you into?" she asks.

Nothing that's on any of the CDs that Larry probably bought ten years ago, that's for sure. Who even keeps CDs anymore?

I think of my dad and his guitar and all the lame '90s cover tunes he plays with his pals at dive bars every weekend. Normally, I hate that stuff. But for some reason, I wouldn't mind hearing it right now. I wouldn't mind just listening to my dad strumming his guitar in the living room when he doesn't think anyone's home.

"No preferences," I say.

She chooses Bob Marley.

Larry comes back with two glasses of wine and some milk for me in a wineglass. God. He may as well've come out with a freakin' Shirley Temple.

"So," he says, motioning for Arielle to sit down. "What are you in the mood for? Chinese? Thai? Mexican? Italian?"

"Why don't we let Josh decide?" she says.

"Oh, um, whatever's fine with me." I sit down on the chair opposite the couch.

"I'll grab some menus and we can narrow it down," Larry says. He dashes off to the kitchen again.

Arielle smiles at me. "Larry says you're staying to do your last year of school at Roosevelt."

I nod.

"That's cool." She studies my face, like I'm supposed to say more. Does she know more? Would Larry tell her? I just sit there, not knowing what to say.

Awkward, awkward silence.

"And you're taking karate with him?"

"Uh-huh."

"Larry's such a great teacher. Did you know that's how we met? We both teach at the Y."

Larry comes back with an enormous stack of menus and some crackers on a plate with a hunk of cheese. "I picked these up at the farmers' market," he says.

We all riffle through the menus and finally decide on Thai. Larry makes the order while Arielle and I try out the cheese. It smells like a goat and I almost throw up. Arielle makes a face, too. We both laugh.

"What's so funny?" Larry asks when he comes back to join us.

"Nothing," we say at the same time.

Bonded. Nice.

"Food will be here in a half hour," Larry tells us. He grabs a cracker and puts an enormous chunk of cheese on it. He starts to chew, then makes a face like he's going to hurl. "Berightback," he says with his mouth full, and races to the kitchen. He comes back with a piece of white cheese. "Cheddar," he says. "Always reliable."

We all crack up.

"So, Josh," Arielle says after we finish dinner. "Tell me more about school. Larry says you want to be an architect? Or do some sort of landscape design? Have you decided which colleges you want to apply to?"

Larry beams at me as if he's my proud dad.

"Not yet," I say. "I have a lot of research to do."

"Well, I've heard Roosevelt has a great guidance office to help students with college applications. And I'm sure Larry can help, too."

"Yeah, Larry's great," I say. Because really he is. Even if he's hands down the biggest dork on the planet.

I decide I should probably give them some time alone, so I clear the table and bring everything to the kitchen. I put all the leftovers away and wash and dry the dishes. As I'm standing there with my hands all soapy, washing more than my own plate, I realize this is the first time in months that I've had a real meal with another person. Sure, my dad and I sit on the couch and watch TV while we wolf down a pizza or something. But this was different. With real plates, not paper. And no TV.

When I turn off the water, I hear them laughing in the living room and decide to slip out for a while. I grab my new keys off the hook by the door and start to leave when Larry calls over.

"Hey, where are you going?"

I turn. They're sitting on the couch, Larry's arm over Arielle's shoulder. They look good together.

"Just for a walk," I say. "I'll be back later. No worries."

Larry studies me for a second, then nods. "OK, just come back before it gets dark."

Before it gets dark? What am I, ten? But I admit, it's nice to have someone care for a change.

I nod. "Be back later." When I step into the hallway, the warm feeling I had earlier slowly drains out of me and I stop and stand there. Alone. I lean back against the closed door and listen to the music on the other side. Larry must have turned it up as soon as I stepped out. I imagine him with Arielle inside. Maybe they're dancing. They seem like the type. I picture them in there, swaying to the music, holding each other. Falling in love. A new feeling starts to seep inside me, starting at my feet. It's cold, and dark, and it feels like if it reaches all the way up to my head, it will simultaneously freeze and suffocate me. So I take the stairs two at a time, and get out and away before it can catch up and swallow me whole.

Chapter 9

Outside, it's still pretty hot and muggy. I take the same path Larry and I took to the park. Lots of people have come here to walk their dogs tonight. Some have picnic dinners spread out on blankets. I head over to the deli and buy an ice-cream sandwich, then go back to the park and find an empty bench.

I used to get these from the ice-cream truck that came to our park when I was a kid. Caleb, Dave, and I would scrounge for change in all the best spots — our parents' coat pockets, under couch cushions, etc. Then we'd each buy whatever we could afford. Usually, it was the lame stuff like a Popsicle or an Italian ice cup because those were the cheapest. But sometimes, if we could find enough money, we'd splurge on a Bomb Pop or Choco Taco and see who could eat it the slowest without getting the drips all over us.

I take a bite and I feel like I'm back there again. When everything sucked, but it was OK because I was with my best friends and we were all in it together. And to be honest, life didn't really suck all that much. We just felt like it did because we wanted a Choco Taco every day. That, and maybe to be playing catch with our dads like some of the other kids in the park, instead of being mostly parentless all the time.

I squeeze the chocolate sandwich so the vanilla ice cream oozes out and lick the sides, just like we used to.

"You keep doing that and you won't have any ice cream left to eat the sandwich with." Stella is standing over me, grinning like I'm something to be amused by. She sits down next to me. She's kind of dressed up, with a nice shirt and a short skirt. She looks really great, actually. If Dave were here, he'd elbow me and say something totally inappropriate about her legs.

"Hey," I say.

"Hey." She looks down at her lap.

"You want one? My treat?"

"Nah," she says. "I'm on a diet."

"You? But you're so—" I realize I just revealed that I've checked out her body. Or at least, that's what it will sound like. “You don’t look like you need to be on a diet.” I finish my sandwich to occupy my mouth and keep it from saying anything else to make me look like an idiot.

“What are you doing out here, anyway?” she asks.

“Larry’s girlfriend is over, and I wanted to give them some space.”

“That’s thoughtful of you.”

“What are you doing here?”

“My boyfriend just dropped me off.”

“Here? Why not at the apartment?”

“I wanted to take a walk before going home. Get some fresh air.” She looks in the direction of the apartment building, as if there’s something there she wants to avoid.

“My mom has this new boyfriend, and she invited him for dinner. I’m kind of avoiding them.” She checks her watch.

“Do you like the guy?” I ask.

She shrugs. “I don’t know. We haven’t really hung out. My mom thinks I scare her boyfriends away.”

“Yeah. I can see that,” I say. “You’re pretty scary.”

“Heh. Yeah. Well, it’s the whole ‘being saddled with a kid’ thing. She doesn’t want to scare them away on the first date. So . . . I keep my distance.”

I nod and try not to think about the phrase she just used.

"Karate practice was kind of fun, huh?" she asks. I swear she could sense I wanted her to change the subject.

"I'm not sure that's the word I'd choose, but —"

She laughs. "Well, I'm glad you're in class. It's nice to know someone who can teach me the ropes."

Right.

"Larry said you stayed with him one summer when you were little and took his class then?"

"Yeah. My dad's in this band, and they traveled around for the summer, playing at different pubs and stuff. My parents couldn't really take me to all the bars, so Larry took me in for a few weeks and made me go to all his classes then, too."

"Your dad's in a band? That's so cool!"

"Not really. They're kind of lame."

"Oh. Well, it must have been fun to hang out with Larry for the summer. He seems like such a kid himself."

"Yeah. We had a good time."

"What's his girlfriend like?"

"She seems pretty cool, actually. I hope it works out. Larry deserves a happy life."

She turns to look at me. "Doesn't everyone?"

"I guess." I don't tell her I think there are plenty

of assholes in the world who don't deserve anything. Including me.

"I wish Britt was more like Larry. He's so serious all the time."

Britt? You've got to be kidding me.

"Why are you with him, then?" I ask.

"Oh, I didn't mean there's something wrong with him. Really. He's great. He's just—never mind. I shouldn't have said that."

"I promise I won't tell him."

She laughs. "You're funny, Sam. You're different."

At this point, I know I should tell her my actual name isn't Sam. But I don't. Somehow, I like being this new me. *Sam.* Sam the so-called smart kid, staying with his uncle and going to school so he can get into a good college. Not Josh the loser, living with his uncle because he can't face the girl whose life he ruined. The girl he got pregnant after a freaking one-night stand.

"Nah," I manage to say.

"You are. I can tell. You're not like most guys."

I cringe as I try to block out the memory I've been trying to forget for almost a year.

No, I'm not like most guys. I'm worse.

"How long are you staying out here?" she asks after we've been sitting in silence way too long. "Do you want to walk back together?"

"Sure." We get up, and I throw out my ice-cream sandwich wrapper.

She nods approvingly, as if she expected me to toss it on the ground.

We walk toward the apartment. It's still hot outside, even though it's dusk. I can feel the heat coming off the pavement. It feels good, though, somehow. It feels alive.

"I still can't believe you left your school senior year just to come to Roosevelt," Stella says. "You must be a really serious student."

Time to perpetuate another lie, I guess.

"Actually, my grades weren't so good, and my guidance counselor thought taking special classes my last year would show colleges I was serious about architecture and stuff."

"You already know what you want to do with your life? That's so great. I have no clue. Not even a remote idea."

All I really know is that I need to get away, and this is the only chance I have. That's all I know about what I want to do with my so-called life. And now I have officially reverted to my asshole ways by not even owning up to this fact. But obviously, I don't tell Stella this. I don't say anything at all.

"Well, thanks for walking me home," she says as we come to our apartment building. "Samurai Sam."

Samurai Sam. That's me.

We go inside, and she takes the elevator while I head for the stairs. "See you tomorrow!" she says just before the door slides closed.

I watch the lights above the elevator door light up as it passes each floor. The light stops on the fourth floor, and I imagine her walking out, going to her apartment, and heading straight to her room to call *Britt*. I know I shouldn't judge the guy by his name, or apparent lack of a sense of humor, but I can't help it. Something about the way Stella talked about him, like she had to convince me he's a good guy, felt strange. Why do girls do that? Why do they go out with guys they have to convince people — convince themselves — to like?

But the second I think that, I see another face. The one I wish I could forget. Looking at me the same way I bet Stella looks at *Britt*. Like I had something for her. Like there was some gift I could give her that was finally going to make her happy.

I remember how I smiled back.

How I played the game.

How I ruined her life.

I stand outside Larry's door and try to take slow, deep breaths. Just try to forget. But even with my eyes open, I see her face, and know I never will.

Chapter 10

That night, I wake up again at two a.m. and hear the familiar crying. Only it's not familiar. It's louder. More desperate. I wait for the footsteps, the *creak-creak, creak-creak*. But they don't come. Then, the cries turn to screeches.

I throw the covers off and stand up. Clover grunts and stretches her legs, then looks up at me in the dark.

"Sorry," I tell her.

I pace back and forth. Where the hell are the baby's parents?

Why is it so hard to breathe?

I want to hit something, but none of this crap is mine.

I pound the wall with my fist instead. Jackie Chan smiles at me on that stupid poster, and I punch his face. He keeps smiling, so I punch it again. Hard. And again.

"What the hell?"

I jump and turn around.

Larry is standing in my doorway in his boxers.

"What's going on?" he asks.

I look down at my fist. "Sorry," I say.

He steps inside the room. "What happened?"

I don't know.

He lifts his head when he hears the cries above us, then looks back at me.

"Oh," he says quietly.

Arielle appears behind him, wearing an oversize T-shirt that comes to her thighs.

"Everything OK?" she asks. She has this sweet, concerned look on her face.

And it's too much.

Too much.

I shouldn't be here.

"I'm sorry," I say.

"No, don't be. I understand." Larry motions for Arielle to go back to bed.

"I'm such an asshole," I say.

"No." He reaches out to put his hand on my shoulder, but I move out of reach.

"I'm sorry," I say again. Because I don't know what else to say. And I am. I'm sorry for a million things. For everything.

"Josh," Larry starts, but there's nothing he can say, either. He knows he can't change the past.

Finally, above us, the crying stops. We both look up, and our eyes follow the sound of footsteps crossing the ceiling. Then the rocking.

Creak-creak, creak-creak.

I feel my body relax, like a balloon deflating. Larry reaches over and squeezes my shoulder. "Everything's all right now. Try to get some sleep."

"Sorry to wake you."

"No worries," he says. "Let me know if you need anything."

He shuffles back down the hall and closes his door.

As soon as I sit down on the bed, Clover pads over to me and leans against my arm, purring. I wipe the side of my face and wonder if I started crying these silent tears before Larry came in, or after.

Chapter 11

Arielle is making chocolate-chip pancakes for breakfast. Larry can't stop grinning, and I can't stop feeling like I am the biggest third wheel in history. Arielle acts like my being here is no big deal, though. And that last night never happened. She sips her coffee and tells Larry, who refuses to eat the pancakes and downs his smelly egg shake, how life is unpredictable and he should enjoy food, especially when she makes it. But Larry says he can make his life more predictable by taking care of his body, and tries to convince her to have one of his shakes.

I'm tempted to remind him of the pint of ice cream he finished off by himself, but don't.

"What is a true karate man?" Larry asks me.

"You?" I answer.

"Should I give you a printout so you can practice?" Larry asks. "As soon as you get the katas down, I'll be testing you for your blue belt. You used to know this stuff, remember?"

"Yeah," I say. "Not really."

"I'll leave a copy in your room. We've got a whole year together. If you practice every day, you could really move up fast. Maybe even make it to brown belt. That'll look great on your college applications, too!"

"Larry, ease up," Arielle says. "He's been here less than a week. Karate may not be his thing."

"Impossible," Larry says. "He's a natural."

Arielle rolls her eyes. "I'm just saying."

Larry stands and leans forward to kiss the top of her head. She reaches up and pats his cheek. He glances over at me and winks.

I take that as my cue to go to my room.

I flop on my bed and check my phone for messages.

Caleb: wuts up? y haven't u called?

Because I don't know what to say.

Dave: ashley wants 2 break up. call me.

Who the hell is Ashley?

Mom: sorry i missed call. love u. next time leave message.

And say what?

I finally decide to text Caleb back: sorry. nothing 2 report

I won't have time to call Dave until after "camp," so I just text: call u l8r.

I decide to delete my mom's message. Is she not capable of dialing my number and calling me herself? Still nothing from my dad. I know what they will say when I finally talk to them: "We wanted to give you some time to settle in."

Right.

The truth is, my parents are afraid to talk to me face-to-face. We all know it. I've become who they were, and it is killing them. It's like looking in a mirror to their past. Who wants to do that when it's filled with one giant mistake?

"Let's go, handsome!" Larry calls from the hall.

I throw my gi in my gym bag and leave my phone on the bed.

In the locker room, I struggle with my new gi. Larry tells me it looks great and helps me with my belt. I feel like I'm eight again. If I didn't know everyone else was wearing gis, there is no way in hell I'd even put this thing on.

When we get to our practice room, people are already doing the stretches Larry taught us. I find a space in the back and start stretching my arms, which are embarrassingly sore. When Larry calls us to line up, I find my place in the yellow-belt row and look for Stella, but she's not here. Larry busily checks everyone off his list, then looks over at Stella's empty place. He shrugs and puts his clipboard down.

After doing the stretches we learned yesterday, we all kneel on the floor and Larry has us take some deep breaths.

"Eric," he says seriously to one of the blue belts. "What is a true karate man?"

Eric repeats the question and starts to lead us in the opening ritual. "What is a true karate man?" he asks.

"What is a true karate man?" we all repeat.

As he continues, the door flings open and Stella rushes over to her spot behind me. Her hair is kind of messy and her face is covered with red splotches, like she's been crying. I'm about to ask if she's OK, but she gives me a look like, *Don't ask.* So I don't.

All morning we go through the first Taikyoku, which involves a series of blocking and punching moves. The moves feel like a strange kind of dance. You have to get your feet and arms in just the right positions or you lose your balance. "Learn how to release your mind," Larry tells us. "Embrace the movements."

After we all demonstrate that we more or less understand the first kata, Larry tells us it's time to spar. He brings out all the protective equipment, and we figure out how to get it on. Predictably, Larry puts me with Stella. He even has the nerve to wink at me. I pretend not to notice.

"Victory relies on your ability to know the difference between vulnerable points and invulnerable ones," Larry says. I'm not sure anyone knows what he's talking about. It's another precept we're supposed to follow.

Stella and I try to go through the moves, but she's totally distracted and I'm too worried I'm going to hurt her, so we make a terrible pair. When Larry comes over to watch us, he rolls his eyes dramatically and tells us to get over ourselves. And then the weirdest thing happens. Stella steps back, looks at me, and starts to cry. Before Larry and I can do anything, she runs out of the room.

"Stop trying to be a matchmaker," I say. "She already has a boyfriend."

Larry makes his hurt-puppy face. "How was I supposed to know?" he asks.

I shake my head and leave him there.

Out in the hall, I look both ways for Stella. She's way down at the end, sitting on the steps that lead to the pool. I walk quietly to her. She has her face hidden in her hands. Her shoulders are shaking.

"Hey," I say quietly. "Everything all right?"

She looks up and wipes her face on the cuff of her gi. "What do you think?" she says coldly.

"No?"

"He's cute *and* brilliant."

She thinks I'm cute?

I sit down next to her. "I'm guessing you don't want to talk about it."

She sighs and fiddles with the end of her belt. "One of Britt's friends saw you and me at the park. He told Britt we were acting like more than friends."

I move away from her a little. "Did you set him straight?"

"I tried, but he wouldn't listen. He said he wanted to come see me, but I told him I had to come to practice. Then he hung up on me! I tried to call him back, but he wouldn't answer. So now he thinks I'm cheating on him *and* I care more about karate than him."

She stands up and starts pacing. "He's so mad at me. I've ruined everything. Why do I have to be so stubborn? I should've just told him to come get me so we could talk. I know if we talked face-to-face, he'd believe me. He's so damn jealous. I know it's just because he loves me, but I wish he would *trust* me a little more. You know?"

She looks at me like she expects me to say something

helpful or reassuring. But he sounds like kind of a jerk, and I'm sure that's not what she wants to hear. So I just keep quiet.

"You two OK?" It's Larry, calling from the doorway down the hall.

I give him a thumbs-up.

"Thanks for coming to check on me, Sam," Stella says. "That was nice."

"No problem."

She smiles at me, and my heart skips. Or beats faster. Or whatever it is your heart does when a beautiful girl smiles at you like that. Only I don't want it to. It can't.

"About this Sam thing," I say.

"What thing?"

"It's just that —" I feel like such an idiot. "My name's not actually Sam. It's a nickname Larry made up a long time ago when I stayed with him."

"What? Why didn't you tell me?"

"I tried, but —"

"Well, whatever. So, what *is* your name, then?"

"Josh."

"Josh. Really? But you look like a Sam to me."

"That's because you thought I was a Sam."

"Josh," she says again. "I don't know if I like that."

"Um. Thanks?"

She grins. "Sorry, Sammy."

I groan. "Please don't turn into Larry on me."

She elbows me. "I'll try."

I stand up and hold out my hand. "C'mon. We better go back."

She wipes her eyes and lets me pull her to her feet. Then we go back to class and spend the rest of the day learning our moves.

For the next three days, Stella and I mostly practice side by side. She doesn't mention her boyfriend again, but the way she constantly checks her phone for texts every time we have a break makes me think they're still together. Larry doesn't seem to care either way, and constantly pairs us off. He makes annoying faces at me behind her back, gesturing at me to *Go for it.* I ignore him.

The thing about doing katas with the class is that it's sort of like a dance, where everyone is in sync. You have to get your stance just right. And your timing. But when we're all moving together, it feels like we're part of one powerful force. I know it sounds lame, but that's how it feels. I never in a million years thought I would be the type of guy who would be into something like this. But when I'm moving with everyone else, I feel like I'm part of something. Like a wave rolling in and back out. It feels strangely peaceful, which is weird, I know, since it's karate. But when I'm moving with the group, I don't think about anything else. I just think about moving with the force. It's like we're all part of something bigger than what we are by ourselves.

Maybe that's what I like about it. For a few hours a day, I don't feel so alone.

Chapter 12

The weekend is predictably uneventful. Larry and Arielle go out with friends, and I stay home and watch way too many Jackie Chan movies. My mom calls me on Sunday and we talk briefly.

Mom: Honey! How are you?

Me: Fine.

Mom: Is Larry OK? Are you getting along?

Me: Yeah, of course.

Mom: Are you eating all right?

Me: Uh-huh.

Mom: Have you met any friends? Are you lonely? Why haven't you called?

Me: I'm taking karate with Larry, so he's keeping me busy.

Mom: That's wonderful! Larry is a good guy.

Me: Yeah. He's great.

Mom: I miss you, Josh. Your dad does, too.

Me: I miss you, too, Mom.

Clover jumps on my bed and I scratch her head. She purrs like crazy.

Mom: It's nice to hear your voice, honey. Call more often to check in. All right? Please?

Me: I will.

Mom: Here's your dad.

My mom and dad are actually home at the same time? There's a first. My parents are masters at avoiding each other. Have been since I can remember. Dave and I used to wonder which of our parents would get divorced first, but for some reason, his parents have stuck together just like mine. Maybe living in denial is easier than actually doing something about it.

Dad: Hey, Joshy!

Me: Hey.

Dad: How's it goin' over there? Larry takin' good care of you?

Me: Yeah, Dad. No worries.

Dad: All set for classes? Do you need money?

Me: I'm all set.

Dad: The house sure is quiet without you, kid.

Like I made so much noise? The house has *always*

been quiet. Because no one in my family actually talks to one another.

Dad: Rosie really misses you.

Me: Give her a pat for me, OK? And don't let her off that diet.

Dad: I won't, bud. She's doin' pretty good.

I pet Clover again and try to swallow down the feeling in my chest that I haven't felt since the time I woke up in the middle of the night during a sleepover at Caleb's when I was in the third grade and wanted to go home so badly I had to cry myself back to sleep.

Dad: All right, then, bud. Let us know how the first day goes. We'll be thinking of you.

Me: Thanks, Dad. Don't worry, I'll be fine.

Dad: We'll talk to you soon. You let us know if you need anything. Just call. Anytime.

Me: I will, Dad. Thanks. Bye.

Clover rubs her head under my hand. *We'll* talk to you soon, he said. *We'll.* As if he and my mom are an actual *we*. Weird.

I decide I should probably call Dave next, but he doesn't pick up, so I leave a message. Two seconds later, he texts me back.

Dave: i was wrong. she wanted 2 tell me she loves me. Dave FTW!

Yeah.

Dave FTW.

WTF?

On the first day of school, Larry makes me a huge breakfast. Luckily, it doesn't involve raw egg. He's so amped up, I swear he's going to get out a camera and take a picture like I'm starting kindergarten. He asks me about five thousand times if I'm sure I have everything I need and if I'm sure I know how to get to the school.

"I don't understand why you aren't getting a ride with Stella," he says, even though I already explained how there is no way I'm going to be a third wheel in that situation. In fact, I'm pretty sure I've explained this at least five times.

"You have to get over that," I tell him.

He hands me a paper bag. "Lunch," he says.

I take the bag, which is oddly heavy. "Thanks. You didn't have to make me lunch."

"It's your first day!" He punches my arm, then gets all serious. "You'll be OK? You can find the bus stop? You know where to get off?"

"Yeah. I'll be fine."

There's a little bit of sadness in his eyes. When he sees me notice, he turns away. Maybe he's thinking about how much it must suck to spend your senior year away from the friends you grew up with, at a new place where you don't know a soul except for a girl who doesn't want to be seen with you. Or maybe he knows all that is nothing compared to why I'm here in the first place.

When I leave the building, Stella's sitting on the stoop with her backpack. She has jeans on, with a tight T-shirt. Her hair's down, which I've never seen before. She looks beautiful. She also looks nervous.

"Hi," I say.

"Hi," she says. "Are you taking the bus?"

"Yeah. You waiting for Britt?"

She glances down the street. "Yeah. I'd offer you a ride, but . . . you know how he is."

"No worries."

She keeps looking down the street, then back at me, until it finally dawns on me that she's not nervous because it's the first day of school, she's nervous about Britt seeing us together and she wants me to get the hell away from her before he shows up.

"Oh," I say. "Right. The jealous thing." I know I sound like a wounded jerk, but whatever. This is so lame. The one friend I'll know at school I have to pretend is a stranger. Perfect.

She doesn't apologize. In fact, she looks annoyed with me.

Whatever.

"Have a good day!" I call over my shoulder, not really meaning it.

"You, too," she says quietly, probably not meaning it, either.

At school, I follow the stream of students inside and check the postcard I got telling me where my homeroom and first class would be, along with my schedule. It feels different here from my old school. A little cleaner. A little more organized. And a lot bigger. When I find the room, I take a desk in the back. The desks are all drafting tables, like the one in my drafting class at my old school, but nicer. There, the tables were covered with carvings and permanent marker about who loves who, who does who, who has a big dick, who has no dick, and who should eat shit. Here, they are smooth and clean. Here, maybe no one cares about who should eat shit.

When the teacher walks in, he clears his throat and everyone gets quiet. He asks how everyone's summer was but clearly doesn't really want anyone to answer, because without even hesitating, he starts to take roll, then passes out our course syllabus and textbooks. We spend the next hour going over what we'll be doing all year and why.

I get out my planner and start writing in the due

dates for projects. I fill them all in, all the way to June. My whole year, all planned out.

Ten months.

Ten months, and then I'll really be gone for good.

All morning, I look for Stella, but I don't see her until lunch. She's sitting at a table in the corner with who I can only assume is *Britt*. He has his arm around her while he eats with one hand. Seriously. That has to be a challenge. But Stella seems to like it. The rest of their table is full of what appears to be "the in-crowd." This is obviously the popular table, and Britt is the leader. Every time he opens his mouth, the table erupts in laughter. They love the guy. Stella catches me watching them and quickly looks away. Clearly, there will be no invitation to join them.

I find an open spot at a table that seems mostly full of people who don't know one another. They all look down at their lunches as if they are searching for some clue to how to get a life. I sit down and take out the lunch Larry made for me. Tofu sandwich. Carrot sticks. A chunk of cheese. An apple. Definitely no clues here. I open a paper napkin he stuck in the bag and a note falls out. I quickly glance around to see if anyone noticed, but everyone seems to be focused on not being noticed themselves. I put the note in my back pocket and start eating.

The kid sitting next to me opens a thermos of what smells like chicken noodle soup. When he spoons it out, I can tell it's the gross kind that comes in a can, with the tiny squares of dark meat that is supposedly chicken. My dad used to make us that soup for lunch on Saturdays, when my mom was at work. We'd make peanut-butter crackers with saltines and dip them in the broth until the crackers got soggy and the peanut butter started to melt. I remember I always left the little chicken squares uneaten and gave them to Rosie.

"So, you're Josh, right?" the kid asks.

"Yeah," I say.

"We're in first period together. I'm Jason."

"Oh. Hey."

He actually holds out his hand to shake. Who does that?

I shake it, feeling like I've just been inducted into the dork table. If Dave could see this, he'd laugh his ass off.

"You know what colleges you're applying to yet?"

I shake my head.

"I can share my list of schools if you want. My parents are obsessed. I have a spreadsheet."

"Oh, uh, that's OK."

"No, really. It's actually kind of helpful. I don't mind."

He takes a huge slurp from his soup, and a little bit of broth dribbles down the side of his mouth.

My life.

"Thanks," I say, and take a bite of my tasteless tofu sandwich.

"No problem. So, you're new here, right?

"Yeah."

He nods. I really wish I couldn't smell that soup. I don't know why it's making me feel sick.

I wolf down my sandwich and stuff the rest of the food back in my lunch bag, then get up to leave.

"See you around!" Jason says.

I force myself to smile and nod. "Yeah. See ya."

I head to my locker and throw my stuff inside. Then I reach for the note.

What is a true karate man?
Remember, and you'll be fine.
—L

I crumple it into a ball and toss it in my locker.

Here's an answer, Larry: A true karate man doesn't embarrass the crap out of his nephew by leaving a note in his lunch on the first day of school senior year.

I know he's just trying to be nice. But did he even think what would happen if someone saw that note? Stupid question, I know. Larry wouldn't care, so he doesn't think anyone else would. Because Larry lives in his own world. Or he did. Now I live in it, too.

What *is* a true karate man? What would Larry say?

It's not just the words we say at the beginning of class. I know that. But what, then? What is the key to being Larry? To being so damn happy all the time?

I wish I knew.

Chapter 13

Back home, Larry is waiting for me, bouncing around the living room with excitement.

"Well? How'd it go? Did you make any friends? Do you have lots of homework? Did you see Stella?"

"Relax, Larry. Don't have a heart attack."

"*Telllll meeeeee.*" I swear he is practically panting.

"It was fine."

"Fine? That's your word for the first day of school? What about your teachers? Did you like them? What are your classes like? Did you have anyone to sit with at lunch?"

"About that," I interrupt him. "No more notes in my lunch. What are you trying to do to me?"

"What do you mean?"

"Guys get beat up for that stuff."

"Nah, that's old school."

"Um. Really?"

"I just wanted to give you some advice. Let you know I was thinking of you."

"No offense, but next time maybe you could just, you know, say it to me in private?"

"OK, Sammy. Sorry." He gives me his kicked-puppy look.

"Never mind. It's fine." I can't believe I am having this conversation. "I'm gonna go get some work done," I say, even though I don't have any yet.

"Great! I'll throw a snack together and then we can head to practice later."

Snack. I swear he really does think I'm still eight years old.

He grins at me. "Cheese and crackers?"

"OK, Lar. Thanks."

I go to my room, shut the door, and breathe. Day One finished. One hundred seventy-nine to go.

Today was Dave and Caleb's first day, too. Usually, the three of us go to school the first day together. We find our lockers and complain about who we got for homeroom. Then we meet up at lunch to bitch and moan some more and listen to Dave's rundown on which girls got hotter over the summer and which ones didn't. I know it sounds totally lame, but I wish I could have been there today. Only I know it would have been different this year. So I guess I didn't miss anything after all.

I pull out my phone and check for messages.

Dave: being a snr rocks! we own this place! wywh!!!

This is followed by a long list of girls who transformed over the summer. I don't even recognize some of the names.

Caleb: how was yr 1st day? call me!

Before I can text them back, my phone rings. It's my mom.

Me: Hey, Mom. How are you?

Mom: Hi, honey! How are *you*? Did school go all right?

Me: Yeah, it was fine.

Mom: Just fine?

This again?

Yes. Fine. What else am I supposed to say? It's school. Let's just be glad it was fine and that I didn't say it totally sucked.

Me:

Mom: Do you think you're going to like it there? Is your schedule OK? Do you like your teachers?

Me: Yeah, Mom. It's all good. No worries.

Mom: Are the kids nice?

Me: Yeah, sure. They seemed nice enough.

Mom: [*Heavy sigh.*]

Me: Try not to worry so much.

Mom: I'm sorry, honey. I can't help it.

Sure, now.

Me: I'll be fine.

Mom: Your dad really wants to talk to you. Hang on.

I get a horrible, awkward image of them standing in the living room together.

Dad: Hey, Joshy! How'd Day One go?

Me: It was good, Dad.

Dad: That's great!

Me:

Dad: Uh, well, we just wanted to make sure things are all right there.

Me: Yeah, Dad. Things are all right.

Dad: You need anything? Money?

Me: I'm all set. Give Rosie a pat for me.

Dad: OK, then. We'll talk again soon. You call if you need anything.

Me: Bye, then.

Dad: Bye, Joshy.

I wait for him to hang up before I turn my phone off. I don't know why hearing him say my name like that makes the back of my throat ache, but it does. I swallow it away, and start to throw my karate stuff together.

"Knock, knock!" Larry calls from the other side of the door.

"Come in!" I call.

He opens the door and holds up a plate of cheese and crackers. "C'mon. Let's carb up and go to the gym."

I follow him back to the kitchen, and we devour the plate of food. Then we walk to practice.

Stella shows up shortly after we do and acts all friendly, as if she didn't spend the day pretending she didn't know me — or even see me, for that matter. I never would have pegged Stella for one of those people who care more about being popular than being a real friend. But I don't even know if that's it. Was she ignoring me for *Britt*'s benefit? Or her own?

When we line up and kneel to begin, Larry asks the question. But this time, he asks me.

"Josh, what is a true karate man?"

I clear my throat, already feeling my cheeks start to burn.

"What is a true karate man?" I ask.

The class repeats my question.

"A true karate man is one with a godlike capacity . . ."

" . . . to think and feel for others . . ."

" . . . irrespective of their rank or position . . ."

I look around me. Everyone else is staring straight

ahead as they repeat my broken phrases. I continue to recite for Larry, who smiles proudly. As I say the words, I try to hold on to their meaning. I think about my life and how I've lived it so far. How I've let down everyone I know. My parents. My friends. And — everyone. And I don't know what to do about it. I don't know how to make up for it. But with every phrase, I realize that I am just about the furthest thing from a true karate man as there can be.

PART TWO
DECEMBER

One who possesses ideals so lofty,

a mind so delicate

as to lift him above all things

base and ignoble.

—Gichin Funakoshi (1868–1957)

Chapter 14

"Hey, Josh! Hold up!"

Jason follows me down the hall after the last bell rings. He's one of the only people I talk to at school. I made it pretty clear within the first week that I'm a loner, but Jason doesn't seem to be the kind of guy who picks up on subtle (or not so subtle) hints.

I turn around.

"What's up?" I ask.

"I was just wondering if you were going to the library."

"Yeah," I tell him. "Why?"

"Oh. Because I heard some people were meeting up to hang out, and I didn't catch where. I thought you might know." This is what I mean about him not noticing things like my social status.

"You mean there's a party somewhere?" I ask.

"That's what I overheard. To celebrate the start of winter break."

"Right." I briefly wonder if Stella will be at this party, but realize it wouldn't matter. She still acts like I don't exist beyond the walls of the Y. On the few occasions we pass in the halls here at school, she doesn't even acknowledge me. Probably because she's almost always physically attached to *Britt* and surrounded by their posse.

"Sorry. Haven't heard anything," I say.

Jason shrugs. Then he just stands there, like he's waiting for me to invite him to hang out with me instead.

"So, I've gotta go study," I tell him.

"Oh, sure," Jason says quietly. He looks so bummed, I feel bad about not being able to help him out with the party. Why he doesn't realize I am not and never will be his ticket to a social life is beyond me. He knows my routine. In fact, half the time he joins me. But I always have to ask. And he seems to always act surprised to be invited. As if we're going to a football game and not the Losers Hall of Fame.

"You wanna come?" I ask.

"Me? Sure!" He rushes toward me. "Thanks. I didn't really want to go to the party, anyway."

Right.

We head to the library together, Jason talking a mile

a minute about some engineering project he's working on. I keep nodding and saying "Uh-huh" like I'm listening. But mostly I'm wondering about the party we aren't going to. And if Stella is there, if she'll wonder why I'm not. Or if she'll even notice.

I spread my stuff out on our usual table. Jason sits across from me and does the same, so our papers get all mixed up. He looks over at me and smiles, like this is going to be so much fun, even though this is it. This is all we do. Basically, every school day is the same. I go to school, to the library, then home. I know I sound like the most boring person on the planet, but I am not normally a good student. I have to work at this stuff. Hard. I managed to bring my grades way up first quarter compared to last year, but now I have to keep them up. It's the only way I'll get out of here.

After about an hour, it's clear Jason is bored out of his mind and not really into doing homework, so he tells me he needs to get home. He looks so damn disappointed that we didn't have a good time, as if he truly believed this could have been a better alternative to the mystery party we weren't cool enough to be invited to. As if I was his one shot at making a friend.

Crap.

"Hey," I say before he goes. "Sorry I didn't talk much. It's just that I have this big project due when we come back from break, and I wanted to get a head start on it."

He smiles a little. He reminds me of Dave and how easy he is to please just by paying a little attention to him. "That's OK," he says. "I get it. See ya over break?"

"Yeah, definitely."

As he walks away, I wonder how desperate he must be to want to be friends with a jerk like me. But I kind of smile, too. Because as much as I don't want to get attached to anyone here, not talking to anyone is pretty damn depressing.

This is my life so far with Larry in eight simple steps.

Step 1: Go to school.

Step 2: Go to library to do homework.

Step 3: Go to apartment to drop off school stuff and pick up karate stuff.

Step 4: Go to karate practice.

Step 5: Go back to apartment, scarf down something for dinner, and shower.

Step 6: Check phone for texts.

Step 7: Try to reply to texts but can't think of anything to say.

Step 8: Pass out.

Repeat.

Six more months to go.

* * *

Later that night, I get out of the shower and grab an ice pack before heading to my room. Stella rarely comes to practice on Friday nights because that's when *Britt* has games, and like a good girlfriend, she never misses one. Larry paired me up with the old black belt, Jacob, for sparring. He may be ancient, but he knows how to kick. He got my left shin, and it hurts like a mother. I press the cold against it while I sit on the bed. Clover comes over to sniff the ice pack, and I give her the usual scratch behind the ears. Then I check my messages.

Caleb: senior yr sux. wywh

Dave: c&c finally did it. stud!

So, Caleb finally had sex with his girlfriend, Corinne, and instead of telling me, he complains about senior year. Interesting. But I know why he didn't tell me. So whatever.

Mom: we're coming 2 get u 4 winter break. cant wait!

Back up. *We* again? And, they're coming to get me?

I don't think so.

Luckily, Larry agrees. He asked me a while ago what my plans were for the holidays, and I said I didn't know, but that I really didn't want to go home. Christmas at my house isn't exactly merry and bright. Normally it consists of my mom leaving the fake tree out with a box of ornaments next to it along with a note for me and my dad to "get festive." And then my dad pulling out a twelve-pack and sitting on the couch while I throw a few ornaments on the limp branches before giving up and having a beer with him. So, yeah. I'm pretty sure they can handle the holidays without me.

Larry says this is my journey, and if I think staying away is important, then I should. Mainly, I think he wants me here because Arielle is going away for the holidays to visit family and he doesn't want to be alone. Either way, I'm glad he's on my side.

Now I just have to explain it to my parents.

The thing is, when I can get into the routine here, I can forget about there. I spend every day focusing on school, and every night focusing on karate. Stella zipped up to yellow belt with me really fast, and then the two of us moved up to blue and now green. Larry thinks if we keep at it, we could make brown before I leave. People don't usually move up so fast, but that's because most people go to karate only once a week. But Stella and I go every night. For a while I wondered how Stella got away with it, what with *Britt* seeming so jealous of how she spends her time and with who. But then I realized he has basketball practice every night, and with Stella at karate, he knows exactly where she is. I am starting to think that Britt is kind of a shit. But what do I know? I'm just glad Stella still comes to practice, with the exception of Fridays. She seems to love karate as much as I do.

Larry says we have "the thirst." Whatever. I just know that when I'm at practice with Stella and Larry, I'm not stressed about school — or anything else.

Stella and I have an unspoken agreement that we don't walk to practice together. We don't hang out on the stoop. We still act like strangers at school. Basically, we aren't seen anywhere together except in practice, and on the walk with Larry back home. Practice is the "safety zone." At practice, we joke around together. We help each other with the katas. We spar. When we demonstrate the katas together, we move as if we're connected. Like we both feel the same energy pulling us through each move, perfectly synchronized. It's more than a dance, though. I don't know what it is, exactly. It's as if we are both feeling the same rhythm, the same power. Everything else in my life disappears, or at least fades away. I don't think about why I'm here. I just think about the moment. Maybe it's the same for her. Maybe for this one time each day, we both get to escape from . . . everything. But as soon as class is over, we go our separate ways. Because for whatever reason (also known as *Britt*), I am not allowed to be in Stella's other world.

Larry says anyone that jealous is extremely insecure. But I say it's none of our business. And then he says I'm only staying out of it because I'm afraid of having a relationship. And then I say I do have a relationship. She's my karate partner. And then he gets all flustered and tells Arielle to talk sense into me.

Arielle practically lives at Larry's now, which is kind of awkward. Or it would be. But they're both so cool with each other and with me that I don't feel like such a third wheel anymore. Since Arielle teaches yoga at the Y, she and Larry both mainly work nights and have their days alone together while I'm at school. Arielle refuses to get involved with my covert non-relationship with Stella. Which is a relief.

Because what I don't tell Larry — what I don't tell anyone — is that I'm afraid if Stella knew how I really feel, she'd quit karate. Because what I really feel is that maybe Britt *should* find out about our secret friendship. Maybe then we could find out once and for all what his true colors are. Would he be cool with Stella being "just friends" with me or not? By the way Stella acts, I'm guessing not. But I still want him to find out. And I'm pretty sure that makes me just as much of a shit as he is.

When I finally call my mom to tell her I don't want to come home for winter break, I can hear the disappointment in her voice. It's even worse than when I told her about Thanksgiving.

Me: I'm really sorry, but I'm just not ready to come home yet.

Mom: What do you mean? What about Christmas?

Me: Well, Larry asked me to celebrate with him.

Mom: But —

Me: It'll be better this way, I think.

Mom: But —

Me: I'll be fine. I promise. Larry doesn't have anyone to celebrate with. I should really stay so he doesn't have to be alone. Besides, aren't you working? You always work on Christmas.

Mom: Well, I just thought —

Me: Don't be mad, OK? I just can't come home. Not yet.

Mom:

Me: I'm really sorry, Mom. I just can't.

Mom: No, it's OK, honey. I understand.

Me: OK, well, I gotta go now.

Mom: Bye, honey. I miss you.

Me: Me, too, Mom.

I know I'm an asshole for making her and my dad spend Christmas alone together. But it's not like my presence is going to make it any better. I know when they look at me they probably think about how, if it weren't for me coming into their lives, everything would have been different for them. They wouldn't have had to get married, for one thing. I wonder if they think about that, too. I wonder if they think about how different their lives would be if my mom had had an abortion instead. Or given me up for adoption. Would they have simply moved on? Or would they have been haunted by not knowing where I was? Or whatever became of me?

Sometimes at night, when the cries above wake me up, I can still imagine his face. And I wonder. What would have happened if he hadn't been "given up"?

When I wake up and hear that phrase in my mind, over and over, I give Jackie Chan a good punch in the face. But Larry doesn't come rushing into the room anymore.

He knows what's going on. It's part of my freakin' journey. I just wish I knew where I was going.

Chapter 15

The first day of winter break, someone knocks on our door at around ten in the morning. "Well, look who's here!" Larry says loudly. I'm still in bed, but my door is open. *"Stelll-ahhhhh!"* Larry howls.

I pull on a T-shirt and a pair of sweats as fast as I can. I'm sure I have morning death-breath.

"Come on in, gorgeous."

They walk into the living room. I wave from my door and head straight to the bathroom to brush my teeth. When I come back out, Larry is showing Stella the box of Christmas ornaments from his childhood. There aren't too many, because he had to divide them with my dad.

"Hey, Sam," she says. I really wish she wouldn't call me that.

"Hey," I say.

"What brings you here on this fine winter morning?" Larry asks in his classic cornball way.

"I'm going to the mall to do some Christmas shopping, and I thought Josh might like to come along."

"Aw, that's so sweet," Larry says. When she looks away, he raises his eyebrows at me suggestively, then disappears into the kitchen.

"Coffee? Tea? Cocoa?" he calls out.

"Cocoa, please!" Stella says.

She looks at me kind of shyly. "So? You up for it?"

"Why me?" I ask. "Aren't you worried we might be seen together?"

She blushes. "Britt and his friends are all at a basketball tournament today."

Figures. I force myself not to roll my eyes. But seriously. Why can't she see how truly pathetic this situation is? Right. Probably the same reason I'm not going to say no.

"Let me take a quick shower first," I say.

"Great!"

I'm afraid she's about to hug me or something and smell my stench, so I step back fast and head to the bathroom.

When I come back out, she's finishing her cocoa with

Larry. They both look at me like they've been talking about me.

"What?" I ask.

Stella smirks at Larry. "Oh, nothing."

Larry grins.

"I know what you're getting for Christ-mas," Stella half sings.

Larry moves his shoulders to the beat in a little happy dance.

How do I even respond to this?

Stella gets up. "Ready to go?"

"You kids have fun!" Larry says. "Be good!"

"What's with you?" I ask him. Larry's always in a good mood, but today he looks like he's going to explode with joy.

"I'm just *happy*," he says. "Christmas is coming!"

"OK," I say. "Just — try not to overdo it."

"How the hell can you overdo Christmas?"

"I don't know. But if anyone could, I'm pretty sure it would be you."

"I'm going to take that as a compliment," he says, crossing his arms over his chest.

Stella grabs my hand, and my heart flips just like it always does when she smiles at me.

"C'mon, Scrooge," she says. "Let's go."

When I turn back to say good-bye to Larry, he winks at me and wiggles his eyebrows again.

Give it up, I mouth.

Never, he mouths back.

"I know what you're getting for Christ-mas," Stella sing-songs again as we walk down the street to catch the bus.

"So you said," I say. "What is it?"

"Like I'd tell."

I realize we're walking in sync, just like we move in karate. We're about the same height, but I'm much heavier. Still, it's weird to know someone's moves so well. To have the same ones. She looks up at me as if she just realized the same thing and pauses midstep, so we go out of sync. But as we walk along, we keep falling back in step together, and every time we do, we grin at each other. I can't remember the last time I felt like this. Relaxed. Happy. But even as I think it, I start to feel a weight bearing down on me again, and we fall out of step for real.

On the bus, we sit next to each other and watch the city go by. The bus is crowded with neighborhood people heading out to do their shopping, too. A little kid in front of us sings "Rudolph the Red-Nosed Reindeer," and his dad smiles at him like he's the cutest thing on earth. They hold hands tight. The boy won't sit in his dad's lap. He wants to hold on to the bar and stand like some of the other people. His body sways and he almost falls every time the bus driver hits the brakes or the gas. Each time this happens, the kid bursts out giggling. I wonder if he will ever know how lucky he is to have a dad to hold hands with like that. And then I start to wonder if my baby has a dad like that now. And then my throat starts to ache.

"Makes me miss Benny," Stella says.

For a brief moment, I wish I could tell her who he makes me miss. But I can't.

"You babysit for him every weekend," I say. "How could you miss him?"

She shrugs. "I just do."

We watch and don't watch the kid until we get to the mall stop and step out into the cold with everyone else.

"So, where to?" I ask.

"No idea. Let's just walk."

When I follow her inside the mall entrance, we're accosted by holiday music, fake trees, and the nauseating smell of scented candles. Stella pauses and turns in a circle, taking it all in.

"Don't you just love the holidays?" she asks.

Um.

"Oh, look! Newbury Comics! I love that place. Let's go there first."

Stella picks up every single gag gift and shakes it in my face. "You should get this for Larry!" She holds up an Einstein bobblehead. Its head shakes all over the place. "I'm so smart. Yes I am, yes I am, yes I am," she says as fast as his head nods.

I laugh.

"Oh, my God!" she yells.

A bunch of people look over at us.

"What?"

"You just laughed!"

I stop smiling. "And?"

"I don't think I've ever heard you laugh. I must have magical powers."

I know this can't be true. I mean, the laughing part. "Funny," I say.

She elbows me. "Sorry. I'm just not used to seeing you look, you know, happy."

"Way to harsh my mellow," I say. Because honestly? She really did. Who wants to hear how depressing they are?

"Harsh your mellow? Wow. Larry is really rubbing off on you." She reaches up and pinches my cheek. "You should laugh more often," she says. "It's good for you."

"Now who sounds like Larry?"

She shrugs.

But she's right. For the first time, I feel like maybe it's OK to feel happy once in a while. It's been so long, I feel like I almost forgot how.

We end up leaving the store without buying anything.

"Who are you buying for, anyway?" I ask as we zigzag through the stream of shoppers. I suddenly have an impression of us going into every single store in the mall and doing exactly what we just did. Picking up a bunch of crap, laughing at it, and putting it back down. Which would actually be fun if we weren't secret friends and we weren't, in reality, probably shopping for crap for her boyfriend.

"Oh . . ." she says. "A bunch of people."

"Like?"

"My mom. And . . ."

"The boyfriend," I finish.

"'The boyfriend'? C'mon Sam, you know he has a name."

"Sorry. I mean, *Britt*." *And you know my name, too,* I think. *Yet you refuse to use it.*

"Don't say it like that."

"Like what?"

"Like his name is *shit,* not Britt."

"Sorry."

"Just c'mon." She drags me into another store and

makes me stand there while she holds up some shirts in front of my chest and squints, as if she's trying to transfer Britt's face onto mine. Seriously.

"Please tell me you're not doing what I think you're doing," I tell her.

"What?" She puts the shirt back on the rack and blushes. "Fine. Tell me what *you* want for Christmas."

I roll my eyes. "Nothing."

She punches my arm.

"Um. Ow?"

"C'mon. If you could have anything, what would it be?" She smiles at me like she genuinely wants to know. And then, out of the corner of my eye, I see a familiar hat. And then, even more familiar long brown hair falling out of it.

My heart stops like I just took a kick to the chest. Then it speeds up so fast I can barely breathe.

It's the unmistakable rainbow hat Caleb's mom gave her last year.

Ellie.

She's two display racks over from us. I swing around fast.

"Sam?" Stella comes around to face me again.

I grab the display rack to hold myself up.

"I have to go," I say. I rush out of the store and start running.

"Sam! Wait up!"

I dart through shoppers and baby strollers. Why are there so many damn baby strollers? I keep running until I find an exit, and then I am heaving into the trash can just outside the door. Heaving and, oh my God, crying. What the hell. I quickly wipe my mouth and face and just breathe and try to calm down. But my heart feels like it's trying to punch its way out of my chest.

Could she have seen me? Was it even her? I can't breathe.

No. It couldn't be. Why would she be at this mall, four hours from home? The hat's crazy, but obviously not the only one in the world. I'm an idiot.

"Sam?" Stella runs over to me. "Are you OK? Ick! What happened?"

She puts her hand on my arm in this caring way that I don't deserve. I shrug her off.

"Look," I say, backing away from her. "I can't help you. I don't know what your boyfriend wants for Christmas, OK? And I honestly don't care. I have to get out of here."

"What? But —"

I start walking away from her.

"Sam!" She runs after me and grabs my shoulder to swing me around and make me face her.

When I do, I see it. That look. That same goddamn

pathetic look. The *Don't leave me here* look. The *I need something from you* look. My eyes start watering up again. I swear if I had a knife on me, I would jam it into my jugular.

"What's going on?" she asks. "You can tell me. I'm your friend."

Really? What kind of friend? The kind that only hangs out with me — will only even be seen with me — when her boyfriend is MIA? What kind of a friend is that?

"Sam," she says, because I am too much of a wimp to ask those questions out loud. "Talk to me."

I force myself to meet her eyes. Her beautiful brown eyes that are boring into me. Trying to see my soul. The real me. I realize hiding who I really am from her is no better than her hiding me from *Britt.* We're both good at deception.

"It's OK," she says, still studying my face.

For the first time, it feels like maybe it is.

I take a deep breath. "You have to stop calling me Sam," I say. "I'm not Sam. I'm not . . . I'm not who you think I am. I thought I could be. I thought I could do the whole 'fresh start' thing, but I can't. I want to be Sam, but I can't be. My name's Josh. All right? My name's Josh."

"All right," she says quietly. "Josh. I'll call you Josh. I'm sorry."

"No! Don't be sorry. Don't you get it? I'm the one who should be sorry."

"But — why? You didn't do anything."

"Yes I did," I say.

Yes I did.

Chapter 16

"What did you do?" This time Stella is the one to step away from me.

"Can we go somewhere? I can't talk here."

She looks uneasy about this. Like she's afraid of me now.

"Forget it," I say. "Listen. I'm a loser. You don't want to hang out with me."

"I know that's not true," she says. But she doesn't seem to want to get any closer, and I don't blame her.

"Let's just go home."

We get on the next bus and ride in silence. When the bus stops by the park entrance. Stella jumps up and says, "Let's get off here."

The park is deserted, since it's December and it's freezing outside. Only the dog walkers racing their dogs out to some unfortunate bush and racing back home again are around. We find a bench and zip our coats up to our chins.

"OK, mystery man," Stella says. "What's your story?"

I don't know why she wants to know so badly. Why she cares. But I'm glad she does.

"I don't know where to start," I tell her.

"You could tell me what happened at the mall," she says.

I breathe in the cold and let it sting my lungs. "I thought I saw someone I knew. From my old school."

"And this person gave you a panic attack?"

A panic attack? Is that what that was? God. I am such a loser.

"I don't know. I guess. I'm sure it couldn't have been her, but —"

"Wow."

"What?"

"She must be some girl to have that kind of power over you."

Power over me? After what I did to her? I wouldn't call it power. I don't know what I'd call it, but not that.

We watch an old woman walk by with an enormous black poodle. She nods at us and speeds up.

Stella waits patiently for me to reply.

"I don't really want to talk about her," I say.

"Was she your girlfriend?"

Did I not just say I didn't want to talk about her?

"No. It's complicated. But — no." I picture her again in the van that night. Looking at me. Waiting for me to say something. Anything. Anything but what I did say. Not that. My hands turn into fists in my pockets.

"Well, there was obviously *something* between the two of you," Stella says.

Obviously.

She waits for me to explain, watching me with her trusting, kind eyes. They are too familiar. And this is all too much.

"It's hard to explain," I say.

She sighs. "Relationships are so complicated."

Understatement.

"Sometimes, it's like, you never really intend for them to get so serious, right? I mean when you're our age. We have our whole lives waiting for us. How many people actually end up with the people they date in high school? But we treat our relationships like they're these precious, infinite things. Like our love is so freaking permanent. When, realistically speaking, they probably have months to live."

"That's very deep," I tell her, relieved to move the focus away from me.

"Thank you. But you know what I'm saying, right?"

"Sure. But if you really think that, why do you stay with Britt? He makes you cry, like, every week. Why stay with a guy who makes you cry all the time?"

"He doesn't make me cry."

"Uh, OK," I say sarcastically.

"I'm serious. I do that to myself. Partly because I get so upset with myself for messing things up."

"How do you mess things up?"

She shrugs. "Just stupid stuff. Forgetting to call and let him know where I am. Things like that. I know what you're thinking. I shouldn't have to call in to report my location every time I go somewhere. But he only wants to know where I am because he loves me and wants to make sure I'm OK."

"And not hanging out with me."

She looks annoyed. "Look. Britt is the best thing that's ever happened to me. I was a nobody before we started dating."

"I doubt that."

"Anyway, I never dreamed in a million years that the cutest boy in school — sorry — would want to be with me. And I don't want to mess it up. He's so great. He's funny, he has tons of friends . . ."

"What about you?"

"Huh?"

"Do you have friends?

"His friends are my friends."

"Don't you have your own friends?"

"Well, yeah."

I wait.

"I have you," she says.

"I'm a secret friend. What about ones he knows about?"

"I have girlfriends, too. Sure. It's just hard to be close with them, because we don't spend a lot of time together anymore."

"Since you started dating Britt."

She sighs. "It's worth it. He makes me happy. He makes me feel good about myself. I like being with someone who wants to put his arm around me, you know? In public. Like he's proud to be with me. I know he's a little possessive, but he's the only guy who ever cared about me. It's, like, he wants everyone to know I'm his."

"His?"

She shakes her head. "You know what I mean."

Sadly, yeah.

"Sorry," I say. "I get you. I wish you didn't feel like he's the only one who cares about you, though. Because plenty of people do. Besides Britt."

She smiles like Larry does when he thinks he's being coy. "Oh, really?"

I feel my cheeks burn.

“That’s not what I meant. Just that, you have friends.”

“I know. Thanks, Sa — Josh.”

“I didn’t do anything.”

“Thanks for being a friend.”

“A karate-only friend, you mean.”

She shifts uncomfortably on the bench. “I’m sorry. I know it’s rude not to pay attention to you at school. But Britt gets so crazy jealous. Besides, you don’t really seem like you’d want to hang out with us, anyway. Britt’s friends don’t exactly seem like your type.”

Because they’re popular? Cool? Normal?

“True,” I say.

“So you’re OK with being ‘karate friends’?”

I shrug. “Yeah, sure.”

She scooches closer to me and puts her head on my shoulder. I can smell her shampoo and wish it didn’t smell so good. I guess I can see why Britt is so jealous. Who’d want to lose a girlfriend like Stella?

“You’re a good guy, Josh. A real karate man.” She gently punches me in the arm. “You’re also good at changing the subject. We were supposed to be talking about you.”

“You’re very violent,” I tell her.

“*Any*way,” she says, rubbing her arms to keep warm. “Are you going to tell me your story or what?”

“What.”

She elbows me the way she always does. "You should, you know. I'm a good listener. It can't be *that* bad. No more pathetic than my story, at least."

"You'd be surprised."

"Secrets will eat you up, Josh. They really will."

"I know," I tell her.

A man rushes past with his tiny dog, urging him to find a spot and go already. I wonder if it's the cold he wants to escape, or if he has some great life to hurry back to.

The truth is, part of me does want to tell Stella my secrets. I want to tell her about the baby. And about what happened. That night. Sometimes I want to tell everyone. Just so I can get rid of it. Because she's right. It's eating me up. But when I turn to face her, when I look in her eyes and see her seem so genuinely interested in my screwed-up life, I can't do it. I can't disappoint her.

I don't want to lose her.

And I know if I tell her the truth, I will.

So I watch the man and his tiny dog instead. The dog walks around a small tree and gets its leash tangled around one leg. The man mutters something about how dumb the dog is as he gets the paw free.

"Just so you know," Stella says after we've been quiet a few minutes, "if you ever change your mind? I'm here."

She gives me her smile, and I feel myself melting, even though it's freezing.

"Thanks," I say. I try to give her my best smile back. One that says I mean it. I really am thankful. For a minute, I think she's going to rest her head on my shoulder again. But instead, she leans her head back and looks at the leafless branches above us. So I look up, too, and just stare through the branches and up to the cold white sky.

We sit there for a while like that. But then Stella starts to really shiver and it's obvious that it's time to go home.

When we get back to our building, she stops before she gets to the elevator.

"Thanks for coming with me," she says.

"We didn't really accomplish anything," I say. "Sorry about that."

"Yes, we did." She turns to come back toward me and puts out her arms, like she wants to give me a hug. But without thinking, I step back. Because for some reason, I feel that same panic I felt earlier at the mall.

"Well, see ya," I say, and turn away from her fast.

What is *wrong* with me?

"Um, see ya," she says, confused.

I start up the stairs before the elevator doors even open, and then I stop and turn around.

"Hey," I call down.

She tilts her head up to look at me.

"Thanks," I say. "You know. For being a friend."

Even though I'm a freak.

She smiles. "No problem." She opens her mouth like she might say something else, too, but before she can, I turn around and hurry the rest of the way up the stairs.

Chapter 17

Larry goes all out for Christmas Eve. He's invited Stella and her mom for dinner, since Arielle went upstate to be with her family. He also invited this old lady who lives on the first floor whose husband died last year and it's her first Christmas alone. Plus a bunch of other people in the building who I haven't met.

Larry, Stella, and I cook all day. We make tons of "finger food" that Larry found recipes for online. We're each assigned three different types. When those are all done, we make Christmas cookies. Larry admits he didn't have time to make cookie dough himself, so he bought the unhealthy premade dough that comes in sheets. He acts like this is the worst crime known to man. But, he says, he made up for it by making the best homemade icing we'll ever taste. He also bought a bunch of cookie cutters in the shapes of Christmas trees and reindeer and other Santa-type stuff. He divides up the icing and shows us how to make different colors with food coloring, and then we sit at the kitchen table and decorate the cookies. Larry blasts old Christmas tunes and sings off-key while Stella and I get carried away making pink and blue Christmas trees.

I know it sounds crazy, but this might be one of the best days of my life. There's something about being here. The smells of cooking. The laughing. The sun coming through the window, making spirits bright . . . OK. Lame. But anyway. It's nice. And way better than being stuck alone in my parents' cave of a house. I bet they didn't even bother to put up the tree now that I'm not coming.

When people start to arrive, Larry directs them to the tree and the box of ornaments waiting to be hung up. He bought a ton of Santa hats and tries to force people to wear them. Somehow I manage to luck out and get away from him whenever he starts waving one in my direction. He makes Stella and me walk around with trays of food to offer people. There's lots of wine and foul-smelling eggnog that Larry spiked to the hilt. "Don't put it near any candles," he jokes to everyone, which gets old fast.

Stella's mom arrives with her new boyfriend. Stella does not look happy to see him.

Her mom's name is Star. She's pretty, like Stella. But

she has that tired look some people have, and she wears way too much makeup to try to cover it up. "I've heard so much about you, Josh! It's nice to finally meet!"

The boyfriend, Calvin, shakes my hand real hard. Then he gives me his card. He's a Realtor at the company Stella's mom is a receptionist at. Star explains that he has convinced her mom to enroll in school to get her own real-estate license. She looks really happy, but Stella looks completely pissed about the whole thing, which seems weird.

Larry cranks up the music, and everyone continues to eat and drink. When all the ornaments are on the tree, Larry turns off the lights and makes everyone sing "Silent Night." Then he plugs in the lights on the tree, and everyone claps.

When Ben and his parents show up, Stella runs over and they give her a huge group hug. I never realized that his parents were both guys. I figured Jean was a girl. But I guess it's Gene. Anyway, Gil has the baby in one of those slings that hangs on your chest, and he walks around, rocking, while he talks to everyone, apologizing for being late and missing the tree lighting. With the baby all covered up like that, Gil looks like he's pregnant. It's kind of disturbing, given that he has a beard.

Every time he starts to come over to me to introduce himself, I pretend I need something in the kitchen.

Everyone else coos over how cute the baby is, whispering loudly.

"Don't worry, he can sleep through anything," Gil says.

"Yeah, except for his internal two a.m. alarm clock," Gene adds. "The kid is wired for two on the dot. It's the strangest thing."

Larry automatically looks over at me. I turn away and bring the almost-full tray I'm carrying back to the kitchen, then sneak off to my room. Clover is cowering on my bed, scared of all the strangers in the house. I pet her to try to calm her down.

There's a light knock. Stella comes in without waiting for me to answer. She's wearing one of the Santa hats.

"Hey, you OK?" she asks.

"Huh? Oh, yeah. Just needed some air."

She sniffs. "In here?"

"So funny."

She sits down at the end of my bed. "Great party, huh?"

"Yeah," I say.

Her eyes dart around the room as she checks out all the Jackie Chan and karate crap. "Nice decorations," she says, grinning.

"Larry, not me."

"Really? I never would've guessed." She winks and reaches over to pet the cat. "So, I have to ask," she says, "because I've been wondering about this since the first time we met."

Clover moves out from under her hand and walks over to me, as if she knows I need her.

"What?" I ask, even though I'm sure I don't want to know.

"Why do babies freak you out?"

My face gets hot. "They don't."

"Right. Every time Gil tried to get near you with the baby, you ran to the kitchen."

"What? I wasn't running."

"Speed walked, then. Whatever. What's up with that?"

"Nothing. I don't know what you're talking about."

"OK," she says sarcastically. She stares at me. Maybe she thinks if she waits long enough, I'll tell her the truth.

"Nice hat, by the way," I tell her.

"You really are a master at changing the subject," Stella says. Then she gives me that smile that makes me feel a way I don't want to. Like my insides are on fire. I turn away.

"Wait here. I have something for you." She comes back a minute later with a tiny gift bag.

Crap. I didn't think to get her anything.

"It's not a big deal, so don't feel bad about not getting me something," she says, like she can read my mind.

I reach inside and take out a small box. It thuds when I shake it.

"You got me a piece of coal, didn't you?" I say.

"Just open it." When our eyes meet again, I feel this crazy sinking feeling in my chest. Good and bad at once. This time, she's the one who looks away.

I quickly open the box to break the silence. Inside, there's a rock. It's speckled orange and polished smooth, like the ones you buy at a museum store or something.

"It's a rock," she says.

"Oh. I wasn't sure."

She elbows me. "Now who's funny?"

I pull out the rock and inspect it. "It's a nice rock," I say. "Very smooth."

"It's a special rock." She moves closer to me. "My grandmother gave it to me when my mom and I moved here. We used to live with her. Anyway, she said to keep it in my pocket, and whenever I felt scared or lonely, to squeeze it. She had one, too, and she said she'd be able to tell when I squeezed it, and she'd send me strength."

"But . . . that's too . . . like, special. I can't take this." I try to hand it back.

"No, no. See, my grandmother died. And now I have both rocks. So, you know. I don't need two. I don't know what's going on with you, and obviously you don't want to talk about it. But . . . we're friends. Maybe you don't want to talk to me about whatever it is you're carrying, but I can still send you some strength when you need it. And . . . maybe you could do the same for me."

"Wow," I say. "This is, like, the nicest thing anyone's ever done for me. But why me? Why not give this to Britt?"

She shrugs. "He doesn't need any strength. He has a perfect life."

"Because he has you?"

She gives me a shove. "No, stupid. He just doesn't need anything. Not like you and me. He lives in a fancy house. He has an expensive car. His parents are still together. He's a natural athlete. A great student. You get it. He doesn't have to worry about stuff the way you and I do." There's a little flicker of sadness in her face when she says that. She covers it up fast, but I see it.

"So how come you don't like your mom's new boyfriend?" I ask.

She sighs. "It's not that I don't like him. He just gives me a bad feeling."

"How come?"

"You've seen how my mom acts around him. She's totally fallen for him. And now she's going to spend all this money that we don't have on going to classes to get her license when, given her past experiences, this relationship will be over in a month and she'll end up quitting her job and going somewhere else and never becoming a Realtor or whatever and all that money will be wasted."

Wow. She's even more of a pessimist than I am.

"What if he doesn't?" I ask.

"Doesn't what?"

"Break up with her. What if they stay together?"

"They won't."

"Why not?"

"Because they never do." She shakes her head. "I will never be like her. I swear."

I hand her the rock.

"What?"

"I think you need to squeeze this," I say.

She laughs. "Sorry. I got a little carried away. Ugh. She *promised* me Christmas was going to be special this year. Just the two of us. But I bet you a million bucks *Calvin* ends up spending the night."

"Sorry," I say.

"Forget it. Let's just go back out and have some fun."

I reach for her arm before she gets up. "Hey," I say. "Thanks for the rock. It's really nice."

She shifts a little closer to me, and I automatically move away just the slightest bit.

She sighs. "Would you relax? I'm not going to try to jump your bones."

"Jump my—" I can't help it. I start laughing.

She laughs, too, and it feels so good. So good to be sitting here with her, and this amazing gift. This amazing girl. Friend.

"Anyway," she says when we stop laughing. "When you need, you know, some strength, you can squeeze this, and I'll know. And I'll send you some."

"I seriously can't believe someone would do something so nice for me," I say.

"Well, believe it," she says. "That's what friends do."

I close my fingers around the rock again and think about Dave and Caleb back home and what a horrible friend I've been to them. I squeeze the rock and promise myself to do better.

"Thanks," I say. "This is really cool. And—you know, if you need strength, I'll send you some, too."

Before I know she's coming, she's got her arms around me and gives me a huge squeeze. I have about two seconds to smell her honey-scented hair before she kisses me on the cheek and runs out of the room. But the smell of her perfume is still here.

I take a slow, deep breath before it slips away.

Chapter 18

After everyone leaves, I help Larry pick up. He hums carols while we wash dishes and put everything away. When we're finally done, we stand in front of the tree and admire the lights.

"That was a nice night," Larry declares. He puts his hand on my shoulder. "I love Christmas Eve."

"Yeah," I say.

"I noticed Stella had a present for you. Anything good?"

"Actually, yeah. It was a rock."

"Like a pet rock?"

"Not exactly."

I'm not sure why I don't want to tell him the details. It just seems like something private between Stella and me.

"Hmm," says Larry. "That's different. I like that. What did you get for her?"

"Nothing. I'm such an idiot."

He shakes his head. "We need to work on that."

"No kidding."

"Well, I guess we should hit the hay so Santa can come."

"Seriously?"

"What?" He paws around in the ornament box next to the tree and pulls out two stockings. "Won't come if we don't leave 'em out." He drapes them over the back of the couch. "G'night, Sammy. Merry Christmas." He walks down the hall, humming "Jingle Bells."

"G'night," I say quietly.

In my room, I check my cell. My mom sent a photo of the Christmas tree set up in our living room. Our dog, Rosie, is sitting in front of it with a big red ribbon around her neck and a pair of fake antlers on her head, as if someone in our family actually found a sense of humor.

I read the message: we <3 u!

Weird.

I check my other messages.

Caleb: merry xmas! y didn't u come home?

Dave: [Inappropriate joke about Mary and Joseph.]

I flip back to the photo of the tree. Poor Rosie looks so embarrassed with that goofy ribbon around her neck. But looking at her like this makes me realize how much I miss her. Even her foul smell. I leave the photo on my phone propped up on my side table and shut off the lights. The glow-in-the-dark stars come to life, and I imagine they're Christmas lights.

Next to my phone, I grab Stella's box and pull out the rock. It slowly warms in my hand as I hold it in my fist. I picture her somewhere in the building above me, holding her own rock. I give it a squeeze. "Hey," I say in my head. "Merry Christmas." I hold the box to my face and smell her perfume again. Then I roll over, the rock still in my hand, and fall asleep.

When I wake up, I'm still holding Stella's rock. I reach for the box and put it back, then wait for the cries to start. They're quiet at first, then louder. I hear the familiar creaks. And then singing. Just muffled, but I recognize the tune from earlier tonight. *Silent night. Holy night.* I imagine Gene or Gil up there, holding the baby. Rocking him. Holding him and loving him. Holding him and being his father.

I cross my arms at my chest and hold the emptiness

there. I feel it as if it is the heaviest thing in the world. As if it is crushing me. And I can't breathe. I squeeze tighter, trying to smother the nothing that is slowly suffocating me.

But there's nothing to hang on to but myself.

Chapter 19

Larry flings open my door and spreads his arms out, like, *Ta-da!* He's wearing red sweatpants, a white T-shirt, and a Santa hat.

I roll over and check the clock. "Larry, it's seven thirty in the morning."

"I know! And also? It's *Christmas*!"

I put my pillow over my head. He pulls it off.

"C'mon," he whines. "Christmas morning! Let's go see what Santa brought."

I groan. "You go see and let me know."

He whips off my sheets in a dramatic tug. The cat goes flying off the bed.

"Oh! Sorry, Clover. I didn't see you there," he says. But she's long gone.

I sit up and rub the gunk out of my eyes.

"On Christmas, mo-or-neen, wake up bright and er-er-lee!" Larry starts to sing.

"I'm up, I'm up," I moan.

Larry grins. "I already made cocoa!"

Maybe he was an elf in a former life.

He semi-bounces out of the room, and I drag myself after him. In the living room, the tree is all lit up. There are presents. And two stockings laid out on each end of the couch. And one tiny one in the middle with a little cat on it for Clover.

"Wow," I say.

"Isn't this great?" Larry comes out of the kitchen with two mugs of cocoa.

"No smoothie?" I ask.

"It's Christmas!"

"Be right back." I go to my room to get the small pile of presents I have for Larry and Clover. I put them under the tree, and Larry and I dig into our stockings. Larry makes us take turns pulling one thing out at a time. There's some pretty crazy stuff in mine, including an Einstein bobblehead.

When Larry takes out gifts from his stocking, he looks genuinely surprised and thrilled about each one. Maybe Arielle gave him a pile of stuff to put in it before she left. Or maybe this year there really was a Santa Claus.

Clover races around the living room with her new catnip mouse while Larry and I finish. I get three chocolate Santas, a candy cane, and a bunch of other gag gifts from the comic store. A lot of them are karate-themed and totally embarrassing. Larry cracks up each time I pull something out, but he refuses to say he bought them. "Santa sure knows you!" he keeps saying.

Ho. Ho. Ho.

When we finish with our stockings, Larry turns up the Christmas classics he's got playing on his stereo and says it's time to stop for breakfast. He's been teaching me how to cook, so I help him whisk eggs for omelets and chop up a bunch of vegetables to go in them. We chow down in the living room, watching the blinking lights on the tree. Clover settles in between us, having wiped herself out from chasing her mouse all morning.

After breakfast, Larry takes our dishes and tells me to stay put when I offer to help wash up. I lean back and close my eyes. Everything about this morning feels right. Like I belong here. I can't remember the last time I felt like this. Like I'm really wanted. But that's how Larry makes me feel. Like he's glad I'm here. Not some mistake. Some burden. I know I should probably check my cell and see if my parents called, but right now, I just don't want to think about them. I just want to enjoy this moment. This day.

And then, as if I summoned it all just by bringing

them to mind, the buzzer goes off and Larry races over to press the button. "Perfect timing!" he yells into the little speaker. "Come on up!"

"Who is it?" I ask.

"Stay put. You have some surprise guests."

"What the hell?" I say. Because I know who it is and I am not happy and suddenly my merry Christmas feeling is gone.

"They miss you, Josh. Now try to look like you're glad to see them. They're nervous, and you'll make it worse."

Shit.

"I thought we agreed this wasn't part of my *journey*," I say, all whiny.

"I agreed you shouldn't go home. I didn't agree you shouldn't see your mom and dad. Now—" Larry puts his fingers to his mouth as if forcing his lips to make a smile, a direction for me to do the same.

"Shit," I say out loud.

"Don't say *shit* on Christmas. It's not nice." He walks over to the door and opens it. "Hey, guys!" he calls down to them.

I stand up and feel sick. One-on-one, my parents are fine. I know they love me in their weird way. Growing up, my mom and I spent time volunteering at a soup kitchen once a week. We had breakfast together on weekends while my dad slept off his hangovers. She made sure

I had money for food when she worked late. Whatever. She was fine. My dad and I spent our time hanging out in the garage while he worked on his van. Or eating crap food together while we watched crap TV. When I got older, he'd let me have one of his beers and we'd stay up late till he passed out on the couch.

Neither of my parents was ever mean to me. They never hit me. But they weren't exactly the model parents. And most noticeably, they spent almost zero time together. In fact, they made avoiding each other almost an art. My dad would be snoring on the couch before my mom got home from work, and then he'd be up and off to work the next morning before my mom woke up. This was just how it always was with them. The three of us in a room at the same time was a rare and therefore extremely awkward occurrence. I can only imagine how much more so this will be now.

Larry gives my mom and dad each a huge bear hug as they step into the apartment.

"Surprise!" my mom says, rushing over to me and pulling me close. She smells different. Her hair is down, which it never is, and she's had it colored or something, because there aren't any gray streaks in it anymore. And she's wearing makeup.

"You look fantastic, Sylvia!" Larry says to her.

She beams at me. "It's so good to see you, honey!"

"Joshy!" My dad gives me a guy half-hug. I notice he doesn't smell like his usual hangover at all. He steps back from me and looks me up and down. "You grew," he says.

"He's bulking up!" Larry says. "I've got him at practice five days a week plus weekends! He'll be a brown belt by year's end if it kills me."

Larry leads my parents into the living room. "Sit, sit," he says.

My mom rushes back over to the door and brings in the shopping bags my dad lugged up the stairs. "Just brought a few things for under the tree," she says. She pulls out some wrapped packages and arranges them with the other gifts.

"Let me make you some coffee and we'll get started," Larry says, leaving me alone with them.

I sit in Larry's usual chair and realize my hands are shaking. My parents sit across from me on the couch, carefully pushing our stocking stuff aside. But there's still so much crap to move, they end up sitting right next to each other. They're so close, their shoulders and legs are touching.

"What?" my mom asks.

"Huh?"

"You're staring at us," she says.

"Oh. Uh, I'm just, you know, surprised to see you." Especially together.

"We couldn't not see you on Christmas!" My mom looks so nervously happy. Like she's afraid I might yell at her.

Part of me wants to.

I don't know why. Not really. It was nice of them to come. To make the four-hour drive, they must have had to get up at, like, five in the morning. On Christmas. But ten minutes ago, I was feeling happy. And right now, I feel like I have a weight in my chest, pulling me back against the chair cushion. Trapping me.

"We wanted to bring Rosie, but she's having so much trouble getting around. We thought it might be too much," my mom says.

"Is she OK?" I ask.

"Oh, sure. She's fine. She's just getting old."

"She really misses you," my dad says. "She sleeps in your room every night."

"Really?"

My mom smiles, then gives my dad a warning look, I think to let him know he's going too far on the Rosie thing. Because I know my eyes are watering up, and I feel like the worst son on the planet for not visiting them all this time. Not even at Thanksgiving, which I spent with Larry volunteering at a homeless shelter, just like I used to do with my mom. I knew it would've made my mom proud, but I never even bothered to tell her. I never bother to tell them anything. But let's be honest. It's partly because in the past, they never asked.

My dad shifts uncomfortably on the couch. "So, you doin' all right?" he asks, changing the subject. "School OK?"

"Yeah," I say. "It's fine. I aced my midterms and everything."

"That's great! Wow. Aced 'em, huh?"

I try not to feel offended by how surprised he is, because mostly, he sounds proud. And that is a first.

"We're so impressed with how hard you're working, Josh," my mom says. "You're doing so well here." She looks happy and sad at the same time.

I'm not sure how to reply. I'm doing well in school, yeah. I'm doing well in karate. But am I doing well in life? Would she say that if she knew about the two a.m. wake-up calls? Would she say that if she knew me well enough to be able to look at me and see beyond my mask? Isn't that what most moms do? Instead, I feel like she's looking at me for the first time. Maybe they both are. At this new me they think they see — hope they see. But I'm not new. I'm the same old me. Why can't they see that?

Luckily, Larry comes back in to interrupt the most awkward conversation ever. "Coffee'll be ready in a jiff."

He sits on the arm of my chair. "How was the drive? Any traffic?"

"Nope. Interstate was dead," my dad says.

Larry nods.

My mom scans the apartment. She looks about as comfortable as I feel.

"So," Larry says. "How's the music goin', Hal?"

"Ah, you know. Same ole, same ole." My dad taps his hands on his knees. For a minute, I see him back home, sitting on the couch on that hot summer day when everything changed.

When I left the hospital that awful day, I walked all the way home. By the time I got there, I was dripping in sweat and all I wanted to do was stand under a cold shower. And maybe drown myself. Before I opened the screen door, though, I heard music coming from the living room. My dad was playing a lullaby he probably thought no one but Rosie could hear. I remember standing outside. Outside looking in. And wishing he would never stop.

"Why don't you open your gifts?" my mom suggests.

"Great idea!" Larry says. He hops up and grabs some presents and piles a bunch at my feet. Then he hands one to each of my parents.

Wait. How long has Larry known about this little secret?

I pick up a smallish box and check the tag: *For Josh From Mom & Dad.*

"Oh, wait," my mom says. "Why don't you save that one for last?"

"Here, open this!" Larry says, reaching over and choosing another package. "It's from me!"

It feels like a book, but when I open it, I pull out a picture frame. *What Is a True Karate Man?* is written in beautiful calligraphy.

"So you won't forget," Larry tells me. "Do you like it?"

I read the words I've finally been able to memorize. The words that define Larry. "Yeah," I say. "Yeah. It's great. Thanks!" I smile at him so he knows I mean it.

"I want you to hang it on the wall near your bed and read it every day," Larry says, getting all serious. "Because that's who you are, Josh. A true karate man."

I feel myself blush. Hardly.

"Let's see," my mom says, reaching for the frame. She and my dad read it at the same time. Larry beams at me.

"That's lovely," my mom says, handing the frame back. My dad nods quietly.

"Josh is making great progress," Larry says. "We should show you some of our moves after dinner."

That is so not going to happen. Karate seems cool when I'm with Larry and Stella. But the thought of doing katas in front of my dad seems totally lame.

"Here," I say, reaching for a package for Larry in an attempt to change the subject. "Open this." And please shut the hell up about karate. No offense.

Larry tears off the paper. It's a set of new white T-shirts, because I am so tired of his sweat-stained disgusting ones and I'm sure he is, too. He laughs, which seems like a good sign.

But all of this feels weird. Larry and I, we've been together for such a short time, but we already have all these private jokes and stuff. My parents and me? Zero. Zero private jokes. I know why they are here. They love me. And I love them. But I wish they had asked. I really wish they had asked. Because, selfish as it is, all I want to do is hang out with my uncle and share a few stupid private jokes and for one freaking day not think about anything else.

But that's not going to happen now.

Maybe it never was.

Maybe I don't deserve that day, anyway.

Chapter 20

I don't have any gifts to give my parents, because I mailed them all home and I guess they didn't arrive on time, because my parents didn't bring them. But of course Larry is prepared and urges them to open the gifts he handed out. For my dad: a set of guitar picks, a couple of CDs, and a new collar for Rosie. For my mom: a book he heard about on NPR, a pillow you heat up and put around your neck to de-stress, and some new slippers. Not bad.

Finally, I only have the one gift left from my parents. They already got me a bunch of great stuff. More than any other year. There are a few moments when I feel like they bought me extra gifts out of guilt, but I decide that's not it. I decide they just miss me. And I feel bad for being so mad at them.

"You guys really went overboard," I say.

My mom smiles at my dad. "It's not much, really."

I tear off the paper slowly and find another frame, similar to the one Larry gave me. But when I turn it over, I see a photo of me, Caleb, and Dave when we were little. Rosie's in it, too. She was just a puppy. I remember this was the day we adopted her and we were all playing with her in the front yard. In the photo, we're laughing like crazy. I've got my arms around Rosie, and she's reaching her head up, licking my face. I feel my mouth turn into a smile, just looking at us. But then I feel this horrible ache in the back of my throat. It's as if the three of us have come back from the past to remind me of how we used to be. What I left behind. What I lost. It makes me feel more lonely than I've felt since I got here.

"I was going through all the photos I never bothered to print," my mom says. "I was thinking of making some photo books, since Irene at work told me how easy it is. Anyway, I wanted to at least sort through the really special ones. And . . . well, I came across this, and I thought you'd like to have it."

"You boys were so inseparable," my dad says. "Little troublemakers." But he says it in a proud way.

"I love it," I say quietly. "Thanks."

"You're welcome." When my mom looks at me, I see something in her face I haven't seen in years. Maybe I've only seen it in pictures. It's not so much what I see, but what I don't see. What's not there anymore. The stress and worry that used to make her knit her eyebrows. She just looks . . . relieved. But I don't know why. Relieved that things turned out different for me than they did for her and my dad when they made the same mistake? Relieved that I'm here and not home, saddled to a girl I don't love and a baby I don't want?

She reaches out and puts her hand on my knee. It feels weird.

"This is so great!" Larry says enthusiastically. "Being all together for Christmas. Too bad Mom and Dad aren't here anymore, huh, Hal? They'd love this, man. Just love it."

My dad nods and gets a sad look on his face. He fidgets with a ribbon from one of my mom's presents. I keep watching them sitting next to each other, as if they belong that way. I can't believe the thought enters my brain, but maybe they do.

"How 'bout some eggnog while we put dinner together?"

"Oh, uh, me?" My dad's face turns a little red. "Nah."

"Since when have you ever turned down a drink, bro?"

My mom gets this really uncomfortable look on her face. It's the way she looked back at home all the time. Maybe things haven't changed that much after all.

"Uh, I'm kinda takin' it easy these days," my dad says.

Excuse me? I'm glad my dad doesn't see my mouth drop to the floor.

"Oh! Wow. Well. That's awesome, man! Hey, you should try these smoothies I make . . ." He grabs my dad's arm and pulls him up and toward the kitchen.

My mom glances over at me, relief flooding her face.

"Seriously?" I ask under my breath.

She nods. "Let's not make a big deal out of it, though. OK?" she whispers.

"But —"

"I know it *is,*" she interrupts. "Obviously. But I don't want him to be self-conscious about it. He's still struggling. A lot."

"Yeah. Of course."

"He's been so — determined. Since you left."

"What do you mean?"

"To be better. To prove to you —" She stops. "Oh, I don't know."

But I can tell she does. "What? Prove to me what?"

"That — that things —" She looks up at the ceiling, as if the words she's looking for are written up there. "That how things were — with your dad — with your dad and me, wasn't your fault. They didn't have anything to do with you. And that your life isn't over, Josh. Things can — things *will* — get better."

I hear Larry laugh in the kitchen and wonder what my dad just said.

"What, seventeen years from now? That's how long it took Dad to get over me ruining his life?"

"Why would you say that?" She looks genuinely hurt. "You didn't ruin anyone's life. Your dad and I were in love. We probably would have gotten married whether or not I got pregnant. Did you change things? Of course! We didn't have the same kind of freedom. But Josh, your presence isn't what pulled your dad and me apart."

"Then, what did?"

"I don't know."

"Yes, you do," I say. "Even if you don't want to admit it."

"You can believe what you want, Josh. But what difference does it make now? Do you know what matters? That we're here. Now. We love you." She wipes her wet cheeks with the back of her hand. "Your dad was heartbroken about what happened, don't you see that? He feels like he failed you. Didn't talk to you enough about how to be careful. It's killing him. We know why you wanted to leave. But that doesn't mean we were happy about it. We miss you. Nothing is the same without you."

"Yeah. Everything is *better.*"

"No!" She cringes at the sound of her raised voice. "No," she whispers.

"Yes, it is," I say. "Dad quit drinking? You took time off from work for Christmas? These aren't normal occurrences."

She sighs. "Fine. Things are getting better. But that's only because you showed us what matters. *You* did that. For the first time in years, we can finally see again. We can see how awful we were to each other and — to you, Josh. We weren't there for you when you needed us the most."

"You couldn't have done anything."

"We could have been there."

"You didn't know."

"Maybe if we'd paid more attention, we would have sensed something was wrong. We could have been there for you sooner. When you needed us."

"It's OK," I lie.

"No. It isn't."

We're both quiet for a minute, mulling that one over.

"But we want to be better now," she finally says. "Your dad is trying so hard. And I am, too. You're right. Things are different. Better. But we have a long, long way to go. And there's still something missing."

"What's that?"

She smiles at me in her sad way. "Isn't it obvious?"

I don't know what to say.

"You, of course. It's terrible not having you home with us." She looks like she's going to cry.

"I'm sorry," I say. "But I can't come home."

"I know, honey. I know." She leans toward me and hugs me and it feels awkward, but good, too.

"Why don't you show me your room?" she asks when she pulls away from me, wiping her eyes.

When we stand up, she puts her hand on my shoulder. "You've grown so much in just four months. I can't believe it." Her eyes get all watery again.

"C'mon, Mom. Get yourself together." I smile to show her I'm joking.

When we go into my room, my mom takes it all in. "I see Larry decorated it for you."

"Yeah, it's kind of like a shrine in here."

"Kind of," she says, looking at all the movies and trophies and other karate crap displayed on the bookcases.

"What happened here?" she asks, touching the rip in the Jackie Chan poster. "Did Larry get carried away?"

I shrug. "I don't know. It was already there," I lie. I'm getting good at this.

She shakes her head. "Your uncle is such a character."

"Yeah."

"But he's been good for you. I can tell."

"Yeah," I say again. "I guess so."

Yeah.

I guess he has.

She sits down on the edge of my bed. "It's so good to see you, honey. To see that you're all right."

I lean back against the wall, feeling her last words choke me.

This lie is just too big.

It's like we're pretending all over again, but instead of pretending that it's normal to never see each other, we're pretending it's normal to be together. Seeing each other. Only maybe we're not. Maybe we're only seeing the pretend us. She doesn't see the real me. She doesn't even know who the real me is.

"What's wrong?" she asks. Her worry line creases down the middle of her forehead.

She touches my arm, but I brush it off.

"I can't do this," I say. I understand now. This is why I didn't want them to come. This is why I didn't want to see them.

"What?" she asks.

"Pretend."

"But I thought—"

"That everything's fine," I say guiltily. "Yeah. I know."

"Josh, what's wrong?" She looks genuinely surprised to learn that maybe things aren't as rosy as she thought. And I feel bad. Because we played the game so well earlier.

Maybe that's what I've been doing since I got here. Except at night. Except when the baby wakes up and I freak out and—

"I thought you of all people would understand," I say. "What it's like. Why I'm here? Why I had to get away?"

"Josh, I—"

"Don't you wonder?" I ask.

"Wonder what?"

"About him," I say. "Your grandson. Don't you think about him? Doesn't it feel weird to know he's out there somewhere?"

She looks away from me, as if I just slapped her across the face. And I feel so bad. So bad when I know she's here because she loves me. But coming here was wrong. She should have asked. She should have talked to me and asked what *I* wanted for once. What I needed.

"Josh, I'm sorry," she says. "I thought you were—"

"*Better?* Right. Look at me, Mom! Where am I? Am I at high school with my best friends, living it up? No. I'm here. Yeah, I'm doing well in school. Whatever. But things are never going to be *fine*. OK? This isn't something I can just put behind me. It's in front of me. It's beside me. It's hanging over me. Can't you see that? It will *never* go away. For the rest of my life I have to carry this. Just like—just like Ellie. And it's all my fault."

She starts to cry.

"Don't!" I yell. And I feel like such a jerk for it. But it's not fair, her crying. She's not even supposed to be here.

"Hey," Larry says. He's standing in the doorway. "Everything OK?"

My mom wipes her eyes and shifts away from him so he can't see her face.

"Josh?"

"Yeah," I say. "Everything's OK. Everything's *fine*."

"It doesn't look fine."

"Maybe Josh is right. Maybe we shouldn't have come," my mom says.

He turns on me. "What? You said that?"

"Not exactly."

"What is *wrong* with you, Josh?" He walks over and sits next to my mom, putting his arm around her.

"I'm an asshole," I say.

He looks at me in disgust. No arguing there.

"Everything all right in here?" Now my dad is standing in the doorway. "Sylvie? What's wrong?"

I swear I haven't heard my dad use my mom's name, haven't heard him address her, even, since I was a little kid. And that's what's wrong. *That's* what's wrong.

"All of this!" I yell.

"Josh, please," Larry says.

My dad steps back, confused.

"Just forget it," I say. "I'm sorry."

My mom wipes her face dry. Larry stands up, then looks like he doesn't know where to go. My dad stays in the doorway.

"Let's just go make dinner," Larry says. So we follow him out of my temporary room and into the kitchen. Only not my dad. My dad sits down on the couch and stares at the Christmas tree as though it is the most fascinating thing he's ever seen.

And now — yeah — *now* it feels like old times.

Chapter 21

"You're *really* harshing my mellow, Josh," Larry hisses at me.

My mom sits at the kitchen table, looking destroyed.

"I'm sorry," I say. I sit down across from my mom. "Really," I tell her. "I didn't mean what I said."

She shakes her head. "Yes, you did," she says quietly. "And you're right, Josh. I could have tried harder." She reaches out to touch my hand. "But I wish you would talk to me. How can I know what's going on with you if you never talk to me? I call and you sound OK. But how can I tell over the phone?"

"I'm sorry," I say again. I know it sounds lame, even though I am. "I'm glad things are getting better for you and Dad. Really."

So why do I feel so pissed off about it?

"Thank you, honey." She pulls her hand back and sits up straighter.

"Well," Larry says, as if that's that. "From now on, Josh is going to talk to Sylvie once a week. *Really* talk. Glad that's settled. Now come here." He spreads his arms out and motions with his hands for us to get up. I roll my eyes.

"C'mon, c'mon," he says.

My mom smiles shyly and gets up, so I do, too. Larry reaches out and grabs our hands, then pulls us together into an awkward three-person hug. God.

"All better," he says, practically squeezing the life out of me. I realize this is a warning.

I slap his back heartily. "Yeah, all better."

"Now, let's get cookin'." He hands us each a red apron with a candy cane on the front. Clearly, nothing is going to stop him from making this the *Best! Christmas! Ever!*

We spend the rest of the morning and part of the afternoon making a huge Christmas dinner together. At some point, my dad falls asleep on the couch in the living room, just like old times. But me, my mom, and Larry continue to cut and chop and stir in the kitchen. At first it's awkward, what with the memory of my semi-outburst hanging over us. But Larry is good at bringing people around. Even me. And pretty soon things get less uncomfortable.

We make garlic mashed potatoes, green bean casserole, butternut squash with butter and brown sugar, carrots glazed with maple syrup, and homemade dinner rolls. Larry even makes roast beef with gravy for my parents and me, even though he's a vegetarian. For dessert, we make gingerbread with homemade whipped cream.

"Larry, you're a miracle worker," my mom says. "I can't believe how much you've taught Josh."

"He's a natural! My little karate-chopper sidekick."

So not funny.

With all the food in the oven and simmering on the stove, the kitchen is hot and smells amazing. My mom's cheeks are pink from the heat. I can't get over how much younger she looks. And happier. Every time she passes me, she touches my arm or my shoulder, as if to be sure of me. Each touch feels like a silent *I'm sorry.* And maybe even *I love you.* It reminds me of how Caleb's mom touches him. I used to wonder what that felt like. To be that close and comfortable around each other. Now I know. It feels nice.

This is probably the most time we've spent together since I was a little kid. No lie. But even though I'm glad it's finally happening, I still feel this annoying seed of anger that won't go away. I want to ask her what took her so long to get here. Not here, in this kitchen, but here in this new *place.* Where she *wants* to see me. Where she wants to be sure of me. Instead of rushing out of the house to go to work. To volunteer. To see a friend. To see anyone but my dad and me. Is it easier to act this way here, in this home that isn't ours, that is only temporary?

That's when I realize why I feel angry. Because her being here is a constant reminder that *here* isn't my real life. My real home. And in a few months, I'm going to have to leave it.

"So, Sylvia," Larry says quietly to my mom after peeking out the door to the living room to make sure my dad's still asleep. "What's with Hal not drinking? Is that for real?"

My mom glances over at me, then taps the whisk she was using to stir the gravy against the side of the pan. The brown sauce dribbles down through the wires. My mom studies it like it's the most fascinating thing in the world. But I can tell what she's really doing is choosing her words carefully, because we both know Larry is asking for me.

"Yes. It's for real," she says.

I smile back at her, because I want her to know I'm glad. I really am. I can be angry and glad at the same time, right?

"He's been walking, too," she says. "Every day. He takes Rosie out when he gets home from work. They've both lost weight. Could you tell, Josh?"

I wipe my hands on my apron. "Yeah," I say. "Definitely." I try to imagine my dad actually walking anywhere. Rosie, too. It seems so . . . un-Hal-like.

"He has a long way to go, of course," my mom adds. She gets a sad look on her face. "But this is a big first step. And I'm trying really hard to be . . . supportive. I know I haven't been much help in the past."

Larry opens the oven to check on the roast beef for the millionth time. "You're the best thing that happened to old Hal, Sylvie. You really are. Well, besides Joshy here." Larry reaches over to ruffle my hair.

My mom smiles weakly. "Things are better," she says quietly. Almost guiltily.

"Better all around," Larry says, reaching over to squeeze my arm. The guy can't seem to stop touching me all of a sudden. Maybe it's contagious.

"Yeah," I say, ignoring Larry's hand. I try to sound more convincing than I did earlier. In so many ways, things actually are. Better. But this day feels so unreal. My parents here. My dad not drinking. My mom not running away from us. It seems too good to be true. And I feel like I'm waiting for the sucker punch that takes it all away.

Chapter 22

The kitchen smells amazing by the time we're finished. Larry brings out a bunch of serving dishes while my mom goes into the living room to wake up my dad. I stand in the kitchen doorway and watch her walk over to him and put her hand on his shoulder. When he opens his eyes and sees her, he looks confused for just a second, then smiles awkwardly. I can't hear what she whispers to him, but he nods and gets up. They are still so formal with each other. Not like you would imagine a longtime married couple would be. It's like they still don't quite know how to talk to each other. I'm glad they're trying. I am. But watching them like this makes me feel so empty and alone. So I go back into the kitchen and help Larry.

Just before we're about to sit down for dinner, there's a knock on the door and Larry announces we're having more surprise guests. That Larry. He's just full of surprises.

It's Stella, Star, and Calvin. Stella looks even more pissed off at her mom than she did last night.

"It smells so gooooood in here," Calvin says.

Star clutches his arm. "Thanks for inviting us, Larry. That was so sweet of you."

Larry introduces my parents to everyone. Then Calvin and Star join my dad on the couch.

"Merry Christmas," Stella says to me. She's wearing the Santa hat again.

"You, too," I say.

She glances toward her mom and Calvin uncomfortably, then back at me. "He spent the night," she mouths, a disgusted look on her face.

I wish I could hug her. She looks like she needs one. Instead, Larry puts his arm around her and whispers something in her ear. She laughs weakly and follows him into the kitchen to help bring out some hors d'oeuvres. We still have some folding chairs from last night's party, so we all squish around the coffee table. Larry turns up the cheesy Christmas music and tries to come up with stuff to talk about. My mom actually tells some pretty funny stories about the old people she works with at the nursing home. And my dad shares a few crazy stories from the body-shop place he runs, about people totaling their cars doing stupid stuff while they were driving. His favorite is the guy who was brushing his teeth in traffic.

I notice that Stella keeps watching Calvin as if she would like to spar with him. I catch her mom giving her warning looks to "behave," but Stella ignores her.

When Larry finally announces it's time for dinner, we load up our plates in the kitchen and come back out to our seats in the living room. The food is delicious, and everyone's quiet while we stuff our faces. Larry doesn't offer any wine or eggnog or booze of any sort, and I think Calvin and Stella seem a bit disappointed, especially when Larry was so generous with the stuff at last night's party. But I'm grateful to Larry for keeping it dry, for my dad's sake.

After dinner, Star and Calvin help clean up and then say they should be going. Stella asks if she can stick around for a while, and they seem eager to let her. When they leave, she leans against the door and takes a deep breath with her eyes closed, like she's trying to keep herself from crying.

"You OK?" I ask.

She opens her eyes and shrugs. "I guess. I just wish she'd sent him home last night so we could have Christmas morning, just the two of us. But of course my mom's so afraid he'll dump her if she disappoints him. It's pathetic. I don't see what she sees in him, anyway."

"He seems to genuinely like her," I try. "Maybe he'll be different from the others."

"He better be." She takes my arm and leads me back to the living room. My mom eyes the hand on my arm and raises her eyebrows. But I act like I don't notice.

My dad gets up from the couch and stretches. "Guess we better hit the road," he says. My mom gets up, too. They seem smaller to me, and not just because I've grown. Not smaller in a bad way, just . . . more like two parts of a whole.

"Are you sure you can't stay over?" Larry asks. "You've already driven so much today."

My dad puts his arm on my mom's shoulder. "Nah, we'll be fine. I got a nice nap in, and we'll stop for coffee at some point. We gotta get back to Rosie. Josh's friend Caleb was going to walk her at lunchtime, but she'll need to go out again tonight."

Larry hugs them good-bye and I walk them out to the hall.

"It was so good to see you, honey," my mom says. "Anytime you want us to visit, just let us know and we'll come. And you know you can come back home whenever you want."

My dad puts his huge paw of a hand on my shoulder. "You need any money, son?"

"Nah, Dad. I'm good."

"Larry says you finished all your college applications," my mom says. "I wish you'd have let me help. I would've been happy to, you know."

"It's fine, Mom. The school has a really good guidance counselor who helped us put everything together."

She looks sad. Like she feels left out. "You didn't even tell us where you were applying. I hope you didn't apply to anywhere too far away?"

I shake my head. I don't want to tell her that's exactly what I did. Especially not now, when she seems on the verge of tears again.

My dad pats my shoulder a few times. "We're real proud of you, Josh," he says. "I know it's rough, bud. But you're doin' good here. I can tell."

"Thanks, Dad. I—I'm proud of you, too."

I think I embarrassed him, because he turns away and picks up their bags. I didn't mean to. I just . . . I wanted him to know.

"Give Rosie a pat for me," I say. My voice cracks just a little as that ache in my throat comes back. I hug them fast, because it is really time for them to go. Really. Time.

I watch them climb down the stairs. They both look up at me from the floor below and wave. "Drive carefully!" I call. "Don't brush your teeth or anything!"

"Merry Christmas, honey," my mom says.

And then they're gone.

Chapter 23

I take my time going back inside. When I finally do, I find Stella and Larry sitting on the couch. Stella is leaning over, her face in her hands, and Larry is rubbing her back.

Stella sits up and wipes her eyes when she hears me come in.

"Time for cocoa," Larry says. He gets up and leaves us.

"What happened?" I ask.

She slides over a bit, so I sit next to her.

"I guess I'm more upset than I thought," she says. "I'll be OK. I just wish . . . I wish for once she'd put *me* first. You know? It makes me feel like she doesn't care."

"I'm sure she does," I say lamely.

She shakes her head. "I know. She just has a warped way of showing it sometimes. Your parents seem real nice, though."

"Yeah," I say. "They're OK."

"At least they came to see you, right?"

"True."

"But?"

"They've got their own issues, that's all."

We both lean our heads back and look up at the ceiling.

"What kind of issues?" Stella asks.

"My dad used to drink a lot."

"Oh. But he stopped?"

"Looks like it. I don't think he was an alcoholic or anything. But he used to drink a lot on the weekends."

"What made him stop?"

Me.

"I don't know."

"Your parents have been married for a long time, huh?"

"Yup."

"That's cool. You're like, one of the only people I know whose parents are still together."

"Me, too, actually. I always thought they would end up getting a divorce, but they're hanging on."

"Why did you think that?"

"They used to avoid each other like the plague. Today was the first time the three of us have spent more than a few minutes together in years."

"Wow."

"Yeah. Guess I should have left home a long time ago."

She elbows me. "I'm sure that's not true."

Well, not totally. But sort of.

Larry comes in with a tray of mugs, and we all take sips of cocoa in silence. Larry leans back on the couch and says, "You know, for the most part, this was one of the best Christmases ever. With the exception of your mom dissing you for that dude. No offense, Stell."

She rests her head on his shoulder and sighs. "None taken."

He pats her knee. "Whaddaya say we watch a movie? I'll make popcorn."

"Larry, how can you even think about eating after that huge dinner?"

He shrugs. "I think it is physically impossible for me to watch a movie without stuffing my face. No matter how sick I feel later."

"Well, I'm game," Stella says.

"As long as it's not Jackie Chan, I'm in," I say.

"What do you mean?"

"Not everyone shares your love for Jackie."

"How is that even possible?" he asks seriously. "Never

mind. I have the perfect choice just for Stella," he says, acting all fake-mad at me. He jumps up and runs down the hall to my room, then comes back waving a *Rocky* DVD in his hand.

"Stell-aah!" he cries, shaking it in her face.

"You do know Rocky's girlfriend's name is Adrian, right?" I ask Larry.

"I know, I know," Larry says. "But I just like saying it. Stellllaaaaa," he cries again, just to prove it.

We all get comfortable and start watching, but after about ten minutes, Stella jumps when her phone vibrates. She reads the message and frowns.

"Uh, sorry guys. I think I'm gonna call it a night."

"Oh, Stell. You're not leaving us for another guy, are you?"

"Cute as you are, Larry. Sorry."

"Say hi to *Britt* for us," Larry says.

"Don't say his name like that," she says.

"Like what?"

Stella looks at me.

"Like *shit*," I explain.

Larry laughs.

"Shut up," Stella says.

"They do sound the same," I try.

"You two are so funny I forgot to laugh." She gets up to go, then turns back. "Merry Christmas, boys. Wish I could stay." The funny thing is, the way she looks at us just then, I think she really does.

"Well, that was a little ironic, don'tcha think?" Larry asks when she's gone.

"What do you mean?"

"Hmm. Stella's mad at her mom for blowing her off for some guy and . . . there she goes doing the same thing to us!"

"It's not really the same thing," I say.

Larry sighs. "Close enough."

When I wake up later, I'm sweating.

The baby was screaming. In my dream. He was crying in his little plastic bed next to all the other new babies, and the nurses were ignoring him, and all the parents smiling through the glass were too busy admiring their own babies to care. I pounded on the glass to get the nurses' attention, but they didn't look up. I kept pounding and pounding. And then I saw her. Ellie. The room had a glass wall on the opposite side, and she was behind it, pounding on the glass just like me. I could tell by the way her mouth was open that she was screaming. "I want my baby!" over and over. Her fists were white crescents against the glass. She was crying. Sobbing. I pounded harder, too.

That's when she saw me. Recognized me. And

screamed, "No!" She shook her head, then pounded on the glass even harder. So hard the glass smashed. Some nurses ran over to her. Someone grabbed her and started pulling her away. I pounded harder on my own glass wall to get them to stop. I pounded and pounded until the glass wall broke on my side, too. I could feel my fist scrape through the shards, ripping the skin open. But they ignored me and took her away.

I woke up and found teeth marks in my hand.

Now, in this room hundreds of miles away from that real place of my dreams, I still hear the screaming.

It is above me. It doesn't stop like it usually does. I get up and pace the floor. Waiting for someone to soothe him. But he just keeps crying. Why the hell doesn't someone help him? I pace faster. I cover my ears. But he's still screaming.

I punch Jackie Chan's face. I punch every inch of that ridiculous poster until I punch one of the thumbtacks sticking out of the wall and cut my hand. Then I punch harder. I punch it and punch it, getting blood all over that stupid face until Larry comes running in and pulls me backward, wrapping his huge arms around me. He hugs me so hard I can hardly breathe. I am sobbing. Choking. But he holds on and tells me it's OK. It's OK. Until finally the screaming stops, and Larry lets go of me. We sit on the floor, leaning against my makeshift bed, panting.

"You can tell me you're fine a thousand times, Josh. But you're not. You need help."

I fall back onto my bed, still shaking.

"I know," I say.

I know.

Larry grabs a tissue from the box on the bookcase and I press it against my hand to stop the bleeding. "Tell me what happened," he says.

"You know what happened."

"Yeah. I do."

"Then what's the point?"

"Maybe I need to hear it from you. Someday, you're going to have to talk about it."

"Why?"

"Because it's the only way to get over it."

"I can't," I say. "I'm not like you. I'm not — good, like you." I see Ellie again. Pounding on the glass. And her mouth, forming the word *No.*

He sighs and puts his strong arm across my back, squeezing my shoulder hard.

"You are in your heart, Josh. I know you are. And I'm going to lift you up. I'm going to lift you out of this."

A true karate man lifts those who have fallen, no matter how low. I can imagine him thinking this as he looks at me. That he's going to be a true karate man and get me out of this mess. But he doesn't know everything that happened. He doesn't know what I did. He doesn't know how low I've gone.

I turn away from him. "I just need to be alone," I say.

"That's the last thing you need."

"Please." I cover my face with my hands.

I feel him hovering nearby. Waiting. Wondering what a true karate man would do.

"Please," I say again.

He sighs. "I'm here when you're ready, Josh. I just want you to know that."

"I know," I say. "Thanks."

When I'm sure he's gone, I pull Stella's rock out of its box and squeeze it. But I don't talk to it. I don't want her to hear what I'm thinking. I just need to feel . . . something. As the rock warms in my hand, my eyes get heavy. Clover climbs up from the foot of the bed and rubs the side of her head against my face, then settles down next to me, purring. I try to go back to sleep, but every time I close my eyes, I see Ellie. Silently screaming. *No.*

If they knew the whole story, they wouldn't be here.

Not Larry. Not Stella. Not even my parents.

None of them would.

Not even the damn cat.

PART THREE

MARCH

Yet one who strengthens his hands
to lift those who have fallen,
no matter how low.

—Gichin Funakoshi (1868–1957)

Chapter 24

"If the envelope is big, that's good news," Jason tells me as we hurry down the hall after our last class. "If it's thin, don't even bother to open it."

For the past few weeks, everyone at school has been obsessed with college acceptances, even though it's only March. You can tell who all the early-acceptance people are, because they walk around without a care. Everyone else seems completely stressed, especially the ones who tried for early acceptance and didn't get it.

"My parents are totally freaking out," Jason says. "I swear my mom's going to have a nervous breakdown if I don't get an acceptance letter soon."

"I'm sure you'll get your top choice," I say.

"Thanks." He hikes his backpack over his shoulder again. It's so stuffed with books, it keeps slipping off.

"What about you?" he asks. "Any news?"

"Nah," I say. I don't add that I'm starting to freak out just like everyone else. Maybe even more so. But not because I care about *which* school I get into so much as whether or not I get into *any* school.

We don't talk for the rest of our walk to the library, where we find our usual table and get to work. This is our basic routine, now that Jason finally accepted the fact that he is never going to be included in the after-school meet-ups with the in-crowd. Sometimes we hang out on the weekend and catch a movie or something. Stella is still seeing *Britt,* and therefore not allowed to be seen with me outside of karate practice. Larry and Arielle spend every spare moment together, and while they always make an effort to invite me to go out with them and their friends, I know they're just being nice. Who wants to hang out with a dopey seventeen-year-old on a Saturday night? I know I wouldn't.

Besides, even though Jason isn't the kind of person I would've been friends with back home, this isn't home. And I'm not that guy anymore.

I spend about a half hour rereading the same paragraph before I decide to call it quits. Stella and I are testing for our purple belts tonight, and I'm really worried about passing. The test requires us to demonstrate bow katas, which are the hardest for me. Stella's bow is smaller than mine, and we just seem more out of sync when we practice them together. Stella says the bow makes her feel like a warrior. She's amazing at handling hers. But mine just feels like this thing I'm wielding around awkwardly. Larry, of course, says we're both naturals.

But the only reason we do so well compared to most of the others is because we come to practice all the time. Most people can make it to class only once a week, so it takes them way longer to memorize and master the katas to earn each belt. Sometimes I worry that we're moving up a little too fast, but it makes Larry happy. Stella seems as crazed about us moving up as he is. It would suck if she passed and I didn't. I would like to say this is just because I'm competitive, but I know there's a lot more to it than that. If Stella moved ahead, we wouldn't stand next to each other in the same row anymore. And I've come to really like being next to her, even if that's as close as we'll ever get. Maybe *because* that's as close as we'll ever get. It's safer that way.

I say good-bye to Jason, who offers to come cheer me on at the test, but I tell him it would only make me more nervous.

At practice, I start stretching while Larry and I wait for everyone else to arrive. Stella comes in late as usual.

Britt brings her to practice now. I don't know why, but I assume it's so he can spend more time with her. I've noticed she brings her karate equipment bag to school with her. This means she must go off with him after school and then he takes her straight to practice. God forbid she spend any time alone with her pre-Britt friends. Or me. I just hope this is her choice as much as it is his. Because otherwise? I would be starting to worry.

"Hey," Stella says, coming up next to me. I can tell she's been crying again. She's always coming to practice with red eyes.

"Hey," I say. "What happened this time?"

"This time?" She's annoyed. She's always annoyed when I ask her that.

"Never mind," I say. "Are you OK?"

"Yes," she says firmly. And we drop it.

Larry comes bouncing over to us in his happy puppy-dog way. "Tonight's the night!" he says. "Purple!"

After we do our stretches, Larry asks each person testing for a belt to perform the required katas. Jacob and some other black belts are there to help judge us and decide if we should pass. When it's time to spar, I get nervous, as usual. Stella and I bow to each other.

"Remember, don't think you have to win. Think you don't have to lose," Larry says, referring to another precept.

“We nod, then start our pivoting dance, waiting for each other to look the wrong way for a split second so we can get a hit.

“Come on, now, someone make a move!” Larry says as he pivots around us.

I feel a sharp pain on my shin. Stella grins at me. Larry blows his whistle and makes us step back.

“Stop treating her like a girl, Sammy,” he says to me. “Show us your skills.”

We go back and forth, each of us getting OK hits on the other after that. By the time Larry finally lets us stop, we’re both covered in sweat. But it’s over. One by one, Larry calls us each up and presents us with our new belts. After all the belts are handed out, we untie the ones we have on, drape them over our necks, and tie on our new ones. Then Larry gives a little speech about how proud he is of all of us, but especially me and Stella, which is embarrassing, but also nice.

I keep thinking about my old life and how I never, ever would have done something like this there. I would have said it was lame and gone out drinking with Caleb and Dave instead. But here, there’s something about Larry that makes me want to try harder. At everything. “You need to strengthen your hands, Josh,” he’s always saying. It’s part of the saying we do at the beginning of each class. I’m supposed to strengthen my hands so that I can "lift those who have fallen, no matter how low." Larry always holds out his own hands when he says this. Just like my dad's, they are enormous. Like baseball mitts. It's like he was born to lift people. Even me.

Larry passes around a plate of brownies he made and we all congratulate one another. Stella punches me in the arm and says, "Great job."

"You, too," I say, punching her back.

"Save that for sparring," Larry says. "Arms are for hugging."

Stella makes a gagging gesture.

"Very ladylike," Larry tells her.

"Don't treat me like a girl," Stella says.

"Touché."

Yes. He really said *touché*. Unbelievable.

After the last kid gets picked up, the three of us finish cleaning up and head for home. At least Stella still walks home with us. Maybe Britt's OK with it because Larry's with us, so it's not like we're alone together. Who knows.

On the way home, Larry's pumped about us getting our brown belts by the end of the year. There isn't a whole lot more to learn to move up, and we both did really well on tonight's test, so we're pumped, too. "You guys are the best students I've ever had," Larry tells us. "I'm not just saying that."

Stella and I goof around, doing a bunch of exaggerated crescent kicks and blocks as we walk down the sidewalk while Larry cheers us on.

"That's because we have the best instructor on earth!" Stella calls over her shoulder.

"Yeah, baby!" Larry yells back

When we get to our building, I notice my face feels weird. I rub my mouth and realize it's because I've been smiling the whole way home.

Larry calls Arielle to say good night, and I head to my room and check my phone.

Caleb: r u coming home 4 spring brk?

Dave: SPRING BRK PARTAY!!!!!!

My mom: Can't wait to c u soon!

No, no, and sorry.

I told Larry I wanted to stay here for break. I expected him to say, "Of course. It's part of your journey," but instead he just said it was my decision. I get the feeling Larry is starting to wonder about my journey and where I'm headed. He tried to get me to start seeing a therapist back in December, but I refused. Then he tried to *be* my therapist, but that didn't really work out, either. He showed me this picture book he loved as a little kid. It's called *We're Going on a Bear Hunt.* It's about all these obstacles these kids come to on their journey to find a bear. Why they want to find a bear, I don't even know. But basically they learn that they can't go over some obstacle and they can't go under it; they have to go through it.

"Josh," Larry said. "This is where you are. You are on a quest to face your bear. You are trying too hard to get over something, but the whole point is that you can't. You can only go through it."

And that ended our one-and-only fake-therapy session.

Because I'm not five.

"Knock, knock," Larry says, standing in my open doorway.

I close my cell and look up at him.

"Just wanted to say good night."

"'Night," I say.

"You doin' OK?"

"Yeah."

He always asks me. And I always answer the same, even when I don't know if it's true.

When he leaves, I open my phone again and find the picture of Rosie and the Christmas tree. I leave it open and put it next to the picture of Dave, Caleb, and me that I keep on the nightstand next to the clock. Then I get out Stella's rock and turn off the light. I stare up at the stars and Larry's smiley face. Sometimes if I concentrate really hard on something — anything — else, I can manage to get myself into a deep sleep and doze through the two o'clock wake-up. That, and Larry gave me this nasty-tasting herbal stuff that helps me sleep. He thinks the baby will start sleeping through the night pretty soon, and everything will get easier.

Maybe.

I close my eyes and picture Stella and me punching the air as we walked down the sidewalk. I picture her laughing at me. And me, finally laughing back. And I think, maybe there's a chance. Maybe she'll wake up tomorrow and realize there is more to life than *Britt*. Maybe she'll see me as more than a karate partner and secret friend she shares a rock with.

Maybe.

But when I fall asleep, it's not Stella I dream of, it's Ellie.

Ellie behind glass.

Silently screaming.

No.

And I wake up the same way I always do. In a cold sweat. Shaking. Remembering that night, and all the awful ones that followed.

No.

The word she should have said out loud.

The word I felt, but ignored.

The word that could have saved us.

No.

Chapter 25

Larry hired Stella and me to help him teach karate camp during spring break. I don't think I'm very good with kids, but Larry says part of being a true karate man is sharing your skills and rising to the challenge. OK, then.

On Monday morning, the classroom is insane. All the little kids are running around, pulling on one another's belts, making karate chops in the "air," but actually making contact.

"There is no first strike in karate!" Larry quotes. But the kids don't listen.

"Accidents arise from negligence!" Stella quotes back.

Larry looks like he wants to hug her. But the scene is still mayhem.

Two kids start crying within the first twenty minutes. Finally, Larry yells, *"Line up!"* in this huge voice I've never heard him use before, and all the kids practically jump out of their skins and start circling around because they have no idea how to line up. Larry explains.

Stella and I are the highest in rank for this class, so we stand in the front row facing Larry. All the kids are quiet as Larry talks them through how the class will run. Then he has us kneel, facing him. "Stella, what is a true karate man?"

"What is a true karate man?" Stella says.

"What is a true karate man?" we repeat. As we say the words, I watch Larry. Larry, the true karate man. I think about my life so far this year. How amazingly different it's been. Back at home, the biggest excitement of the week was stealing beer from the fridge, picking up Caleb and Dave, and driving to some parking lot and getting wasted before we set out to find a party. For a while, that seemed to be all that mattered. Until last winter. Then it was all about finding a place where we could be alone. To drink and think and — in my case — forget.

Since I came to Larry's, I haven't been wasted once. I haven't even missed it.

"The ultimate aim in karate, therefore," Stella says, "lies not in victory or defeat, but in the perfection of the character of its participants."

Larry beams at all the kids, like their characters are getting more perfect at this very moment. He grins at me, as if to tell me mine is, too.

Larry claps his hands, and we get to our feet. Then he has me and Stella demonstrate some basic moves from the first kata for all the kids to practice. Larry has us walk around the room and assist the ones who need extra help. One kid gives Stella a high block to the chest, and she falls over backward. Larry goes running over, but she's OK. I make a point to keep my groin and the rest of my body out of whacking distance.

During lunch break, we sit on the floor and eat. The room smells disgusting once the various bologna and tuna-fish sandwiches come out. The few girls in the class all pile next to Stella and watch her eat as if she's the girl version of Jackie Chan. Only one kid bothers to sit next to me. A little boy with glasses and a sniff.

"I have a pet rat," he tells me. *Sniff.*

Gross.

"That's nice," I say.

"No. He got his tail bit off from my cat." *Sniff.*

"Oh. That's too bad."

"My dad likes rats."

"Hmm. But I don't think your cat does."

"Nope." *Sniff.*

As we discuss the length of the rat's tail, Stella looks

up from her groupies and winks at me, like she approves of my sitting with the creepy kid. When she does that, it feels worth it.

For the second half of the class, Larry tries to liven things up by having the kids take turns sparring. All the safety equipment is way too big for them, and they look like backward Ninja Turtles behind their chest protectors. A few kids seem to have a pretty good natural talent, but most are so wound up from the cookies Larry shared with everyone at lunch that they kick and block like maniacs.

Finally, Larry tells me and Stella to suit up and show them how it's really done.

We get our gear on and face each other. "Ready to go down?" Stella asks.

"Are you?"

She grins.

Larry gives us the signal and we start to pivot in a tight circle, watching each other for the "tells" we've both learned to look for. As soon as Stella's eyes go to my fists, I know she's going to swing. If she looks at my shoulder, I know that's her target for a kick to the solar plexus. I block several attempts before I make a move.

"Remember what the outcome of battle depends on!" Larry shouts at us.

"How we handle weakness and strength!" recites Stella, then kicks at my head.

"Go after her, Josh!" Larry says. "Get some kicks in!"

I make a feeble attempt to get a kick at her side, but she easily blocks me.

"You won't hurt me," she says. "Just do it."

But I don't want to. This is the one part of karate that I really can't stand. The only person I think I would get any enjoyment out of sparring with is *Britt*.

The little kids start to chant our names. "Stell-a-Stell-a. Jo-osh-Jo-osh." The *Stell-a*s are way louder.

Stella nails me in the knee with a kick when I'm distracted by Rat Boy pumping his fist in the air and screaming *"Go, Josh, go!"*

Larry separates us and lets us catch our breath.

"See what happened here?" he asks the kids. "Sparring is all about anticipation and determination." They stare back at him blankly.

"It's not about fighting," he says. "This isn't fighting. Karate is an aid to justice." Larry is a master at sneaking in the precepts today.

But the kids aren't really listening. You can see the hunger for a fight in their little eyes.

"OK, you two, let's go again."

Stella lifts her fists and nods at me. "Just try," she says.

We pivot back and forth in a jerky motion.

"C'mon!" she says, egging me on. The kids pick up their chanting.

The second Stella pauses to acknowledge her groupies with a cocky nod, I take the opportunity to get a nice kick to the hip. Only it feels like I kicked too hard.

"Sorry!" I say, without thinking.

"Remember, accidents arise from negligence!" Larry yells. He separates us again, and explains how I got that one off because Stella wasn't expecting it. She let herself get distracted. The little kids who were cheering for her look at the floor, shamefaced.

Finally, we get to stop. As we're taking off our gear, Stella punches my arm. "You need to get some balls," she tells me. "I'm not some fragile bird. I can take it."

I know that. I know it.

But I don't want to hit her. Or kick her. I just want to move with her like we do when we're practicing katas. Like we're dancing some dance only the two of us know. A dance that brings us closer than if we were holding each other in a slow dance. There's no touching. No danger. No risk. And even though there's no music, there is a rhythm anyway. We are the only ones who can hear it. As we move, it's like we're gathering power together. Like we could take on the world.

It's the only time I feel like that. Ever. Like I'm strong

enough to take whatever comes next. Like I could be a true karate man after all.

But maybe Stella doesn't notice all that.

Maybe it's just me.

Maybe that's for the best.

Chapter 26

Stella, Larry, and I spend the rest of the week getting the kids in shape. On Friday, Larry plans a ceremony for the parents to come to, and the students demonstrate the moves they've learned. They're not ready for their yellow belts yet, but you can bet all of them are begging their parents to sign them up for classes now. This is how Larry stays in business, I'm sure.

Larry gives all the kids special little trophies for their efforts. He calls each one to the front of the room, and when they bow to him to receive their reward, I have to admit, it's pretty cute.

After class, Larry says he's taking us out for dinner to thank us for helping him all week.

Stella looks uneasy. "I'm not sure," she says, fingering her cell phone.

"Give me that thing," Larry says, pulling it away. "You're always racing over to check it. Who are you messaging, anyway? Friends? A boyfriend?"

"None of your business."

"But you'll come?"

"I'm not sure . . . I told Britt . . ."

Larry rolls his eyes. "There's nothing wrong with letting your karate instructor take you out for a thank-you dinner. Tell him I have a girlfriend, and anyway, I'm not a pervert."

She slaps him lightly. "Britt doesn't think that."

"Then what's the problem?"

She glances over at me. "Nothing. It's just . . . Never mind. You'll think it's stupid."

Larry looks shocked. "I would never!"

"We have a phone date every night."

Larry's mouth drops open. "TMI!"

"Not phone *sex*! God, Larry. Just . . . to talk."

Larry makes a big deal of sighing with relief. "I'm sure *Britt* can miss one little phone date. Can't he?"

I doubt it.

"Stop saying his name like that," Stella says.

Larry sighs dramatically again. "I can't help it!"

I stifle a laugh.

Stella shakes her head at us, then shoves her phone in her bag. "Fine. Take us to dinner. I hope you have a lot of cash, because you just convinced me to order the most expensive thing on the menu."

"Yay!" Larry hugs her.

We walk a few blocks to this cool Spanish place that serves tapas, and Larry orders a bunch of things for us to try. Every dish is incredible. Larry makes a big deal of trying to come up with new ways to describe each one and makes Stella and me crack up.

But every five minutes or so, Stella checks her phone, and I can tell it's driving Larry nuts.

"What does he text you, anyway?" Larry asks.

"Oh, nothing," Stella says. She flips her phone closed and puts it back in her bag.

"Come on, tell me one thing."

Stella blushes. "No. It's private."

"Does he say he loves you?"

"Sure."

"Does he say . . . Hope you're having fun?"

Stella looks at me.

"Drop it, Lar," I say.

He throws up his hands. "OK, OK. I'm sorry, Stell. We can't always choose who we fall in love with. Love is a crazy thing."

He glances from me to Stella in an embarrassingly obvious way. He just can't seem to help himself.

"Speaking of love," Stella says, "how are things going with *your* girlfriend?"

Larry gets all dreamy. "She's working late. She had a private class with some company downtown that wants their employees to be less stressed. She was doing a two-hour session with them, and then she's going to train a few select employees so they can run yoga sessions a few times a week. Cool company, huh?"

Stella nods.

"Aaand . . ." Larry says, motioning for us to lean forward so he can tell us a secret. "I've made a big decision."

"What is it?" Stella whispers loudly.

Larry smiles his goofy smile.

"We've been going out for almost a year now, and, well, I've never felt this way about anyone before. Ever. So . . . I'm going to ask her to marry me!"

Stella squeals.

I raise my hand to give him a high-five, but he jumps up and pulls me into a classic, squeeze-the-air-out-of-you Larry embrace.

"That's great, Larry," I manage to squeak out.

"You guys will help me, right?" he asks when we sit back down. "To pick out a ring? It has to be perfect. And we have to figure out a really cool way for me to ask her. You know. Something super-special."

"Oh, like putting the ring in a champagne glass!" Stella says. "Or hiding it in a cupcake!"

"But what if she chokes on it?" I ask. "Or breaks a tooth? That would suck."

"Nah, nah, nah," Larry interrupts. "I'm not doing something cheesy. Sorry, Stell, no offense. This has to be all class. I've got to show her how mature I am. And romantic."

"Maybe you should take her away for a weekend," I suggest.

"Ooh, yes!" Stella says. "Take her to New York and go to a show!"

"Eh, she doesn't really like the city."

"Maybe a nice place in the country," I say. "Where you could go hiking or something. She's always saying how much she loves nature."

"I like it!" Larry claps me on the back.

Stella gives me a look. I think she's hurt that Larry hasn't liked any of her ideas. "Maybe you could propose on top of a mountain," she tries. "Although March isn't the best month for that."

"Now you're talkin', though!" Larry starts taking notes on his hand.

"Uh, Einstein? You better remember to wash that off before you see her," I say.

He laughs. "Josh, you are such a kidder. I love this lighter side of you."

"He's a real romantic," Stella says.

"Oh, really?" Larry asks in an exaggerated voice.

"I just meant because he has good ideas," Stella says quickly. "About you and Arielle."

Larry leans back in his seat. "She's so wonderful, isn't she?" It's not a question we need to answer. Obviously.

"What kind of ring will you get?" Stella asks.

"Something different. You know, not like the traditional thing. Something artsy. Meaningful."

"In other words, you have no idea," I say.

"Not really, no. I was thinking maybe you guys would go shopping with me. I'm not telling anyone else about the engagement, by the way, so don't mention it to any of my and Arielle's friends. They all have big mouths. And don't tell Gil or Gene, either. OK, Stell? Not even your mom."

"Don't worry. There's no way I'd tell her."

"Why not?" I ask.

"Because it would only make her depressed that she hasn't 'moved to the next level' with Calvin. She's been taking these Realtor classes to get her license, and spending all her free time with him, but . . . he hasn't popped the question yet."

"It takes time," Larry says reassuringly.

"Tell that to my mom. You'd think she was an old lady the way she talks. Like time is running out."

Larry sighs. "Poor Star."

"Anyway," Stella says. "What kind of ring are you going to get, Lar? Silver? Gold? Titanium?"

Larry looks totally overwhelmed. "I don't know! Ugh. Maybe I should propose without a ring and let her pick it out herself? I just want everything to be perfect."

"Calm down, Larry," I say. "You look like you're about to have a heart attack."

He pats his chest. "Sorry. I can't help it. Whenever I think about asking her, I get all excited and freaked out at the same time."

"Don't worry, Lar. We'll help you," Stella says. "Definitely."

"You guys are the best." He flags the waiter over to get our bill.

On the walk home, we move slowly, like none of us really wants this time to end. It's a cool, crisp night, and the people on the streets rush by, clutching their coat collars to their necks or tucking their faces into their scarves. When we get to the park, Larry suggests we walk through it and take the long way home, but Stella admits she needs to get back and call Britt.

"Oh, Britt," Larry says.

"Don't start, Larry." Stella hurries ahead of us. "Besides, I'm cold!" she calls over her shoulder.

"You two make the cutest couple," Larry whispers to me.

"Shut it, Larry," I hiss.

"I'm serious," he hisses back. "That other guy's a creeper. Always texting her and having to know where she is every second. That's not love, that's . . . possession. C'mon, Sam Man, you know you like her."

"I don't want a girlfriend," I say.

"Why not?" Larry stops walking.

"Come on, we should keep up with Stella. It's late."

"We'll catch up. Just tell me why not."

"Because I'm not ready, OK?"

"When will you be ready, Josh? Don't be like me. Don't be single too long. Life's too short to be alone."

"Then why were you?"

"Eh, I wanted to play the field. Not get tied down, you know? But the thing is, after a while I realized that of all my friends, I was the only single one left. Thank God Arielle came along. I swear, Sammy. I was one lonely fool."

Way ahead, Stella stops and turns to wait for us. We

pick up our pace and Larry drops the subject. But I keep thinking about what he said about being alone. Larry runs ahead and grabs Stella's hand. They skip along the sidewalk like little kids. I follow behind, wondering what it would feel like to take Stella's hand from Larry's and skip like a fool down the sidewalk beside her. My hand tingles. I would love to give them both a shock. Show them I know how to have fun.

But instead, I stuff my hands in my pockets and walk after them, falling farther and farther behind.

Chapter 27

It's 11:33 p.m. and I can't sleep. Larry and Arielle are in the living room, watching *Project A*. This has to be Jackie Chan's corniest movie of all time. But they're in there laughing their heads off. It seems impossible to me that there could be more than one person on this planet who loves Jackie as much as Larry. Maybe Arielle just does it to humor him. Or maybe she does it just because she loves him. Either way, clearly she's perfect for him.

I'm glad Larry is so happy. I'm glad he found someone who makes him laugh. But when he's happy like this, with Arielle, I feel like I don't belong here.

I flip open my cell.

Caleb: missed u @ break. d crashed his dad's truck but he's OK.

Dave: dude! come home i need a driver!

I text them back, then flip to the Christmas photo of Rosie and prop my phone next to the picture of me, Dave, and Caleb, like I do every night. I get out Stella's stone, glance over at Jackie Chan's beat-up face, and turn out the light. As the stars come out and the stone warms in my hand and the laughter down the hall fades to quiet, I listen to Clover's purrs and think about how I am surrounded by happiness. How lucky I am. And how I don't deserve this.

I squeeze the rock harder and try for the thousandth time to get the memory of that night out of my head. The way Ellie looked at me when she realized I wasn't going to stay. That I'd just used her like so many other assholes. And then the next memory. The way Caleb looked at me when he showed me the note that changed my life forever. And the words themselves, blurry from Ellie's tears, that made me realize I'd gotten her pregnant. And the worst memory of all. The image of the baby. My baby. The tiny little face behind glass. The small angry fist dangling outside his blanket. I try to ignore the feeling that burns in my chest now, just like it did then, when I left him. But it doesn't go away, no matter how hard I squeeze the rock.

When I wake up to the crying, I stay put and stare at the ceiling. I listen to the familiar soothing voice calm the baby back to quiet. I close my eyes and make a low humming sound to drown out the noise. But when I do, I see him again, just like always. Alone. Waiting for someone to come and hold him. And now I see the Ellie from my dreams, silently screaming at me. *No.*

I sit up. Clover rolls over and purrs, stretching out all four paws. I lean forward and scratch her belly. The noise above finally goes away, and I lie back again. Clover creeps up the bed and plops down next to my head. I rub her ears and put my face against her fur, letting her purrs lull me back to sleep.

Chapter 28

Jason comes rushing toward me the minute I get to my locker on the Monday after break.

"Did you hear anything?"

He looks too happy to see me. "Did *you*?" I say, since that has to be why.

"NYU. In." He breathes out as if he's been holding his breath for a month.

"Awesome," I say.

"How 'bout you?"

"Nah. Not yet."

"I'm sure you will soon."

"Yeah, eventually," I say. I try to make it sound like I'm not too worried. But now that people are starting to hear from schools, I feel even more on edge than usual. I applied to schools all over the place: San Francisco,

Chicago, Dallas, Philly. Everywhere that's too long to drive to and from my hometown in one day. That was my rule. Now I'm wondering if I aimed too high.

The whole day seems to be about people sharing college news. High-fiving. Consoling. It's as if everyone's life but mine changed over break.

By the end of the day, I can't wait to get out of here. I'm heading to the library when I turn the corner and see Stella and *Britt* at the end of the hall. They're hugging and laughing. I step back and am about to go the other way, but I can't help risking another look. Stella's familiar laughter echoes in the empty hallway. I peek around the corner again. Britt picks her up in a hug and swings her around in a circle, her legs flying out behind her. When he puts her down, he cups her face in his hands. "This is the best day ever," he tells her.

"I know," she says.

They're both holding letters. I'm guessing college acceptance letters.

"Why did you wait all day to tell me?" he asks.

"I wanted to tell you when we were alone."

He hugs her again. She looks so small, buried in his arms. I've never seen them alone together. I always figured they fought most of the time, since whenever Stella shows up after being with him she looks upset. But they look so . . . comfortable. Happy. Like they belong together.

"I love you so much," he says.

And then he looks up and sees me.

I step back quickly and practically run down the hall. I can't believe I didn't just turn around the second I saw them. God. What is *wrong* with me?

"Hey, Josh."

I swing around and see this girl, Kelly, who's in my homeroom and a few classes with me. Where the hell did she come from?

"Uh, hey," I say, out of breath.

"Are you OK?"

"Huh? Yeah. Why?"

She looks at me funny and shrugs. "Anyway. A bunch of us are heading over to Joe's. Wanna come?"

"Joe's?"

"Cuppa. You know, the café on Main? Big white coffee cup for a sign?"

I wonder what she means by "a bunch of us" and if that includes Stella and Britt. I can't exactly ask. Obviously. But there is no way I want him to see me now. He probably thinks I'm some sort of stalker.

"Thanks, but I have too much work to do."

"Oh."

"Sorry." I start walking away. Then I stop and turn around. She's still standing there. "Thanks for asking, though."

"Sure," she says. "See ya."

I spend two hours at the school library on my own. Jason never shows up. Maybe he got invited to Joe's, too. The whole time I'm there, I keep thinking about how Stella and Britt looked. Happy. Maybe he is a bit possessive, but the guy clearly does love her. And she loves him. So yeah. That's good. Whatever.

On my way out, I run into my guidance counselor.

"Josh! How're you doing? Any news?"

"Nah, not yet."

"Well, these next few weeks, the acceptances will start rolling in."

I nod.

"How's everything else going? You holding up? This time of year can be pretty stressful."

"Yeah, I'm doin' pretty good."

He pats me on the back. "Good."

Right.

Outside, the sky is a grayish blue. It's windy, too. I wait for the bus with a bunch of other students. Some I recognize, some I don't. They nod to me but don't talk to me. It's like I'm almost invisible but not quite.

At Larry's apartment, I dump my stuff in my room and head to the kitchen to make dinner. Clover follows me, since she knows I'll give her a treat. Larry will already be at the Y, teaching. I only have a few minutes to scarf something down, so I make a sandwich and sit alone at the kitchen table, with Clover rubbing against my legs.

While I'm eating, the phone rings.

"Hi, Joshy, it's me," my mom says. "I tried calling your cell, but you weren't picking up."

"We can't use phones in school," I say. "Remember? Sorry. I always forget to turn it back on."

"That's OK, honey. I just wanted to check in. I'm so glad I caught you. It's been a while."

There's an awkward pause. My mom tried keeping up with her pledge to call me once a week to make sure I'm "fine," but she always seems to call when I'm at practice. Or out. Sometimes I wonder how much she really wants to know.

"So, I have some good news," she tells me. "I got a promotion at work!"

"Hey, that's great!"

"It's such good timing, with you starting college next year."

"I can take out student loans, Mom. You don't have to pay."

"Of course we'll pay! I mean, as much as we possibly can. We'll take out the loans if we have to. Have you heard anything yet, honey?"

"No, not yet."

"Well, I'm sure you will soon."

"Yeah, hopefully."

Awkward silence.

"So, in addition to my promotion, I also got a nice little bonus, and your dad and I decided to go away for a long weekend."

"Wow," I say.

"I know. Crazy, huh? Your dad and I have never really gone away like this before. Just the two of us. It's a big step."

"That's great, Mom." I mean it. I do. Even if it's a little weird. I knew things were better at Christmas, but I didn't realize we'd reached, like, second-honeymoon level. If someone told me a year ago they'd be like this, I would have laughed.

"Actually it was our therapist's suggestion. He thinks going away might help us . . . you know. Rekindle . . . things. Between us."

Oh, God. I so don't want to hear about them rekindling anything. And also, therapist?

"Is everything OK with you guys? Why are you seeing a therapist?"

I listen to her take a few slow breaths before she answers. "We're trying, Josh. But it's hard. We thought a therapist could help."

"Oh."

"Don't worry, honey. This is a good thing! Anyway,

we'll be staying at a little bed-and-breakfast place in Vermont. I wanted to let you know, in case you needed to reach us. I don't know what the cell coverage will be like there."

She gives me the name and phone number of the place, and I write it down.

"How's Dad doing with — everything else?" I ask. I can't seem to bring myself to say the drinking. I don't know why, since we're talking about them going somewhere to "rekindle" things.

"He's fine," she says, stealing my word. "He has his struggles, you know. But he's trying really hard. And the walking has been so good for him. Rosie, too!"

"Tell them I said hi," I say.

"It's good to hear your voice, honey. School is still going all right?"

"Yeah, everything is fine." I imagine her cringing at the word, but she doesn't seem to miss a beat.

"All right. We'll call when we get home."

"I hope you guys have a good time," I say. "Really."

"Thanks, sweetheart."

I hang up the phone and look down at Clover, who's staring at me with her big, wondering eyes.

"Crazy," I say to her.

"What's crazy?"

I jump about a mile.

"Jesus, Larry, you scared the crap out of me."

"Sorry, Sammy. I had a break, so I dashed home for a bite before class. That your mom on the phone?"

"Yeah."

"And?"

"She and my dad are going away for the weekend. Together."

"Nice!"

"You mean crazy."

"No-oh, I mean nice."

"Nice and crazy."

"Why crazy? They're married, right?"

"Well, yeah. But they've been married for seventeen years, and they never wanted to be alone before. At least not in my memory. It's just — crazy."

"Seventeen years? Really? Wow. Time flies."

Yes. Seventeen years, Larry. Do the math.

"So, what's the special occasion?" he asks.

"My mom got a promotion. And my dad is stone-cold sober. And they have a therapist who thinks a weekend away is a good idea."

"Wow."

"I know."

"Why aren't you more excited? You should be happy for them, right?"

"I am."

"You don't sound like it."

"I am!"

"Well, you don't have to get all upset. Jeez."

"I'm not upset. I'm just . . . never mind. I just wonder what made them change, that's all." But I feel like I know. And I guess it's not such a bad thing. Maybe something good *should* come out of the mess I made. At least something good for other people.

"So, where are they going?"

I motion to the piece of paper on the table.

"Oooh, Vermont! Maybe they can scope the place out for me."

Give me strength.

He makes himself a smoothie and downs it in about three gulps.

"Ahhhh. OK. Ready to hit the Y?"

"That's all you're having for dinner?"

"I'm going to meet the little lady after practice for a late meal."

"Little lady? Seriously, Lar?"

"Aw, lighten up."

I shake my head.

"You should be happy about your parents, Josh. You know? It's cool they're getting help to make things work. It means they still love each other. That's awesome!"

"I didn't say I wasn't happy for them. I am! If I'd

known what a positive effect my absence would have on their marriage, I would've left a long time ago."

"Come on, that's not true. And hey, it's you who kept them together in the first place."

"What do you mean?"

"Hell-o-oh? You know what I'm talking about. Shotgun wedding?"

Oh. So he does know.

"Do you know what the chances are of those kinds of marriages surviving? But look at your parents. After all these years, they stuck it out. And they're still dedicated to making it work."

"So you think they did the right thing?"

He looks at me and hesitates. Like he knows he has to be careful now.

"Every situation is different. All right? They made the best choice for them. You made the best choice for you."

"I didn't have a choice."

Larry's quiet.

"Never mind," I say. "It doesn't matter."

"No," he says sarcastically. "Obviously not."

But I don't reply. I go to my room, grab my karate stuff, and follow him out to the hall, down the stairs, and all the way to the Y in silence.

Chapter 29

First thing Saturday morning, Stella, Larry, and I head downtown to look at rings.

"Can't you leave that thing at home?" Larry asks Stella, who is madly texting and walking at the same time. "I can't stand how everyone's always buried in their phones. Hello! Pay attention to the people you are *with*."

She ignores him.

"What are you typing, anyway?" he asks.

"A love letter." She elbows him, finishes texting, and drops her phone in her purse.

A love letter. Fantastic.

We check out the mall first, but Larry says all the rings there look the same. He says we need to go somewhere off the beaten path. Finally, we find a shop downtown that's an artists' co-op, which means a bunch of different artists all sell their stuff at the store.

We lean over case after case until we finally find an artist Larry likes. Someone who works there comes over to help us.

"Would you like to see a few of these?" she asks, gesturing toward some artsy-looking silver bands Larry has his eye on.

Larry leans closer to the glass. "I think so," he says. There's sweat forming on his forehead.

The lady smiles and opens a glass door on her side of the counter.

"It has to be really special," Larry tells her.

"Don't they all?" she asks.

Larry looks embarrassed.

"I'm Grace, by the way."

"Larry. And this is my nephew, Josh, and our friend Stella."

"Nice to meet you." She pulls out a bunch of gold and silver rings and sets them in front of us. A lot of them look like the usual diamond ring, just with slightly different designs on the bands.

Larry picks one up that has tiny diamonds all the way around it rather than one big one.

"Oh, that one really is unique," Grace says. "Look."

She takes the ring from Larry and shows how the diamonds are on some sort of inner ring that turns. She puts it on her finger and spins the ring of diamonds with her thumb. "Isn't that fun?"

Larry takes the ring back and puts it on the tip of his pinkie. He makes the diamonds spin. "Cool," he says. "What do you guys think?"

"Let me try it," Stella says. She puts the ring on and holds her hand out, fingers splayed apart. She moves the inner ring and the diamonds sparkle as they spin around her finger. "It's beautiful, isn't it?"

"It is," I say.

Her cheeks turn pink. My own face feels warm, too.

"It's very unique," Grace interrupts. "It's lovely on you." I think she is going in for the big sale, because obviously this ring, with all the diamonds, is going to be a lot more expensive than the others.

Larry steps back and squints at the ring on Stella's finger, tilting his head at different angles. "I just don't know," he says. "Maybe too flashy."

Stella slides it off her finger and carefully hands it back to Grace.

"Is this a surprise engagement?" Grace asks. "If not, why don't you bring your fiancée here to see what she likes. An engagement ring is an important purchase. She'll be wearing it for the rest of her life."

"It's a surprise," Larry says hopelessly. "Crap. I don't want to screw this up. I want it to be romantic."

He sounds like a little kid.

"You don't have to decide right this minute," I say. I take him by the arm. "Come on, let's check out a few more places."

Stella hesitates at the counter a little bit longer, looking at the ring in a dreamy way. She's probably daydreaming about getting engaged to *Britt.*

"C'mon, Stell," I say, pulling her away from the counter.

Grace gives me a dirty look, like I just blew her chance on a giant commission. I give her what I hope is an apologetic look. Because I do feel bad. But this is Larry. We have to make sure he's happy.

We go outside and walk down the sidewalk until we find a café, where Larry buys us all hot chocolate.

"This is hopeless," Larry says when we sit at a tiny table in the back. "Maybe that lady's right. Maybe I should just ask Arielle first, and then let her pick out a ring."

"No," Stella and I say at the same time.

"I think Arielle will love whatever you pick out," I say. "It's not about the ring. It's about you, you know, telling her you love her and want to spend the rest of your life with her."

Larry clutches his chest and pushes back his seat

dramatically, as if I just said the most earth-shattering thing he ever heard.

Stella laughs.

"What?"

"I do believe my nephew is a hopeless romantic. Who would've thunk it?"

Ha. Ha.

"Right. Whatever. All I'm saying is, I think you're getting way too stressed out over this."

"Josh is right," Stella says. "If someone proposed to me, I wouldn't care about the ring. I'd just care about the proposal. And what the guy said. Like, how he would always love me."

Larry sighs. "I know, I know. In the ideal world, you're right. But I'm so afraid Arielle will say no. I mean, it's like you said. It's the rest of our *lives*!"

I don't point out that, in fact, statistically, marriage is only for the rest of your life fifty percent of the time.

"Look," I say to Larry. "Do you really think she's going to say no because she doesn't like the ring you pick out? Get a clue. If she's that shallow, she doesn't deserve you."

"She's not," Larry says, all defensive.

"I know. That's what I'm trying to tell you. Don't sweat the ring."

We finish our drinks and decide to call it a day. Larry seems kind of withdrawn as we walk home.

"Through the park?" he asks hopefully when we get to the entrance.

"I gotta get back," Stella says. "But you two go." She looks like part of her really wants to stay with us. But she's already reaching in her purse for her phone.

"You sure?" Larry asks.

"Yeah, it's daytime. No worries." She gives Larry a big hug and whispers something in his ear. We watch her hurry down the sidewalk and disappear around the corner.

"You guys would make the cutest couple," Larry says.

I give him a shove.

"I'm serious!"

"I know," I say. Well, not about the cute part. But she's with *Britt.* And after seeing them together in the hall that day, I know she's happy. "You gotta let it go, though, Lar. She's got a boyfriend."

"Yeah, yeah."

It's sunny, and warm for March, and there are quite a few people out walking their dogs. We go a ways without talking, then Larry grabs my arm and stops.

"I'm going to do it next weekend," he says, as if he just decided. "If I don't do it soon, I'll go nuts. This whole thing is causing me way too much stress."

"OK," I say.

"That's it? Just OK?"

"Um, would congratulations be premature?"

"No!"

"Just kidding! I'm really happy for you, Lar. I mean it."

"Hey," he says, facing me. He puts both hands on my shoulders. His fingers press through my jacket and squeeze.

"Easy," I say, looking around and hoping no one sees this strange act of affection.

"Be my best man," he says. "Will you?"

"What? *Me?* Why?"

He lets go. "Because you're my man! Samurai Sam!"

I stare at him.

"My *man*!" he says again.

I really wish he wouldn't say that. Especially in public.

"What about my dad?" I ask.

Larry rolls his eyes. "You know Hal and I have never been close. Plus, can you see him in a tux? C'mon. Say yes, Sammy. Pleeeeeeease?"

Anything to make him stop calling me that.

He waits, peering into my face like a puppy waiting for me to toss him a ball. I smile, realizing how much I love my uncle, sappy as that seems. He took me in when he hardly knew me. He brought me into his life and got me into a sport I never would have imagined being able to do, much less like. He makes me laugh. He makes me feel like I'm not a loser. Like I really could be someone or do something good with my life. He makes me feel like I matter. I can't believe I spent the past few weeks obsessed with what school I'd get into and my ticket out of here instead of facing what I know now: It's going to be really hard to leave.

"Of course I will, you big dope," I finally say.

He jumps up and down and runs circles around me. Then he gives me a huge bear hug and lifts me up in the air.

"Easy, easy," I say, trying to pull away.

He punches me in the arm. "I'm so happy," he says.

"I can see that."

"I really hope she says yes."

"I'm sure she will."

"Really?"

"Yes," I say. "She will."

And God. For his sake, I'm hope I'm right.

Chapter 30

Just as we're leaving the park, Larry's phone starts playing Jackie Chan singing "We Are Ready." I really wish I was kidding.

"Heh-ay beautiful," he says, beaming. *Arielle,* he mouths to me, like I couldn't figure that out.

He walks over to an empty bench and sits down. I stand nearby to wait, but he motions for me to go on without him. I leave him in his state of bliss and head home.

When I get close to the apartment, I see Stella standing outside talking to *Britt.* He's leaning against his freshly buffed BMW. It's the sporty kind my dad calls a penis extender. Of course. Perfect boyfriend would have a perfect car. I comfort myself by thinking about my dad's joke.

I stop walking and sit on the nearest stoop to wait for them to leave before *Britt* sees me. I hear Stella say something, but I can't make out the words. Britt leans toward her and yells in her face.

She cowers and steps back.

What the hell? I get up and start walking toward them. Even from here, I can see that Britt's hands are in fists.

"I wasn't doing anything!" Stella says.

"Then why didn't you return my texts!"

"I was busy! That's all!"

He grabs her arm.

"Hey!" I yell, coming up to them. "Get off her."

He turns to me. "Do I know you?"

Stella looks at me like she wants to kill me. What did *I* do?

"Let go of her. Now."

Britt lets go, then steps closer to me.

"You're the guy from her karate practices, aren't you?"

"Yeah."

He studies my face. "And you're the freak who was spying on us the other day."

Great.

"What?" Stella says, looking at me.

"I wasn't spying," I say. "I just—" I don't know what

to say. Whatever comes out of my mouth will sound completely lame.

"Stay away from us," Britt says, like I really am some kind of stalker.

Stella is looking at me as if for the first time. And not in a curious way. More like a totally creeped-out kind of way.

"Stella has a boyfriend. Got it?"

"I know that. We're just friends. Relax."

"No one is just friends. Unless you're a fag."

"Are you kidding me?" This does not sound like the same Britt I've overheard laughing with his friends at school. This guy is the asshole I secretly hoped he'd be. But I never wanted him to hurt Stella. I just wanted her to dump him. I guess that makes me just as bad.

I glance at Stella again, because I honestly can't believe she'd let him get away with saying this crap. But instead, she crosses her arms at her chest and glares at me like this is all my fault.

"Just stay away from her from now on," Britt says.

"I told you. We're just friends."

"No. You're not friends. You don't talk to her."

"What the hell?" I ask Stella.

"Go away, Josh," she says.

"Wait. You're really going to let him tell you who you can hang out with?"

She doesn't answer.

Britt keeps glaring at me. His jaw clenches and unclenches.

"So this is who you were with when I tried to call," Britt says. "The stalker. Unbelievable."

"I was helping our karate instructor," she says.

"Right."

"We were helping him pick out an engagement ring for his *girlfriend*."

"What did you need him for?" he asks, jerking his elbow toward me.

"He's Larry's nephew," she says.

I hate how her voice sounds. All pleading in some "Please forgive me" way. And like I am just some throw-away loser who *happened* to be there, too.

"Just go home," Stella says to me. "Please."

Britt grabs her arm again. "C'mon. We're leaving." He starts to pull her toward the car. For a brief moment, Stella looks down at his hand, like she isn't sure what to make of it holding her that way. She pulls away, but Britt grabs her back.

"Britt, cut it out," she says.

"We're getting out of here. Now." He pulls harder, and she almost falls.

I feel rage build in my chest. Every cell in my body is saying to beat the crap out of this guy. When Stella tries to break free again and he seems to squeeze harder, I go for it.

All the karate moves I've learned and practiced for the past seven months go out the window, and I'm just grabbing the guy, pulling him away from Stella. He gets free, and before I know it's coming, he punches me in the face. For a few seconds, I can't see, the pain is so blinding. Then I punch back. I manage to block a few of his punches and then nail him in the stomach. He bends over and coughs, then straightens again. He looks like a bull about to charge. Stella is screaming at both of us. Then Larry appears out of nowhere, pulling Britt backward.

"What the hell is going on here?" Larry yells, holding Britt's arms behind him. With his arms held away, exposing his chest and stomach, I have the supreme desire to kick him in the gut and put us all out of his misery. But Stella walks over to me and slaps me across my already bruised face. It hurts like hell.

"You asshole!" she says. She's crying.

"Me?" I say, trying to ignore the searing pain.

"Yes. You!" She strides over to Britt and Larry. "Let him go," she says to Larry. He does.

Britt shakes out his arms as if he just broke free. Right.

Stella walks around to the passenger side of his car and gets in.

"You better hope I never see you around her again," Britt says to me. "Freak."

I have nothing to say to that.

Larry runs over to Stella's side of the car. "Maybe you should stay here, honey," he says. "Please." But she just faces straight ahead, her arms crossed at her chest. Britt gets in the car and peels out of the parking space, down the street.

"Jesus, Sammy," Larry says to me. "You're bleeding."

I feel my face. It's sticky.

"Come on. Arielle's on her way over. We decided to eat in. Let's get you cleaned up before she has a heart attack seeing you like that."

"What about Stella?" I ask.

"We did what we could for now."

"That's it?"

"What do you want me to do? We'll talk when she gets back."

"But he was hurting her," I say.

He looks at me doubtfully.

"What?"

He puts his hand on my arm, and I realize I'm shaking all over. "She'll be OK," he says. "She's smart. She knows how to take care of herself."

Before we go inside, I look down the street one more time, hoping they'll come back and Stella will get out of the car and slam the door and come running over to me and . . . Right. Never gonna happen.

"C'mon," Larry says, and drags me inside to patch me up at the kitchen table.

"You might want to avoid mirrors for a while," he says as he presses an alcohol-soaked cotton ball against my open cuts.

I wince every time. "Do I really look that bad?"

"I may change your name to Rocky."

I roll my eyes, but even that hurts.

"Go lie down. I'll make dinner."

I go to my room and lean back on my bed with an ice pack pressed to my cheek. I look over at Jackie Chan's torn face and wish I could have done that to *the Shit.*

But instead, I feel like I just beat the shit out of myself.

Chapter 31

Stella doesn't show up at our next practice. We start ten minutes late, waiting. Some of the little kids who fell in love with her during camp start to whine about Stella not being here. I tell them she'll come. But the more time goes by, the more it feels like a lie. All I can think is that she chose *Britt* over karate. Over me.

Jacob, the old guy, gives me a disapproving gaze. Some of the other students around my age keep stealing glances at me. I'm sure they're all dying to know if I was in a fight and if I won.

"What happened to your face?" this little kid, Clara, finally asks me. "Did you get in a fight?"

I look to Larry for help on how to answer, but he ignores me and claps his hands to get everyone's attention. He tells us it's time to spar and to get our gear on. Clara motions with her pointer finger for me to bend my head closer to hers. She smells like peanut butter. She reaches up and touches my bruised face with her pointer finger. "That hurts," she tells me.

"Kind of," I say.

She shrugs and walks off to get her sparring gear on.

OK.

Halfway through class, Stella walks in. She goes over to Larry, and they talk in the corner so no one can hear. When she finally takes her place next to me, she doesn't say a word. A few of the little kids run over to hug her before Larry yells at everyone to line up again. He makes his way through the group, asking each of us to demonstrate the latest moves we've learned.

"Remember," he says. "One of the precepts in karate is to know yourself before you try to know others." He looks over at me as if to make sure I know that little gem of advice was for me. Whatever.

The whole time, Stella avoids looking at me. As soon as class is over, she bolts for the door instead of waiting for Larry and me to walk home together like always.

When Larry and I step outside, I search down the street for her, but she's gone.

"She'll come around," Larry says. "She just needs some space."

"Who?" I ask.

He shakes his head, like I'm pathetic. "Come on, let's go home."

As we start walking, Larry puts his arm across my back and squeezes my shoulder.

"I don't get why she'd go out with a guy like that," I say. "She could be with anyone."

"Judging from his car, I'd say that dude has everything Stella doesn't have."

"Stella's not that shallow."

"I didn't say she was shallow."

"You said she's into that guy because of his *car.*"

"I just meant, maybe his financial situation is a bit more stable than hers, that's all. Maybe the idea of not having to worry about money for the first time in her life is appealing."

"That can't be it," I say. I think of how much Stella resents her mom going out with all those guys she thinks will make her life so much better. I know Stella's not like that. She's too smart for that. So what *is* the *Britt* appeal? It's not just Stella who seems crazy about him. Everyone at school seems to love him, too. Maybe they just haven't seen the side of him I have. But Stella has. So . . . I don't get it.

Larry turns and looks at me in this sad way. Like, why would girls go out with any of us losers?

That's when I have an image of myself that day last year. At the party that changed everything. I see myself taking Ellie's hand. Pulling her toward me. Opening the door to my dad's van . . .

I start walking again. Fast.

"Hey!" Larry yells, trying to keep up. "What did I say?"

I wave my hand at him so he'll leave me alone and keep walking. But he runs up to me and puts his hand on my shoulder to stop me. "What is it?" he asks.

"Forget it," I say, pushing his hand away.

But he won't leave it. "You can tell me, Josh."

"There's nothing to tell." I turn and start walking away again.

"We both know that's not true," he calls after me.

I'm the loser. I'm no better than Britt. I'm probably fifty times worse.

I keep walking, trying to break away from Larry. But he's a way better speed walker than me, and he's by my side, taking my arm again, forcing me to slow down.

"Look. We haven't talked all year about why you're really here. That's my fault. I didn't want to push you. But I think it's time, Josh."

Me:

He sighs impatiently. "I know Stella's situation is upsetting you," he says. "But there's more going on here, and we both know it. Maybe, you know, we should start talking about the elephant in the room."

"What elephant?"

"You have to say it, not me."

"I don't have to say anything."

We reach our building and go inside. I go to my room, hoping to escape the whole situation. But Larry follows me.

I sit on my bed and start to check my phone while Larry stands in my doorway.

"Josh," he says. "Talk to me."

I toss my phone on the bed. "What do you want me to say?" I sound like an ungrateful jerk and hate myself for it.

"Whatever you want. But I think it's time you tell me what happened last year."

"Obviously you know already. Haven't we been through this?"

He frowns and walks over to sit at the foot of the bed. "I know you don't want to talk about it. I get that. But . . ."

"You're right. I don't."

"Why not?"

I glance up at Jackie Chan's ripped face. "Why do you think?"

"Jesus, Josh. Would you cut the bullshit?"

I think that's the first time I've heard Larry swear.

"Jesus, Larry, what do you want me to say?"

"The truth! Just say it!"

"How is that supposed to help? You already know the truth!"

Larry moves closer to me. If he tries to touch me right now, I will punch him in the face. I don't care if he tries to block me. I will punch him.

"I care about you, Josh! I love you! And I don't want to see you hurting so bad. You're carrying this huge weight on your back, and I can see how much it's hurting you. But you won't let anyone help you. You can't bear it forever. You have to talk about it!"

"Why?"

"To get it out of you, that's why. You have this . . . this *thing* festering inside you. I think if you talked about it, if you just got it out —"

"Don't you get it, Larry? This isn't something to get out of my system. What I did? What happened? It is *never* going to go away."

"Then you have to claim it, Josh. You have to take ownership of whatever happened and learn how to live with it. And you start by saying —"

"I got a girl pregnant!" I scream in his face. "All right? Are you happy now? I hope so, because I don't feel any better."

Larry nods. "I already know that. And I know how

awful it must have been. But there's something else, isn't there?"

"What do you mean, something else?"

"I think there's more."

"More what?"

"More to the story. I'm right, aren't I?"

I swear I'm going to punch him. I'm going to smash that optimistic, I-never-cry-or-do-anything-bad-because-I'm-such-a-perfect-true-karate-man face in.

"Aren't I," he says again. It's not really a question.

My hands are in fists. Jackie Chan's ripped-up smile taunts me. *I'm right, aren't I?* I hear him say in his accent. I swear I am going to rip that poster to shreds.

"Josh —"

"What do you want, a freaking medal? So what if you're right?"

He ignores my outburst. "Tell me what happened."

"You're so smart — don't you know?"

"You got a girl pregnant," he starts. "And what else?"

My hands are in fists.

"And she had the baby! You know that! She had the baby and she gave him up for adoption. Can we move on now?"

"I already know that, too. Keep going."

"God, Larry. What do you want me to say? I'm a father. Do you know what that's like? I don't even know who my kid is. I don't know *where* he is. I don't know who his parents are. Somewhere out there, my kid is being raised by strangers. I'll never meet him. I'll never know what he looks like or who he'll become. I don't even know if he's happy! His parents could be total assholes! But I don't know. I will *never* know!"

I press my fists to my temples and feel myself start to rock. When I touch my face, it's wet. I know I'm crying like a baby, but I can't help it.

Larry moves closer to me. "Let it out," he says. "Just let it all out."

"I can't!" I yell. I shake my head. I choke, I'm crying so hard. I stand up and start punching Jackie. I tear the poster down and rip it to pieces. Larry doesn't move. I punch the wall again. Over and over until my knuckles are bleeding, and then I just fall on the floor and curl up in a ball.

"Josh," he says. "Josh, it's OK."

But I don't listen. It's not OK. Nothing is OK. I can't let it out, because "it" is a part of me. Something I can never forget. Never change. Never take back.

When I finally stop shaking, Larry moves closer to me.

"What else?" he asks.

I shake my head.

"You've never told me about the mom."

I keep shaking my head. "There's nothing to say about her. It was a one-time thing."

He waits a while, then tries again. "Tell me about her anyway. Tell me what happened that makes you hate yourself so much."

I sit up and lean against the bed and close my eyes.

And I see her.

I see me. And I see her.

I see me reaching for her hand.

I see her telling me she's not sure.

I say, *Come on, it's nice outside.*

She follows me into the dark—

I open my eyes. Larry is watching me intently. "I can't do this," I say.

He's quiet for a long time, as if he knows if he waits long enough, I'll give in. Like he's a goddamn shrink.

"Tell me about her," he finally says in this quiet, obnoxious voice. "Tell me what happened."

"I already told you!" I scream at him.

But he keeps sitting there calmly. "You only told me about the baby. You didn't tell me about 'the one-time thing.'"

I see me opening the door to the van.

She smiles at me.

I tell her how pretty she is.

We kiss.

I remember her mouth and how soft her lips were.

How she pressed her body against me.

How smooth her skin was as I slipped my hand under her shirt.

I told her she was beautiful.

She let me do whatever I wanted.

She didn't say a word.

She didn't move.

It was just like my friends said it would be.

She didn't seem to care.

No.

Maybe she cared.

But she didn't try to stop me.

She just let me touch her.

Reach inside her.

Fuck her.

That's what I did.

I didn't make love to her.

I just fucked her.

Not because I thought she was hot

Not because I liked her.

Not because she was beautiful.

But because I wanted to get it over with.

I did it because I didn't want to be a virgin anymore.

And I think she knew that.

I think she knew.

And she still didn't stop me.

When I opened the door and the van's roof light flicked on automatically, I could see her face.

I could tell, by the way she looked at me, why she didn't tell me to stop.

I could tell what she wanted.

Me.

Love.

But instead of giving it to her, I walked away.

I wipe my face again. Shake my head.

"I can't do this," I say to Larry. "I can't . . . I don't want to remember."

"You already do," Larry says. "You just did." He puts his strong hand on my knee. "So tell me. Right now."

And finally, I do.

Chapter 32

"I was such an asshole," I say when I finish.

"That's true," Larry says. "But you didn't force her, Josh. If she'd asked you to stop, would you have?"

"Of course! But — I shouldn't have taken her to the van in the first place. It's all my fault."

"Don't you think she knew what you were going to try when she left with you? Don't you think she knew what you wanted?"

"I don't know. Yeah. I guess."

"Look, I'm not saying what you did was right. It wasn't. But you didn't rape her."

"No. I just took advantage of her."

"Why do you think she went with you if she didn't want to have sex?"

"I don't know. I think she wanted . . . more. I think maybe she hoped it would be more than just sex. Maybe she was hoping that after, I'd stick around. Be her boyfriend. Tell her I loved her or something. The way she looked at me after, as I was leaving — yeah. I think that's what she wanted. She wanted more. And I just left her there."

"So she was using sex to get love?"

"No! I mean, I think she was hoping sex would get her love. I don't know. It's so screwed up."

"And why did you keep going when it was obvious she wasn't into it?"

"Like I said, I was an asshole."

He frowns.

"And it felt good. Even though she wasn't into it. Obviously. But — yes. I should have stopped. My whole life, her whole life, the baby — everything would be different if I'd stopped. I wouldn't be here. There wouldn't be a baby. Her life wouldn't suck. And it's all my fault."

"How do you know her life sucks?"

"You really have to ask?"

He shrugs. "I'm not saying what happened wasn't awful. But maybe she's different now. Maybe she changed for the better."

"I doubt that."

"Why?"

"Do you think it changed *me* for the better?"

"I don't know. Did it?"

I stare at him.

"I'm just asking. Look at all you've accomplished since you got here. Would any of this have happened if . . . You know."

"Screwing up someone else's life is hardly worth anything good that happened to me."

"Again. You don't know if you did that, in the end. And also, it's not *all* your fault. She played a part, too."

"No."

"Why no?"

Clover walks in and rubs against me.

"I talked her into it."

"Listen, Casanova. You're cute, but you're not that powerful. She was looking for something just like you were. Only different."

"It was still wrong."

"Yeah. It was. But if she hadn't gotten pregnant, would you be thinking that now?"

I see her face again. That sad, expectant face. It was already haunting me way before I found out she was pregnant. "Yeah," I say. "I think I would."

He nods. "That's right. Because you're a good person, Josh. You have a good conscience."

"Right. If I was so good, this never would have happened. I'm no good. Never have been."

"Yes. You are. You made a mistake. A huge, horrible mistake. But you didn't intentionally hurt anyone. You've paid for it big-time. So has she. That night will probably stay with you both for the rest of your lives. But you don't have to punish yourself forever. You know that, right?"

I don't say anything.

"Josh, you can have a girlfriend. You can have sex again. You can live again."

I shake my head. "I know. I guess. But whenever I start to feel happy, all I can think about is what happened. And how I don't deserve to feel good."

"Ever?"

"I don't know! I can't figure out how to move beyond it. Or carry it with me, like you said. I can't get her or the baby out of my head. Every time I hear Benny cry, I see him."

"See him?"

"Well, who I think is him. I don't even know. That's what's so crazy. That day I found out she went to the hospital to have the baby, I went there. And there was this one baby in the nursery, you know, who didn't have a name or people all gaga over him, and something just told me that was him."

"Why didn't you ask the mom if you could see him?"

"Right."

"What?"

"I ruined her life, Larry. I couldn't do that to her."

"I'll say it again. How do you know you ruined her life? How would her life be different if this whole thing didn't happen?"

I think about my two a.m. wake-ups. My panic attacks. The way my heart hurts every time I see or hear a baby. If it's this hard for me, I know it must be worse for her. She had that baby inside her for nine months. And then she had to give him away.

I shake my head. "I dunno."

"Maybe you should try to talk to her," Larry says. "Find out what happened to the baby. Maybe you should try to see him, even."

I picture the Ellie of my dreams, silently screaming *No.*

"I can't," I say.

"There are ways. We could get a lawyer. We could talk to the adoption agency."

"No," I say again.

"But—"

"I've thought about it, all right? It's all I thought about last summer. Every day. I even wrote a letter to her. To apologize, and find out what happened to the baby. But every time I got close to sending it, I panicked. The thing is, I don't want to put her through any more pain. And, it's like, the baby's not really mine, you know? He never was."

"What do you mean?"

"It's like, when two people want a baby, the minute they get pregnant, the baby is theirs, you know? They start thinking of names and all that stuff. The baby is a he or a she. A member of the family already. But when you don't want the baby, all you think about is *Oh, my God, what the hell am I going to do?* The baby is an 'it,' and all you do is think about how you can get rid of it. You pray that will be the girl's choice. You might even hope that she has a miscarriage or something. Anything to make it go away. When you think like that, you don't deserve to see that baby. If you hoped for that, you don't deserve to see him. You don't get to be a part of his life."

"Josh, that's crazy talk. You know that, right?"

"Why is it crazy?"

"Because people get scared! They think and say all kinds of stuff. There's nothing wrong with changing your mind!"

"I don't want to see him. OK? I don't."

"I don't believe you."

"You don't have to. Just . . . drop it, OK? Please."

Larry watches me for a long time.

"I only want to help you," he says. "I know you're

hurting, and it hurts me to see you in so much pain. You wear it on your sleeve, Josh. I can practically feel the pain coming off you."

"I can handle it," I say.

But we both know that's a lie.

Chapter 33

The next day at practice, Larry and I are helping the younger kids tie their belts when Stella shows up. The little girls and a few boys swarm her with hugs, as usual. She smiles as she hugs them back, but there's a sadness in her eyes. All through practice, she avoids me. Larry doesn't ask us to spar. Instead, he gives us each a different group of kids to work with. When we demonstrate the katas together, I don't feel like we're moving in our usual deliberate, dance-like way. I feel like we are puppets dangling from the end of a string that is slowly shredding to a single, thin strand.

After practice, Stella is the first one out of the room. Larry notices and gestures to me to run after her in his unsubtle Larry-like way, mouthing, *Go!*

I rush out to the hall and see her turn the corner.

"Stella!" I yell. I sprint down the hall and practically plow her over when I round the corner.

"What?" she says.

"I just wanted to . . . uh . . . talk to you."

"OK," she says. When she sees my face up close, she cringes and looks away.

"I'm sorry about what happened," I say. "Really. But I was afraid he was going to hurt you."

"I can take care of myself."

"I know you can, but . . ."

"Listen. You're a sweet friend. I know you were just looking out for me. But I think for a little while, we need to take a break. Britt's feeling jealous and a little freaked-out about you spying on us and–"

"What? I wasn't spying on you. God. I came around the corner and saw you. That's all."

"That's not what he said."

"Of course not. He wants you to hate me."

"That's not true."

"Right."

"Why can't you tell him we're just friends?" I ask. "Just tell him he has nothing to be jealous about."

"You don't get it," she says.

"What?"

She puts her hand on my arm. "He has a reason. To be jealous."

My arm tingles where she's touching me. I pull away. Not because I don't like her touching me. I'm just surprised.

"That's what I thought," she says quietly.

"What? No, I—" *I just didn't think you felt the same way about me.* Say it. Just say it.

"Stella—" I start.

"Forget it. I have to go." She turns, and takes off down the hall again. I stand there, touching my arm. Realizing I am the biggest idiot in the world.

On the way home, Larry tells me I look like my dog just died.

I explain what happened.

"I knew it!" he says, all excited.

"You don't get it," I say. "Nothing's going to happen."

"*Why not?* Are you *crazy*? She likes you! She really likes you!"

"She's staying with Britt, Larry."

"But—she *likes* you! Go after her!"

"No. I'm not that guy."

"What guy?"

"The guy who steals other guys' girlfriends. She made her choice. It's probably for the best, anyway."

"Why would you *say* that?"

"You really have to ask?"

"Oh, Josh. C'mon. You made one mistake. Sure, the stars were misaligned and it happened to be a pretty dang big mistake. But you can't live your life by it. You can't let that one night own you forever."

We walk on in silence for a bit, then Larry puts his hand on my shoulder.

"You know what you need? Closure. You have to figure out how to move on from this. You have to forgive yourself. But only you can figure out how to do that."

I wish I knew what it meant to move on. I wish I could remember what it was like before everything happened. When I was just this guy who partied with his friends. Talked about girls. Listened to music. Didn't worry about the future. Couldn't care less about the past. But now, it's like I'm stuck in this void where I can't go back and change what happened, I can only bring it with me, just like Larry said. It's like this shadow, following me everywhere, that keeps getting bigger and bigger. Sometimes, I think it's going to overtake me and swallow me whole.

Sometimes, I wish it would.

"Here's what's going to happen," Larry says. "When we get home, you're going to call her and tell her you need to talk. And then you're going to tell her how you feel.

You won't be stealing her. You'll be helping her make an informed decision. And believe me, when she knows how you feel, she is going to jump in your arms and declare her love for you. Got it?"

"Right."

"C'mon!" He tugs my arm and makes me walk faster. But as we near the building, it turns out I don't need to call her, because she is sitting on the steps, madly texting something on her phone.

Larry elbows me and whispers, "Good luck," then bounds up the stairs and into the building.

Stella keeps texting.

"Hey," I say. I sit down next to her.

She stops and slides a few inches away from me. "Um, Britt is going to be here any minute."

"Oh." I start to get up, since I know this is my cue to get lost before he sees us together. But then I stop.

"Look," I say. "I really am sorry about what happened."

"Just forget it."

"No, I—I can't. I mean. I want you to know—"

"Just forget it," she says again. "Please."

"I like you," I blurt out.

She stands up. "Please don't do this."

"What?"

"Get me all confused. I'm not breaking up with Britt,

OK? I know you think he's a jerk. But I swear. He's never acted that way before. He just got really jealous. He was worried about me when he couldn't reach me. That's all. You don't know the other side of him."

"What side is that?"

"His kind side. He loves me."

"Wanting to know your every move isn't love. It's — ownership."

She peers down the street.

"See? Right there. What you did just now. Don't you get what he does to you? You're always watching out for him, as if you're going to get in trouble for something."

"That's not true."

"Whatever."

"Look," she says. "You're a great guy. A great friend. But you're temporary, Josh. You're leaving as soon as school gets out."

"So are you."

"It's not the same. I still have to come back. And Britt will, too. We live here. But we also applied to the same colleges. We —"

"The same colleges? Really?"

"Yeah. And we both got into one of them, so —"

"But what if you break up? You're the one who said high-school relationships don't last."

"He loves me. He wants us to last."

"What about you? You keep saying how he feels and what he wants. Where do you fit in?"

"I want us to last, too. I don't want to be like my mom, always getting dumped. Always acting desperate. In the time I've been dating Britt, do you know how many boyfriends she's had?"

"No."

"A lot."

"Just because you and Britt break up doesn't make you like your mom."

"I'm not breaking up with him. Besides, me being with Britt is one of the only things that makes my mom happy. She thinks we're going to get married! If she had her way, we'd already be engaged."

"Why?"

"Because she wants a better life for me than she's had. Or provided."

"And Britt will give you that?"

She shrugs. "My mom thinks so."

"What do you think?"

Instead of answering, she scans the end of the road again, then looks down at her phone. To me, those two gestures say it all. But she doesn't get it. She really doesn't see what he's done to her.

"Why did you even give me that rock?" I ask.

"Because I care about you. We're karate partners."

"What happened to 'friends'?"

"Please don't make this so hard."

Now I'm the one looking up and down the street.

"Do you want it back, then?" I ask.

"What?"

"The rock."

She bites her bottom lip. "No. I want you to keep it."

"Why?"

"Because I still care. Look, he's going to be here any second."

"And?"

"Just forget it, OK?" She gets up and starts down the stairs. If Larry could see how this has unfolded, he would probably hit me over the head.

"He doesn't deserve you!" I call after her.

She doesn't turn back.

"Stella!" I call.

But she keeps on walking.

PART FOUR

JUNE

The ultimate aim in karate, therefore,
lies not in victory or defeat,
but in the perfection of the character
of its participants.

—Gichin Funakoshi (1868–1957)

Chapter 34

"Hey, Josh! Check it out!" Jason waves a yearbook at me. "You gonna pick yours up?"

"I didn't order one," I tell him. It's the last day of school, and all day long I've been avoiding people spontaneously hugging and crying in the halls. You'd think this was the end of the world, not the end of senior year. But I guess some of these people think those are the same thing. People like *Britt* and his posse, who will never again experience being able to reign over an entire group of popular-table wannabes. They know this way of life is over. At college, they will have to start from nothing again, and there is no guarantee they will ever achieve the same level of greatness. Me? I'll just go on being invisible like always. Nothing to lose.

"How could you not order a yearbook?" Jason asks, stunned. But I can see the reason slowly dawn on him.

I shrug.

"Well, will you sign mine?"

"Sign it?"

"Yeah, you know. Say some brilliant thing, and when you're famous, I can sell it."

"Don't hold your breath," I tell him. I drop my bag at my feet and take his book and the pen he's already pulled out.

I think for a minute. Then write:

Jason, Thanks for making what could have been a hellish year not be. —Josh

I close the book so he doesn't read it in front of me.

"Thanks! Are you going to the graduation party?"

"No, I have to go to my uncle's wedding."

"That sucks! Can't you get out of it?"

"I'm the best man."

"Oh. Guess not. But you'll still be at graduation, right?"

"Definitely."

"Cool."

I pick up my stuff and head out the school doors for the last time.

It feels pretty damn good.

* * *

As soon as I get home, I check my phone and find about a million texts from my parents. They're coming for my graduation, which they refused to let me skip, and for Larry's wedding, of course. For some bizarre reason only Larry can explain, he thought it would be a brilliant idea to get married the same weekend so it can be, in his words, "A Josh and Larry Extravaganza!" Such. A. Bad. Idea.

Caleb and Dave have been texting like crazy, too. They want me to come home and party with them when they graduate (a week after me), but I keep making excuses for committing to any solid plans. I don't know why. I guess I'm kind of in denial that I actually have to go back home for the summer before I leave for Philly. I got into my third choice, Temple University, which is pretty good, considering how lousy my GPA was before I came here.

About the only person who isn't on my case every day is Stella. But that's because Stella doesn't talk to me anymore.

We still go to karate, but we don't walk home together. Britt picks her up. At practice, she avoids me. And when we're doing our katas side by side, I feel like I'm dancing with a shadow instead of a friend. Sometimes when I catch her looking at me, it's like I'm looking at that other disappointed face. Like I failed another test I never understood the rules for. When we finally tested for our brown belts — and got them — Larry wanted to take us both out for dinner to celebrate, but Stella said no. And at that moment, I realized we really weren't friends anymore.

Larry thinks this is all very tragic. But I did exactly what I set out to do last year when I arrived. I went to school. I studied hard and brought up my grades so I could get into college. I earned my ticket out of Dodge in the form of an acceptance letter to Temple University. I did it. Every goal met. But somewhere along the way, they didn't seem all that important anymore. And then I lost the one thing that was: Stella.

So that's where I'm at. Soon, my parents will come. I'll put on some stupid bright-green-and-purple graduation robe because, yeah, those are the school colors, and I'll shake some dude's hand and get my diploma, which basically represents my *real* ticket out of here. And then I'll stand next to Larry and give him the rings, and he'll walk down the aisle a new man, with Arielle at his side. And then we'll party it up at the reception and then wave good-bye as they drive away.

And then I'll wave good-bye to this life, too.

It feels like I'm always waving good-bye.

Chapter 35

A few days before graduation, Larry and Arielle are off meeting a caterer while I pick up the place in anticipation of my parents coming. Clover follows me from room to room, purring in a sad way. It's like she knows our days are numbered.

When the landline rings, I almost don't pick it up, but then I figure it could be my parents. I say hello, but no one replies for a few seconds. Then I hear a baby crying in the background. I feel my heart start to race.

"Hello?" I say again. "Who is this?"

"J-Josh? Is Larry there?"

"Stella?" I ask.

"Yeah. Can I talk to Larry?"

"He's out with Arielle."

"Do — do you know when he'll be back?"

Her voice sounds weird. I think she's crying.

"I'm not sure. Are you OK?"

"Um. Not really. Can you come outside?"

"Where are you?"

"On the stoop. Could — could you hurry?"

I race down the stairs. Just outside, I find her sitting on the stairs, hugging her foot. Benny is screaming bloody murder from his stroller.

"What happened?" I yell, rushing to her. Her left foot doesn't look right. Her shoe is all smooshed-looking. As soon as she sees me, she starts sobbing.

"Can you help us get to the hospital?" she chokes.

"How did you do that?"

"It kind of got run over. It was an accident."

"An accident?"

"Yes. I swear. But I think I might have broken my foot."

"Shouldn't I call an ambulance?"

"No! It's too expensive. Can you hail a cab? I tried to call my mom, but she's not picking up. And Gil and Gene aren't answering their phones. I figured I'd take a shot at Larry being home. I'd go myself, but I've got the baby and . . ."

"No worries," I say. "Just hang on." I run to the corner and start waving my hands at the traffic to hail a cab. By some miracle, I see one two blocks down, and he flashes his lights to show me he's on the way. I race back to Stella.

The cab pulls to the curb. Stella holds out her hand, and I pull her up and help her over to the door. She winces as she gets in. "The baby," she says, gesturing toward the stroller. He got so quiet all of a sudden, I forgot he was there.

"Oh, uh . . ." I wheel the stroller over to the door.

"You'll have to hand him to me," she says.

"Huh?"

"Pick him up. You can fold the stroller and put it in the trunk."

The driver stands next to the stroller, waiting.

I force myself to look down. A round face with brown eyes and wet cheeks cranes up at me. Pudgy hands reach out, as if they know what my job is.

I breathe in and try to stay calm. I unclick the little straps connected at his waist.

"OK," I say. "OK."

I reach out and put my hands under his tiny arms, around his middle. When his hand touches mine, I feel a chill run up my arm.

"Hurry up, eh?" the driver says.

"Yeah, yeah," I say. I get a hold, and gently lift him out. He's surprisingly solid and heavy. He grabs my nose as soon as he can reach. My heart is pumping against my chest so hard it hurts.

I swivel around and hand him to Stella as fast as I can. But even after I let go, I feel the weight of him in my hands. And the pain in my chest is still there.

I help the driver get the stroller folded up and climb in next to Stella and the baby.

"Can you hold him?" she asks. "My foot . . ."

She passes him over to me.

"I don't know," I say. "I've never—"

But she's passing him over, and he's reaching for me again.

He leans his head back against my chest and looks up. "Gah."

"Hey," I say. His little body is warm and heavy against mine.

"Hospital," Stella tells the driver.

"I figured," he says.

Benny points out the window as we pass a big dump truck. "Duh!" he says. He lifts his head and thuds it against my chest again.

Stella sucks in her breath and flinches when we hit a dip in the road.

"Are you all right?" I ask.

"I think I broke something," she says. "I'm afraid to look."

I peer down at her shoe. There's a black streak across the top where the tire must have gone over.

"You might be OK," I say. "The shoe doesn't look too squashed."

She winces. "I hope you're right."

"How did this happen, anyway?"

"It was an accident," she says again. She turns away from me when she says it. "And I don't want to talk about it."

"Fine," I say.

"Digh!" Ben points as we pass under a green light.

And that's about the extent of our conversation.

At the ER entrance, we all climb out and I get the baby back in the stroller. The driver goes inside and comes back with a wheelchair and a nurse, which is pretty nice of him. Then I realize I ran outside without any cash, and he freaks out because Stella doesn't have any money, either. "Listen, if you come by the same address tomorrow I'll pay you. I promise," I tell him.

He looks like he doesn't believe me, but what else can he do? Plus, the baby's crying again.

He walks away, shaking his head and mumbling.

"I promise I'll pay you back!" I call. He waves his hand at me in disgust.

When I turn back, the nurse is already wheeling Stella toward the ER entrance. I grab the stroller and try to catch up. "Ella!" Ben cries, pointing.

And he reminds me again.

Of Ellie.

Chapter 36

Ben starts crying as we go through the huge sliding door and into the busy waiting room. There's a long line just to check in with the receptionist. There are other babies in the waiting room, too, and it's as if Ben's cries urge them all on. Pretty soon there are three babies crying their heads off. I push Ben's stroller up next to where the nurse left Stella so she can comfort him, but she's looking more and more pale.

"Could you take him out of that thing?" Stella says through gritted teeth. "He probably needs a new diaper."

"Uh . . ."

"We should check," she says.

I unbuckle him and lift him up. He stops crying right away and reaches for my nose again.

"He likes you," Stella says. "I guess he just wanted out."

I stand there holding him under his arms, his legs dangling, my heart pounding all over again. He feels so . . . real. It's the strangest thing, holding this small body. This living thing. With big, innocent eyes. And drool. And hands that reach for your nose, even though you're a stranger.

"You've never held a baby before, have you?" Stella says, almost laughing.

"What gave you that impression?"

Ben smiles at me and swings his legs in the air.

"If you hold him against you on your hip, it's a lot easier," Stella says. "Like that." She motions to a woman ahead of us with a baby teetering on her hip.

"Oh, OK." I try to hold him the right way, and it's true, it's a lot easier once his weight is resting on my hip. Ben pats my shoulder and makes a *ga-ga* noise, then leans his head against me.

You've never held a baby before.

No. I never have.

"Next!" A lady behind a window in the wall calls. We move up in line, and pretty soon we get called over. Stella provides her insurance card and answers a million questions. A nurse comes over to us and gives Stella's foot a quick look. "Can you take the shoe off?" she asks. Stella starts to try, but then yells in pain.

"OK," the nurse says. "Let's get you taken care of. Is this your baby?" she asks. "He's a cutie." She winks at me.

"God, no," Stella says. "I was babysitting when it happened. This is just my friend. He can watch the baby for me."

Back up. First, I'm glad she referred to me as her friend, at least. But more importantly, I can what, now?

The nurse nods. "All right, honey."

Before I can object, before I can say, *Hey! I don't know how to do this! I only just learned how to hold the kid, for Christ's sake!* the nurse is wheeling Stella away, leaving me alone with Ben.

He pats my chest with his chubby hand again. "Ba," he says. I smell this powdery smell that's sweet and different from anything I've smelled before, and I know it's coming from him. Suddenly, his weight feels like more than I can hold. This life, in my arms. He squeezes my sleeve in his fist.

"Easy, there," I say.

He smiles at me. His eyes are deep, dark brown. When I look in them, I know he is seeing straight into my soul. Seeing who I really am. This baby. This life holding on to me. Needing me.

I look around, thinking maybe someone can help me find Stella. Because I know I can't do this. I can't. Even though it's not the same hospital, it looks the same. It smells the same. It sounds the same. And I know somewhere, down some corridor, there is a nursery. Just like —

"Ga," Ben says. "Da." He touches his tiny pointy finger to my cheek. It's wet. I quickly wipe my eyes before anyone can notice.

I carry him into the waiting area, pulling the stroller behind me. I find a place to sit in a corner, where some other mom is holding a baby and talking to another little kid who keeps banging a plastic doll against his mom's knees. "Stop it, Kenny," she says. But he doesn't.

When I sit next to her, she gives me a dirty look, like I'm invading her space. I shift Ben on my lap and glance around. Two other babies are still crying. One mom looks frazzled and scared; the other one looks bored. There are a lot of old people, too, staring blankly at the TV screen on the wall. It smells in here like sweat and Dave's feet. There's a drunk guy on the other side of the room who yells out every few seconds, then closes his eyes again.

As far as waiting rooms go, this one pretty much sucks.

Ben squirms for me to let him down. He teeters on his fat little legs, holding on to my knees to balance himself. He smiles up at me, like he's all that. "Pretty good," I say. He wobbles some more and then almost topples over, but I catch him. He laughs and tries again.

And again and again about a million times. But at least he's not crying.

After a while, there's a new smell in the room, and right away I know what it is and pray it's not coming from Ben. Because, hello? I've never changed a diaper before, and I don't even know if there are any clean ones in the stroller.

The lady next to me wrinkles her nose. "You need to change him," she says. "That's nasty."

Shit.

I pick him up again and check out the stroller for a diaper bag, but I don't see anything like that in there. Ben starts to cry. "Hey, it's OK, bud," I say.

The lady's kid starts to cry, too, but this kid is surprisingly smart and actually pulls at his pants as if to tell his mom he's the one with the problem.

"Really, Kenny?" the mom asks.

He has a pacifier in his mouth, so he just nods. She sighs and heaves herself up.

"Want me to save your seat?" I ask. She gives me that same dirty look. What the hell? It's not my problem her kid needs a new diaper.

Ben is still crying, tugging at me and fussing. Finally, I realize he's just trying to get comfortable. He pulls himself onto me so we're chest to chest, then rests his head on my shoulder, squirming a bit until his head nestles into the side of my neck. I feel his warm breath against my skin. I take my own deep breath. But my throat is tightening up in a familiar ache. I think of the rocking chair creaking above me back at Larry's and gently try to rock him. He makes a satisfied noise. I pat his back a little until he gets heavier and heavier, and then his breathing gets steady and I know he's asleep. I shift so I can lean farther back in the chair. He feels so heavy on top of me. So solid. And warm.

The drunk guy yells out. People come and go. But Ben keeps still, breathing in his steady way. His heartbeat thumping against my chest. My own heart.

Is this what it would be like? Is this what I missed?

Ben must be close to a year old. About the same age as — as my baby would be.

I see him again in the tiny plastic bed with all the other babies. His small fist poking out of the blanket. And I see me walking away. Over and over, I see me walking away.

Ben makes a noise in his sleep. I shift and smell his baby-powder smell again. Feel the solidness of him pressed against me. Trapping me in the chair.

Yes. This is what I missed.

I breathe in again, and close my eyes to keep from crying, it hurts so much.

This is what I missed.

Chapter 37

I wake up to the touch of someone's hand on my shoulder.

"Sir? Your friend is ready to go." It's the nurse from earlier.

I sit up slowly, the weight of Ben hot and heavy on my chest.

Stella waves from the other side of the room. She's sitting in the wheelchair with a pair of crutches across her lap. I stand up awkwardly, trying not to wake Ben, but it doesn't really work and he starts to cry. I reach for the stroller but the nurse says, "Let me get that, hon," and pushes it ahead of us.

"Is he OK?" Stella asks when we've finally made our way through the maze of people and kids in the waiting room.

"Yeah. Are you?"

She shrugs and looks down at her foot, which has an ice pack bandaged around it. "Good thing brown-belt tests were last week," she says. "And I need a new pair of shoes. But other than that, I'm fine. No broken bones, at least."

I put Ben in the stroller and right away my chest feels cold where he was against me. And empty. I follow the nurse as she wheels Stella outside and helps us find a bench to sit on. When the nurse leaves us, Stella checks her phone.

Some things never change.

"Phew," she says. "Gene's on his way. I was hoping he'd get my message."

Oh.

"So, how did this accident happen again?" I ask.

Stella turns away from me just like she did before. But this time, her shoulders start shaking because she's crying. I'm not sure if I should try to hug her, or pat her back, or what. So I don't do anything. As usual.

"I'm such an idiot," she says.

I pick at a scab on my arm.

"Thanks for disagreeing."

"Sorry." I watch a trickle of blood slowly seep out from the newly exposed cut. "Why are you an idiot?"

"Isn't it obvious?" She turns back to me.

I cover the cut with my hand. "Britt went crazy, huh?"

"Kind of. Yeah."

"What tipped him over the edge?"

"He found out I applied to a school he didn't."

"That's it?"

"I told him I'm going. It's my dream school. I never thought I'd get in. That's why I didn't tell him. I just wanted to see, you know. If I could do it. I wasn't even planning to go if I got in. But . . . they offered me a scholarship. A good one."

"That's great!" I say. "Wow! What school?"

"Sarah Lawrence. In New York."

She smiles when she says it, like she can't stop herself, she's so pleased.

"I'm psyched for you, Stell. That's really amazing."

"Thanks."

"So . . . Britt wasn't too thrilled, I take it."

"He totally freaked out. He can't believe I don't want to go to school with him."

"So he ran over your foot?"

"That really was an accident. I was trying to make him stay so I could talk to him. I had my hand on the door handle, and he took off and happened to roll over my foot."

"Wow."

"Yeah. It's so over. He'll never talk to me again. Not after this. He really feels betrayed."

"But . . . he should be excited for you! You got into your dream school. And you got a scholarship!"

"He doesn't see it that way. He thinks I should sacrifice my dream so we can be together." She says it in a sad way. Like she really is disappointed in him.

"Are you going to be OK?"

"Me? Yeah. I think something like this was bound to happen."

"Why do you say that?"

"Because you were right. He's too controlling. I was blind to it for a long time. But I get it now. I didn't want it to be true. He seemed like the perfect boyfriend for so long. But things just kept getting more and more intense. I felt like I was drowning, and he was the one with his hand on my head, holding me underwater."

I'm not sure what to say to that, so I just lean back and squint at the sky.

"I don't even know why I'm crying. I feel so . . . relieved." She wipes the tears from her cheeks and looks up with me. "I'm sorry," she says. "I was the worst friend ever. I can't believe you don't hate me."

"Only a little," I say.

She elbows me in her usual way. "And thanks for watching Ben for me. I know how you feel about babies and all, so thanks."

"What do you mean, 'how I feel about babies'?"

"How you freak out around them?"

Oh. That.

"What's that all about, anyway?"

"I don't know what you mean."

She rolls her eyes. "Right."

I look out at the parking lot, down at my filthy sneakers. Anywhere but in her direction.

"Hey," she says. "Sorry to bring it up. I know it's none of my business."

My hand sticks to my arm where the blood is drying. I pull it away and look down at the palm print of blood left there.

"What did you do?" Stella asks, inspecting my arm.

"Just broke a scab," I say. I wipe my hand on my jeans.

"You're so weird."

"I know."

We sit there quietly, awkwardly, until Gene pulls up in his car. He jumps out and runs over to Stella. "Are you OK? Oh, my God!" He hugs her, then inspects her foot. "Is it broken?"

"No, just bruised."

"Aw, Stell. How did this happen?"

She shrugs. "It was an accident."

I wonder how long it will take for someone to dare to say, "Yeah, right."

"Well, let's get you home." Gene scoops Ben out of the stroller and hugs him before he puts him in his car seat. Ben's whole face changes when he sees his dad. He looks at him like kids look at presents.

I help Stella into the back. We're all pretty quiet on the ride home, except for Ben's happy *ga-ga* noises in the backseat.

"How you doing back there, sweets?" Gene asks Stella.

"Never been better," Stella says.

"That was some accident, Stell. How the heck does someone get their foot run over by a car?"

"Just lucky, I guess," Stella says sarcastically.

Gene leans his head toward the rearview mirror so he can see her face. "Hey," he says. "Are you OK?"

"I'm fine," she says quietly.

Gene focuses back on the road.

"So, Josh, you're graduating soon, too, right? We're so bummed Stella's leaving us. Don't you want to do a gap year, Stell? Stick around for a while?"

"No chance," Stella says. "I've got a ticket to New York

and it's one-way." She turns to me. "What about you?"

"Temple," I say.

"Nice!" She looks genuinely happy. "I've heard Philly is a really cool city."

"Yeah," I say. But it's not New York. And I realize it's very likely we will never see each other again.

Gene pulls up to the curb in front of our building, and I help Stella out. "Can you make sure she gets in safely?" he asks me. "I have to go pick up Gil."

"No problem," I say. I look in the backseat and notice that Ben is watching me. He reaches out his hand and points his little finger at me. I reach through the window and gently squeeze it. "Nice hanging with you," I say.

"Ga."

"OK, we'll see you later!" Gene says, cutting off our deep conversation.

When I let go of Ben's finger, my own are wet with his drool. But it doesn't gross me out. I feel the familiar hurt in my chest and force myself to shrug it off as the car pulls away.

Stella glances up at the steep steps to the front door and groans. "This is gonna be fun."

"Want some help?" I ask.

"If you don't mind . . ."

I take her crutches and stoop down so she can put

her arm around me. As soon as she gets close, I smell her familiar scent. Her laundry detergent and shampoo, mixed with the perfume she wears.

"Ready?" I ask. She nods, and I help her hop up each step on one foot. When we go inside and get in the elevator, she presses two instead of her own floor.

"Do you mind if I crash with you for a while? I don't think I can face our empty apartment. And who knows when my mom will get home?"

"Where is she?"

"Calvin's, most likely. They're still together. All the time, in fact. If she's not staying out late to take a class, she's crashing at his place. It's like she's already said goodbye to me, and I haven't even left yet."

"Oh."

She shrugs, like it's no big deal, but I can tell just thinking about them hurts her somehow. "Anyway. Can I hang at your place for a while?"

"Yeah. Sure," I say. But I wonder if this is the best idea. I wonder if I should be so forgiving. *Britt* screws up and I'm supposed to have been waiting around all this time so we can be friends again?

The elevator door opens, and she leads the way to Larry's on her crutches. When we get inside, I help her prop her foot up on the coffee table and we read through her discharge instructions to figure out when she can take the next round of pain meds and stuff.

"Thank God I'm eighteen," she says. "I never would've gotten out of that place." There's a sadness about her, though. She shouldn't have had to go through that without her mom. An adult who could take care of her. Not me.

I wish Larry would come home. He would know what to say. How to make her feel better. He would call her *Stell-aaaaaaah* and make her laugh. It feels like too much time has passed since we hung out, and now being with her here feels awkward.

I bring her a glass of water and sit next to her on the couch.

"So, what do you want to do?" I ask.

She sighs. "I don't know. Want to sign my bandage?"

"I thought people only signed casts."

"Humor me? I always wanted a cast when I was a kid. You know. So my friends could sign it and draw funny pictures and stuff. Of course, I never really had that many friends, so that was a total fantasy. I probably would have ended up drawing on it myself in different colors and handwriting to make it look like I was popular."

"You haven't always been popular?"

"Nah. That's all Britt. After today . . . well, we'll see.

Who cares, anyway? School's over. It's time to move on. My school friends were all his first. Not mine. They're not the true kind. Not like you."

"Is this your way of guilting me into signing that thing?"

"Yes?"

"That's just sad."

"Oh, come on, please? Think of the honor of getting to be first."

"Fine." I find a marker in the junk drawer in the kitchen. "What do I write?"

"Your name?"

"That's so lame."

"Be creative, then. Surprise me."

I just sit there holding the marker and staring at her foot. "Wait a minute. What if Britt sees this?"

She stops smiling. "He won't."

"Why not?"

"Because it's over."

"For now."

"Forever."

I raise my eyebrows. "For real?"

She sighs. "Just sign this thing, will you? Be clever. I know you can."

I draw a stick figure doing a karate kick and write

True Karate Man and then an arrow pointing up, so it's aimed at Stella.

"Nice," she says. "You know, that whole thing is pretty sexist."

"Maybe you should tell that to Larry."

"Maybe I will."

It feels weird to be talking to her again, just like old times. Weird and pretty great. But it's awkward, too. And I know we're going to have to figure out how to acknowledge the fact that all this time has passed without talking, and how stupid that was. But for now I guess we're both just silently relieved that we *are* talking to each other, so neither of us brings it up.

We decide to order takeout and watch a movie, but before the food comes, Larry bursts through the door.

"Oh, thank God!" he yells, running over to Stella. "I didn't get your message until after class. I tried to call back, but you didn't answer your phone! I ran all the way here!"

He's completely out of breath, sweat pouring in huge droplets down the side of his face. He's still wearing his gi.

"Are you OK? Oh, my God. Look at your foot! Poor Stella!"

"Relax, Larry. I'm fine. I turned my phone off when we got here."

She did? I wonder if she turned it off so Britt couldn't reach her.

Larry turns to me. "Sammy, you took care of her?"

I roll my eyes.

"You're such a good boy." He reaches out to ruffle my hair.

"Easy, Larry," I say.

The buzzer rings, and I take the cue to escape. When I come back with the food, Larry's already setting the coffee table.

"We were going to watch a movie," Stella tells him. "Want to join?"

"Oh! Yes! Can I pick? I have the perfect choice. Just let me take a quick shower."

"You never should have agreed to let him pick," I say as we eat. "You know it's going to be another Jackie Chan."

Stella shrugs. "I like Jackie Chan."

I lean back on the couch. "You're only saying that to annoy me."

"That's because you're so cute when you're annoyed."

My face burns. I get up to clear the table and escape to the kitchen to do the dishes as fast as I can. Larry joins me just as I'm finishing up. His skin is still wet from the shower. His T-shirt is all wet, too.

"Ever heard of a towel?" I ask him.

"I was in a hurry!"

Pathetic.

"I'm making Stella a smoothie," he says. "Want one?"

"No, thanks."

"Hey." He motions for me to come closer. "How did it happen, anyway?" he whispers. "Did the boyfriend do it on purpose?"

"No, it was an accident. But she's lucky she wasn't hurt worse."

"He really is a shit."

"I know that."

"I can hear you, ya know!" Stella calls from the living room.

Larry grimaces. "Oops."

I shake my head.

"Sorry, hon! But you know it's the truth! We only say it cuz we love you!"

Larry elbows me and mouths, *Now's your chance.*

Shut up, I mouth back.

Larry makes a face. *Now,* he mouths again.

I push him away.

When the smoothie is made and we're all settled on the couch, Larry pulls up his movie choice.

Stella groans. "*The Karate Kid*? Really?"

"It's the remake with Jackie!" Larry says. "I've been wanting to watch it for years. I heard it's actually pretty good!"

"From who, the Jackie Chan Fan Club?" I ask.

He waves his hand dismissively. "This is the Jackie Chan Dis-Free Zone. Hush."

So we sit there and watch. And it's kind of agonizing sitting here with Larry making noises through every fight scene and even getting up a few times to mimic the moves, and Stella sitting so close our arms keep touching. And me wondering if she's doing it on purpose or not, because it feels like torture trying to figure out what it all means.

When the movie is finally over, Larry sniffs and wipes his eyes. "See? Great, right?"

Stella and I exchange looks.

"Oh, come on, guys! You loved it. I know you did."

"I preferred the original," Stella says.

"But that one didn't have Jackie!" Larry whines.

"Why is it called *The Karate Kid*? They don't even do karate. They do kung fu."

"Who cares! That's what makes it so great!"

"Because it has a stupid title?" I ask.

"No, because it's just like me! Karate dude in love with kung-fu dude."

"So . . . *confused* dude?" Stella grins when Larry reaches over to swat her.

"Not that kind of love," he says. "It's admiration. No. Awe."

"Awe," I say. "That's one way to put it."

"You two are impossible. Jackie is the Man. He doesn't have to be a karate man to be the Man. Get it?"

Um. No?

Stella shifts on the couch and winces. "There we go with 'the Man.' We need to talk about that, Lar."

"What do you mean?"

She wiggles her foot at him, then cringes.

Larry inspects my drawing. "I don't get it."

"What is a true karate *man*?" she asks.

"Well, that's just traditional. It means woman, too."

"Then we should say that."

"But 'What is a true karate man or woman?' sounds so awkward," he whines.

"Not to me."

"Fine. We can add 'or woman.' "

"Really? You're the best, Lar!"

"That's true. Now. Admit you liked the movie. Please?"

"It was cute," Stella says. "Jackie was awesome."

"Thank you. Josh?"

"Adorable," I say.

Larry mopes, but then starts doing a bunch of blocks and kicks around the living room, so clearly he's not really that upset. If only we could all get over ourselves so easily.

Chapter 38

It's late by the time we bring Stella up to her apartment. Larry insists on going because he wants to talk with Star about what happened. When we step inside the place, though, there's no sign of Star. The apartment feels empty and unlived in. There's not much furniture or anything on the walls. I cringe, realizing this is what Stella comes home to every day. To loneliness. I can imagine the contrast she must feel when she visits the house of *Britt* with the BMW. Is that why she stayed with him so long? Because of the promise of something better?

Stella's bedroom is just as spare as the rest of the house. There are no posters on the wall, just a black-and-white photo of a dirt road leading to some unknown place in the distance. On her nightstand, there's a photo of Britt, which she turns over as soon as she gets close enough to reach it.

"On second thought," she says. She picks it back up and dumps it in the wastebasket next to the nightstand.

"Oh," Larry says, touching a light-green dress hanging on a hook on the back of the door. "Is this your dress for prom?"

Stella frowns. "Was. Good thing I have the wedding to wear it to."

"Oh, Stell," Larry says. "I'm so sorry. Can't you go without him?" He eyes me in his Larry-like way, as if to say, for the hundredth time, *Here's your chance.*

I pretend I don't get the message.

"It's fine," Stella says. "I don't want to go. Not like this." But it's obviously not fine, because her eyes start to water.

"What can we do to help?" Larry says. "I hate to leave you like this."

"I'll be fine. I'm just gonna brush my teeth and crash."

"Do you think your mom'll be home soon? Do you need help getting into some pj's?"

"She's not five, Lar," I say.

Stella laughs. "I can manage."

Larry gives her a big hug. "Call if you need anything, hon. *Anything.*"

"I will."

We turn to go.

"Hey," Stella says before we shut the door. She hobbles forward and gives me a hug. She feels surprisingly tiny as my arms go around her. It's only for a second, but it's enough to know just how small she is. But muscular. Strong.

When we pull apart, she smiles at me in her old way, before things got crazy. My heart melts the same way it used to. But then she turns away.

"C'mon," Larry says, and drags me out of the room.

I follow him back through the apartment and realize why it's so empty. Because Stella's mom believes it's temporary. She believes she'll marry someone, maybe Calvin, who will take her away from this place. This life. Maybe that's what Stella believed about Britt. Until today. I wonder if she believes she can still escape without him.

"You think she'll be OK alone in there?" I whisper. "Maybe we should have her stay with us."

Larry winks at me. "You'd like that, huh?"

"Shut up, Lar. You know what I mean."

"She'll be all right. Stella's a survivor. If she thought she needed to stay with us, she would have said."

"Still. It must suck to be alone all the time."

"I bet that's why she offers to babysit Benny so much."

I hadn't thought of that.

We walk to the end of the hall and take the stairs

instead of the elevator. But instead of going down, Larry goes up.

"Where are you going?" I ask.

"Just follow me."

I shrug and follow him up the stairs until we go beyond what I thought was the top floor. We reach a door that opens up to the rooftop and step out into the warm summer-night air. The tar-covered roof radiates heat as we cross to a few ratty-looking lawn chairs. Beyond us, the neighborhood lights cast a hazy glow.

Larry pulls the chairs closer together. "Take a seat," he says.

We both sit, facing the neighborhood and beyond.

"Come here often?" I ask.

"Not so much. But sometimes." He stretches his arms out. "I like how open it feels up here."

I lean back in the chair and look up where there should be stars. "It's nice," I say.

"Yeah." Larry's quiet for a while. We listen to the traffic and the occasional dog barking.

"I'm worried about Stella," he finally says. "I wish her mom would step up and be around for her. Especially now."

"Me, too."

"And I'm worried about you." He reaches over and squeezes my arm, then lets go. "I wish I could be more like Mr. Han, you know? I wish I could teach you both some real survival skills."

"Mr. Han?" I ask.

"From *The Karate Kid.* You know. Jackie Chan."

"I like to practice nonviolence," I tell him. "No worries."

"You know what I mean. You two . . . you're great kids. But . . . you've got issues."

There's an understatement.

"I wish you didn't. You know? I wish you weren't carrying such heavy loads. I wish I could be Mr. Han to both of you." He swishes his hands through the air. "Jacket on, jacket off."

"Um, yeah. I think we would've both killed you if you did that to us."

"You know what I mean," he says, annoyed.

"Sorry. You've been great. I promise. Way better than Mr. Han."

"Nah. I should've done more. I never thought Stell would let things go so far. Her boyfriend *ran over her foot,* for God's sake. That's crazy. That's what it took for her to break up with the guy? I should have seen something like this coming." He gets up, paces, sits back down.

"Stella really believes it was an accident," I tell him.

"Doesn't matter. He still did it. Because he was driving away from her."

"True," I say. "He really is a shit."

"And then there's her mom being MIA all the time, chasing after Calvin. No wonder Stella was attracted to that Britt guy. He pays more attention to her than her own mom."

"Except that he's an asshole."

"Yeah, except for that."

"But she's getting out now. Just like me."

Larry's quiet for a minute. I think about my year living with Larry, which I've been doing a lot of lately. I think about how I haven't had a single beer since I moved in with him. I haven't gone out. I haven't partied. In fact, in some ways it has been the lamest year of my life so far.

The crazy thing is, it's also been one of the best.

"Yeah, you're both getting out," he finally says. "Man, everything's gonna be so different without you two." He stands up again. "I'm going to make your final days here the best days of your lives! I swear."

"You're getting married in a week, Larry. I think you should focus on your future and how those days will be the best in *your* life."

"Oh, Sammy," he says. "You're a good kid."

We look up at the sky again and listen to the traffic.

"Stella told me you held the baby today," he says after a while. He sits down again. I swear, he cannot be still for five minutes.

"You really have to bring that up now?" I ask.

"Yup."

I shake my head. "Yeah. I held him."

"Are you OK?"

I remember Benny's weight against me. How it felt good and hurt like hell at the same time.

"Yeah," I say. "I'm OK."

He waits for me to say more, but what else is there? I'm OK. It's enough.

"You've been avoiding that baby all year, and suddenly you hold him for what, two hours? And all you have to say is 'Yeah' and 'I'm OK'? I know it had to be hard, Sam."

I automatically put my hand on my chest, where the baby's heart beat against mine.

"What are you feeling? Talk to me."

I think for a minute. I'm not sure. "I'm feeling . . . lighter, I guess."

"What does that mean?"

I breathe in the hot-roof smell. Search for the stars again. Fidget with the loose armrest on my lawn chair.

"I had to take him out of his stroller because he was crying, you know? And I was surprised at how heavy he was. I mean, he was really solid. He held on to me. He practiced standing up. And then he got really tired and nestled against me and went to sleep. It felt so strange to have this life, this small but heavy and warm living thing, depending on me. I'm a total stranger, but he trusted me. He just snuggled his head into my neck and fell sound asleep."

Larry shifts in his chair. "I bet he could sense your goodness."

I laugh. "Yeah, that's it."

"Hey, I'm serious! Babies are real smart. They can tell if someone's trustworthy."

"Maybe. He did give me a long stare."

"See?"

"Anyway. It made me think about what it must be like, you know, to be a dad. To have to do that every day. To be that responsible for someone else. For a minute, I thought, *Yeah, I could do this.* But then I realized I probably couldn't. Not yet, anyway."

"You did the right thing, Sammy . . . Josh."

"I didn't do anything," I say. "It was never really my choice."

"Well, I think it was for the best. What the mom did. What was her name again?"

"Ellie."

"Ellie. That's nice."

I see the Ellie of my dreams when he says that. Not silently screaming. Just standing there. On the other side of the glass. Trying, like me, to get in. I wonder if she got to hold the baby — our baby — before they took him away. I wonder if she was allowed to be with him for a while. To feel the weight of his life against her the way I felt Ben's today. I wonder if she got to feel his soft, fuzzy hair against her cheek. And I wonder which would be worse? Holding him and then letting him go? Or never knowing him at all?

"I feel different about everything after today," I say.

"How so?"

"I'm not sure. I guess part of all the not-knowing was . . . not knowing what it would be like. What it would feel like. To hold the baby. To be responsible for it. Sometimes when I wake up in the middle of the night and hear Ben crying above me, I wonder if my baby is crying somewhere. If he needs to be held and loved. If he's OK. There's this helplessness. Because I don't know where he is. I don't know who is taking care of him. I don't know if he's healthy. There's just so much I don't know about him. But today, when I was holding Ben, I realized one reason I was so worried was because I wouldn't know how to take care of him myself. Today, I realized I would. Somehow, I would just know. And I thought my baby's parents would know, too. And they must love him. How could you hold a kid like that and not love him? Not feel completely responsible?"

Larry doesn't answer. Maybe he's thinking that there are plenty of asshole parents in the world who don't love their kids. Who let their kids cry through the night. I guess I know that, too. But something in my heart tells me that's not the deal with my baby. Something tells me he's OK. People who adopt babies do it because they want them. Right?

"I'm so glad you're going to be my best man, Josh," Larry says. "I'm really proud of you." He reaches over and puts his hand on my arm.

"You're more like him than you think," I add. "You know that, right?"

"Who?"

"Mr. Han," I say, as if it's obvious. "Jackie. I mean, you took me in, just like he took that kid in. You showed me how to live again. Just like him. You showed me how to be happy. To have goals and work toward them. You showed me plenty of survival skills, Larry. You saved me."

"Nah, you saved yourself," he says, but I can tell by the grin on his face he's pleased with himself.

"You're going to be an amazing dad," I say.

He leans back in his chair and sighs happily. "You're a good boy, Josh. A true karate man. I'm really going to miss you."

And since I can tell he's all choked up, I lean back in my own chair and sigh happily, too.

We stare at the dark sky together, not needing to say anything else. Just being grateful to be here together for a little while longer, before everything changes.

Chapter 39

That night, I wake up to the sound of Ben above me. He cries out, waits. Cries out, waits. I look up at the ceiling and wait with him. Clover chirps in her sleep at the foot of my bed when I roll over on my side. Then she stretches and walks up the bed to sniff my face and purr at me. I hold out my hand, and she rubs her head against my fingers in her usual way.

Cry out. Wait. Cry out. Wait.

How long does it take to get up and walk down the hall, for Christ's sake?

Finally, I hear the floor creak and, a few seconds later, the familiar sound of the rocking chair, back and forth.

I didn't realize my heart was racing again.

Now that I'm wide awake, I look around the room. The ceiling stars are faded to a faint glow. I reach for my phone and read the last set of messages I haven't replied to.

Mom: c u nxt wk!!!!!!

Caleb: dave's date 2 prom dumped him. send beer.

Dave: I'm going stag 2 prom. YAAAAAAAAA

I realize these messages are from a couple of days ago and prom is already over. I toss the phone back on the nightstand. Prom. Man. It's a disappointment for everyone. Except Caleb, of course, but that's no surprise. He probably went with his girlfriend, Corinne, and got engaged or something insane.

It must suck for Stella, though, since she bought a dress and everything. I should have asked her to go with me instead. As friends. But I'm sure she'd probably say no. Who wants to hobble around in a fancy dress for prom? She wouldn't even be able to dance. Besides, what if *Britt* showed up? I'd have to kill him or something.

The creaks above me stop, and footsteps cross the room. Then quiet. Quiet, quiet, and I know he must be asleep.

I close my eyes and listen to Clover's purrs next to my head.

It might have been nice, though. Taking Stella to prom. Dancing with her.

But we have our own way of dancing.

And I like ours better.

Chapter 40

Larry pokes his head through my doorway and grins so wide it looks like his mouth is going to split his face in half. "Rise and shine, Sammy! This is it! The Josh and Larry Extravaganza! Are you ready?" He is glistening in sweat but doesn't seem to notice.

"Dude, did you shower yet?" I ask.

"Twice. I can't stop sweating! It's crazy!" He's smiling like a maniac, so I guess it doesn't matter.

"Hey," I say. "I want to give you your present before things get crazy."

"You got me a present?"

"Of course! Well, I mean I got you and Arielle something, too. But this is just for you. You know, to say thanks. For everything."

I sit up and reach under the bed for a long tube.

Larry grins at me and pulls off the plastic cover at the end and dumps out a rolled-up poster. It's not the same movie poster I ripped up, but I hope he likes it.

"No way!" Larry yells after carefully unrolling the paper. He jumps up and down. "I love it! I love it!" He pins the new poster up where the old one used to be, then steps back to admire it. "*The Karate Kid*. That's you, man. That's *us*. Oh, yeah. This is perfect."

"Well. You know. Thanks for being my Mr. Han. I really appreciate it."

He tousles my hair like I'm a little kid again. "This has been a great year, Sammy. The best." His eyes water up.

"Yeah," I say. "It has."

"You better get up and shower. This place is about to become a madhouse."

He practically bounces out of the room, singing his off-key rendition of "I Gotta Feelin'."

After my shower, I put on my only pair of dress pants and a white button-up shirt and tie. Larry picked out the tie. It's supposed to match both my insane graduation robe *and* Arielle's maid of honor's dress. Arielle isn't going to make it to the graduation, obviously, since she's getting ready for the wedding, which is approximately one hour after I walk down my own aisle. I still think this makes Larry a nut job, but he seems to think it was the best idea ever and will help him keep his mind off being nervous. I don't point out that since he has now sweated through two shirts, it doesn't appear to be working.

"Lookin' good!" he says when I walk into the kitchen to make some breakfast. I'm still scarfing down my toast when the buzzer rings and Larry races for the door to let my parents up. They were going to spend the night here last night, but got a hotel instead. Larry was all, "They wanted their privacy, wink, wink." I explained that you aren't supposed to *say* "wink," but he just laughed. "Be happy for them," he said. "I am," I told him.

My dad is wearing a tie and looks like he dropped about thirty pounds. My mom is holding his hand. I almost make a joke about asking them who they are and what they've done to my real parents, but I stop myself. Why remind them of what they used to be, when what they are now is so much better?

Instead, in my best Larry impression, I tell my dad he's lookin' good. He makes a funny face because he doesn't get it. Oh, well. When my mom hugs me, she smells different. Like she got some new kind of shampoo or something.

"You guys look amazing," I tell them. "Wow, Dad. You've lost some serious baggage."

He taps his stomach where his giant beer gut used to be. "Not bad, huh, Joshy?"

"You look so handsome," my mom tells me. "Oh, Josh. You're all grown up. I can't believe this day is here." And then she starts crying.

My dad pats her shoulder awkwardly. So much for *wink, wink*. They're clearly still working on the touching/togetherness thing. I can't imagine how awkward their weekend in Vermont must have been. I try not to cringe at the thought. Even so, while it still feels weird to see them together like this, it also feels good. Really good.

When we're finally ready to leave and are heading down the stairs, Larry says he forgot something and runs back inside. My parents climb into the van, and I slide the side door open. It smells like Rosie and pine air freshener. I sit on the middle seat and start to sweat.

And remember.

That night.

Here.

When everything changed.

"Hey!" Larry says, banging on the window. "Look who I found!"

Stella waves shyly. She's wearing the dress she was supposed to wear for prom, and her hair is all done up in a way I've never seen. She is stunning.

"Surprise!" Larry says. "I brought you a date."

They squeeze in next to me on the seat and lay Stella's crutches over our laps. "I thought you two could help each other with your caps and gowns when we get there," Larry says. He's sitting between us and has his sweaty arms around our shoulders. I try not to breathe.

"My mom was supposed to take me, but she stayed at Calvin's last night and said she'd meet us there." She says *Calvin* the way Larry and I say *Britt*. "I hope you don't mind me crashing your party."

"No," I say. "No, of course we don't mind! God!"

"Nice to see you again, Stella," my mom says, turning back to face us. "What happened to your foot?"

Stella blushes. "It's fine. Just a little mishap."

My mom smiles and faces forward again.

When we get to the school, we all pile out and Stella and I put our caps and gowns on over our clothes. I feel like a complete tool in mine, but Stella says I look smart. When my mom starts to cry into my dad's chest and my dad makes this face like he is going to pass out from discomfort at this open display of affection, Stella and I decide to escape as quickly as possible.

"Never thought I'd be graduating on crutches," Stella says.

"You gonna be OK?"

"Yeah. Fine." She glances around. "Do you see him anywhere?"

I scan the sea of caps and gowns and shake my head. "Why?" I ask.

"I don't want a scene. I almost wish I just stayed home. Why bother be here, since my mom cares more about her precious time with Calvin than helping me get ready? Me graduating and getting into college used to be the most important thing to her. Now it's like she knows I'll do all of those things with or without her, so why waste the energy?"

I reach for her arm. "She'll come. And besides, we're here for you. Me. Larry. You have other people who care about you besides your mom and what's-his-name."

"What's-his-name?"

I give her a Larry smirk. "Hey, it's not like I'm crazy about being here, either. My parents forced me. Let's just get through it together. Misery loves company, and all that."

"Thanks. We better go find our places in line, I guess."

"Yup."

We move closer to the other grads, and Stella gets swallowed up by a circle of girls from the *Britt* crowd who act shocked to see her crutches but probably already heard through the grapevine what happened.

Jason waves me over to our section, and we line up together. He tells me a bunch of guys bet each other to go commando under their gowns. It reminds me of something Dave would do, and I realize our big dream of all graduating together and going out after to get shit-faced never happened. I didn't even make it to their graduation. Some friend I turned out to be.

A bunch of teachers walk around whisper-yelling for people to be quiet as some lame marching music picks up and we all start to slowly improve our line and walk forward. I follow Jason up onto the stage and sit in the third row. The sun is already baking in the football stadium, and people in the audience are using the programs to fan themselves. I scan the sea of people in the audience and try to find Larry and my parents, but there are way too many people to pick them out. Instead, I glance around me and spot Stella a few rows back. I still don't see any sign of Britt.

Once we're all seated, we have to sit through about a million announcements and then this long-ass speech about how we're standing on the edge of our lives or some crap and how it's up to us what happens next. How we'll be leaving home, going to college, getting jobs. How we're the future. Some people in the row behind us are passing a flask around. Yeah. We are the future. Awesome.

Finally, it's time to receive our diplomas. I feel the mood around me change. People sit up more. Our row stands, and we follow the line of people with the same first letter in our last names.

When they say Jason's name, there are some polite claps and a few woots from Jason's family. He steps forward, shakes the guy's hand, takes his diploma and waves it in the air, then heads back to our seats.

Then they say my name, and my dad's distinct, ear-piercing whistle cuts through the applause. I swivel my head around.

No.

Way.

Dave and Caleb are way in the back of the audience, standing on chairs, screaming their heads off.

I wave like an idiot, because I just can't believe they're here. I can't believe they came. After everything.

There's a tap on my shoulder. The guy with my diploma says, "Let's move it along."

I shake his hand, grab my ticket out of here, and run to catch up with Jason. When I get back to my chair, I realize my mouth hurts, I'm smiling so big.

After they read the last person's name, the principal addresses us as graduates and everyone moves their tassel from one side of their cap to the other. The audience claps and the lame music starts up again, and a bunch of people throw their caps in the air. But I just pull mine off and thank God it's over, because I really just want to get the hell out of here and be with my real friends — my family. But first, I find Jason and tell him thanks for hanging out with me all year and good luck at school. He shakes my hand and runs off to find his own family.

I see Stella chatting with her friends and push my way over to her. I feel the invisible line that always separated us at school begin to shrivel away. "Hey, guys," she says. "You know my friend Josh, right? We take karate together."

They all say hey and give Stella hugs good-bye, telling her where the best graduation party will be happening later tonight. Once they're gone, she nods toward the crowd. "Ready for act two?"

"Definitely."

I help clear a path through the maze of people until we spot Larry and crew. At first they don't notice us. Caleb is talking to my mom, Dave is checking out some girl who looks way too young for him, and Larry and my dad are busy fixing Larry's tie. Star and Calvin are standing nearby. Star is craning her neck, clearly looking for Stella, which seems like a good sign. Calvin looks bored out of his mind, which is not.

I check my watch and realize we need to be in the park in about twenty minutes. I push my way through the last remaining people to reach them.

"Dude!" Dave says when he sees me. He and Caleb run over and hug me as if I'm their long-lost brother.

"Man, you're, like, super-stud now," Dave says, squeezing my upper arm.

Caleb rolls his eyes.

"It's great to see you losers," I tell them. "How the hell did you get here?"

"We drove," Caleb says. "We decided a road trip was in order."

"Plus your uncle invited us!" Dave adds.

Larry practically skips over to us. "OK, boys! We gotta jet! I have a wedding to get to!"

"Come in our car," Dave says.

"But—" I gesture toward Stella, who is hugging her mom, at least.

Dave checks her out up and down and nods approvingly.

"She'll come with us," Caleb answers.

"Definitely," Dave says.

"Just don't get pulled over," I say. "I have to be there on time."

"We know, we know, Mr. Best Man."

So I ask Stella if she wants to join us, and she gives her mom one last hug before we follow my best friends off the field.

"I'm Caleb, by the way," Cay says when we get to his car. "And this is Dave." They shake hands with her.

"It's great to meet you," Stella says. "I've heard all about you guys."

"I assume that means you'll be wanting to sit in back with me?" Dave asks.

She laughs. I nudge Dave away from the back door, and Stella and I squeeze in. As soon as we're sitting down, I take a deep breath and remember the smell: Caleb's mom's paints, fast-food wrappers, and Dave's crappy cologne. It brings so many memories of hanging out with these guys flooding into my head. The good and the bad. But right now, mostly the good.

I roll down the window and breathe in the fresh air blowing in my face.

Stella smiles at me and leans over to whisper in my ear. "I like your friends."

I catch Caleb's eyes in the rearview mirror, and he smirks at me.

Dave turns around and grins at us. "So, what's up with you two? Are you, like, a couple?"

Caleb punches him.

"What?" he says, pretending it hurt. "You know you want to know, too."

"We're just friends," I say.

"Yeah," Stella agrees.

But I feel my face prickle, and when I glance over, she's blushing, too.

When we reach the park, we all get out.

Stella stops me before we find Larry.

"Let me fix your tie," she says, balancing herself on her crutches. She reaches up and ruffles my hair, too. "Cap head," she tells me.

When she's done, she steps back and hobbles on her crutches. "Does my hair look OK?" she asks. "I should've brought a mirror or something."

"You look great," I tell her. And then, it just pops out. "You look beautiful."

She blushes again, and I feel like an idiot for saying that out loud.

"C'mon, we're gonna be late," Caleb says.

I take Stella's crutches from her and turn around, then crouch down. "Piggyback," I say. "It'll be faster."

She jumps on my back, and we race down the path toward the gazebo where Larry is standing with my parents and a bunch of his friends. When we reach them, Stella slides off and grabs her crutches. Larry's face is wet with sweat again. I wish I'd thought to grab some napkins or something for him. It seems like something a best man should have thought of.

"It's gorgeous, isn't it?" Larry asks.

Arielle and her mom and sister have totally outdone themselves. The gazebo has strings of flowers all around it. The entrance is completely covered with pink and white roses. I peek inside and see Arielle talking to her dad, who appears to be crying. But Arielle is laughing, patting his shoulder. When she sees me, she comes rushing over to hug me. "How was graduation?" she asks excitedly. "Congratulations! Did Larry scream like a goofball?"

"Hey, I resemble that remark," Larry says.

Arielle rolls her eyes. "We know, Larry. All too well." She turns to me. "Well, you look very handsome. The perfect best man."

Then the justice of the peace arrives and has us all cram into the gazebo and stand in a circle around Larry and Arielle. She asks me and Arielle's sister to step forward and stand inside the circle with Larry and Arielle. Larry's eyes are already watery. "Calm down," Arielle whispers. She winks at him.

Searching the circle, I see all the people of my two lives. My life before, and my life after. My parents. My two best friends. Stella. Gil, Gene, and Ben. Star and Calvin. Even the old lady from Apartment Two. Plus a bunch of Larry and Arielle's closest friends. Everyone's smiling. Everyone's happy. A year ago, I never would have believed I could feel like this. Like I belonged. Like I was worth something. Like I was loved. A sappy, warm feeling fills my chest. Like it's filling up with something good. I think Larry's corniness is rubbing off on me.

After Larry and Arielle read their vows, the JP turns to me and asks for the rings. I pull them out on the little pink ribbon Arielle tied them to. On the rings, there's a pattern of pine needles, to remind them of the place they got engaged, on a wooded trail in Vermont. They slip them on each other's fingers. Tears stream down Larry's cheeks. "Don't make my mascara run, you goof," Arielle says. But it's too late.

At this point, practically everyone is wiping their eyes. It's like a gush fest. But that seems appropriate, given this is all about Larry and Arielle's big day. Finally, the JP announces they're married, and Larry whoops before he grabs Arielle and dips her back and gives her a romantic kiss. Everyone laughs, and then we all move in to hug them. And then, as Larry would say, it's time to party.

Chapter 41

We're like one big crazy parade, following Larry and Arielle through the park and down the road to their favorite Spanish tapas restaurant. It's the same one Larry took me and Stella to the day he told us he was going to ask Arielle to marry him. There's a roof-deck dining room they rented out, so we have the whole place to ourselves. Larry and Arielle arranged a big, long table with enough settings for all of us. A crew of waitstaff bring tray after tray of dishes for us to try. Another waiter is in charge of keeping wineglasses full, but Larry already told him not to give any to me and my friends. I notice that my mom and dad stick to water, too.

After everyone is completely stuffed, the waiters come out with champagne and pour everyone a glass. Even me and my friends, though we get noticeably less than everyone else. But no one takes a drink. Instead, they all look at me expectantly and wait. Stella leans over and whispers, "I think you're supposed to give a toast."

"Me?"

"Best man."

Crap. Why didn't anyone warn me?

Stella motions for me to raise my glass and stand up.

I take a deep breath and lift my glass. Larry and Arielle glow up at me.

"Uh," I say. I clear my throat.

"He's speechless," Larry says.

"Quiet, Larry." Arielle nudges him.

"Most of you know, Larry has been letting me stay with him this past school year so I could go to Roosevelt."

"And he just graduated today! Woo-hoo!" Larry shouts.

Dave woots.

I think they *are* long-lost brothers.

"Anyway. Thanks, Larry. It's been a great year."

"It was my pleasure," Larry says. He wipes his eyes.

"When I met Arielle," I continue, "I knew she was perfect for Larry. There aren't many people who can put up with his kind of crazy."

"Hey!"

"I mean it in the best way, Larry." I turn to Arielle.

"Thanks for giving Larry a chance," I tell her. "I hope you guys have a life filled with all the things that make you happy. And since that's each other, I think you're well on your way."

I raise my glass, and everyone else does the same. "To Arielle and Larry. I hope you have a lifetime of happiness."

"Hear, hear!" my dad yells, and everyone echoes him.

Then we all drink. Except for my mom and dad, who put down their glasses and drink from their water.

"Wow, man," Dave says to me when I sit back down. "You've turned into a real sap."

Caleb elbows him.

"Ow! I didn't say that was a *bad* thing!"

I drain my champagne. Before I can refill my glass with the bottle the waiters left on the table, Larry pulls it away. "Save room for cake," he says. Like that makes any sense.

As if on cue, the chef comes through the door, pushing a cart with a big cake on it. The cake has a gazebo on top that looks just like the one at the park. Everyone *ooh*s and *ahh*s over it, especially Larry and Arielle. Arielle's sister gets up with a new glass of champagne. "My turn," she says.

"Larry and Arielle, I knew the minute I first saw you together, you were meant to be that way always, just like

Josh said. You make each other smile. You make each other more beautiful. When Arielle asked me to be in charge of the cake, I decided to take a day trip over to the park and get some photos of the place where you'd say your vows. Now, I know Arielle asked me to be in charge of the cake because we both think Jackson at Cake Tops is super cute."

"Oh, *really*?" Larry asks, looking at Arielle in this ridiculously jealous way.

"Oh, stop it," she says.

"*Any*way," Arielle's sister goes on, "Jackson and I decided that it would be really amazing to make a gazebo to go on the top of the cake. And Jackson has a friend who's a glassblower. And it just so happens that this glassblower friend is even cuter than Jackson. Don't you think?" She motions to the guy sitting next to her, who blushes. Larry whistles.

"*Any*way," she says again, "thanks, Arielle, for the excuse to visit Jackson. Which led to me meeting Andy. Who made the most beautiful gazebo I think I've ever seen." She raises her glass. "To Larry and Arielle!" she says.

We all lift our glasses again. Unfortunately, mine is empty.

"And to Andy!" Larry says.

He and Arielle get up to cut the cake just as a group

of people walk out on the deck with guitars and hand drums and start playing music. People eat and dance, and it's like this never-ending party. Larry and Arielle dance the whole time. Every so often, they move close to the table and grab up someone who looks bored or who hasn't been humiliated on the dance floor yet. I make a big effort to look very busy anytime they get near.

I keep catching Stella looking at the dance area hopefully, until Star and Calvin start making out as they slow dance.

"Someone needs to get a room," Dave jokes.

But we all saw Stella's face when she noticed them, so no one thinks it's funny.

Dave and Caleb have spent the last hour filling me in on all the crap that's been happening for the past year that they couldn't really elaborate on in e-mail and texts. Mainly, that Caleb is still seeing Corinne and that Dave and his girlfriend may be getting back together. I can feel the dance we're doing. It's kind of like sparring. They keep throwing punches of info at me, and I keep waiting for the big knockout punch. The thing maybe they want to tell me about most. About how Ellie's been doing.

But I'm not going to ask. And they won't say anything unless I do. So I'm safe.

Safe.

"Yo, man, you should really ask her to dance," Dave

whispers to me when Stella turns away from us to talk to Arielle's sister.

"She's on crutches," I say.

"You could carry her," Dave suggests.

"Oh, please," I say.

"C'mon, dude. She's hot!" Dave says.

"We're just friends."

"So? She's still hot!"

I sigh. "If you get me a glass of champagne, I'll do it."

Caleb reaches under the table with both hands. A minute later, he's passing me a water glass with a mysteriously bubbly substance inside. I down it before Larry can stop me.

I sit for a minute, letting the warmth settle into my chest.

"It's time," Dave says, just as Stella turns back to us.

"Time for what?" she asks.

"Time to dance?" I ask.

She blushes. "Finally!"

I stand up, and she takes my hand. The minute our skin connects, I feel that familiar jolt I always feel when we touch. I purposely do not turn back to see what Dave and Caleb are doing, because most likely it involves annoying expressions and exchanges of money, since I'm sure they bet on whether or not I'd have the balls to ask Stella to dance.

"Um, how are we going to do this?" I ask her, looking down at her injured foot.

"I have no idea. Let's just see what happens."

She leans on me and we kind of hobble forward on three legs until we make it out to the dance floor. Stella reaches for my shoulders, and I put my hands around her waist, then we kind of pivot around slowly, her on one foot.

"Thanks," she whispers in my ear.

"For what?"

"This. I always wanted to slow dance like this."

"You never have?"

"Missed prom, remember?"

"But there must have been other times."

She shrugs and rests her head on my chest.

"I hear prom is the top overrated event of all the big life events," I tell her.

"You made that up."

"No, really. This is way better. We get to be with the people we want to be with. Not all those losers who care where your dress came from and how much it cost and whether you hired a freakin' limo or not."

"Wow."

"What?"

"I never thought you'd have given so much thought to prom."

"Just how to avoid it."

"Well, you're probably right," she says. "This is pretty nice."

"I'm really sorry you had to miss yours, though," I tell her. "I should have, like, asked you. But I was too chicken."

"I would have said no, anyway."

"Oh. Um — thanks?"

"Not because of you. Just because . . . it would have been too awkward. All my friends would be like, 'What happened with Britt?' and it would end up being a stupid gossip fest."

"Well, I'm still sorry you didn't get to go."

"We're here now, so let's not stress about it. It's the thought that counts."

We turn and turn. Slowly. Barely to the music. This moment could last forever. Just like this. Just us here. But I can feel the music slowing down and ending. And I don't know what to do next. Because in a week, I'll be leaving. And at the end of the summer, we'll be going to different cities. And all I'll have left to remind me of Stella is a rock I'm supposed to talk to.

"What's wrong?" she asks, looking up at me.

"Huh? Oh, nothing," I say. "I was just thinking."

"About something sad?"

I hold her a little closer and force myself to smile. "Nah," I say. "No worries."

She rests her head on my chest again and holds me back.

"Liar," she whispers.

Chapter 42

As the next song starts, I know before I turn around that it's my dad playing. And when I see Larry's face, I realize I'm not the only one my dad used to play the song for. Tears slowly slip down Larry's cheeks as he stands there, staring at my dad and his guitar. My dad. Playing this slow, sad lullaby with a voice that sounds different from the one I remember. My mom walks over to Larry, and they start to slowly dance together.

"I thought you said your dad's band was lame," Stella says quietly. "I think he's really good."

"He doesn't play like this with his band," I say. "At least, he didn't used to."

She rests her head on my shoulder again and I try to hold her close like before, but somehow it suddenly feels so much harder. For some reason, she feels so heavy. I look over at Gil and Gene, who dance together holding Ben between them. He reaches his pudgy hand for Gil's glasses and laughs. Gil smiles, and Gene gently pulls Ben's hand away, so gently that Ben doesn't mind, but laughs again. The three of them move to the lullaby like a rocking chair, back and forth. My mom reaches for Larry's face and wipes his cheeks dry. Arielle is dancing with her dad, and she does the same for him.

"What's wrong?" Stella asks. But she doesn't reach up and wipe my face, thank God. I close my eyes and listen to the music. Feel the weight — the life — of Stella against me, knowing that soon I will have to let her go.

My dad keeps playing, and we all keep slowly rocking to the lull of his deep, steady voice. He sings about love and heartbreak and closing your eyes, and promises of what will be when we wake up. I imagine those dreamed promises to be true for everyone listening. But for me, there's a void there. An emptiness.

When the song ends, everyone claps like crazy and begs my dad to play more. Larry comes over and asks if he can cut in, so he takes Stella away, and my mom comes over and forces me to dance with her, which isn't really that bad, even if it feels awkward.

"Dad's incredible," I tell her. "He's really improved."

"It's the drinking, mainly," she says. "He's so much better when he's sober. And —"

"What?"

She glances over at him. "Oh, I don't know."

But I can tell she does.

"What?" I say again.

"Do you know he told me he was afraid he couldn't play sober?"

I shake my head.

"He was scared. He thought he was going to have to give up both."

"What changed his mind?"

"I asked him to try."

We listen together for a while. Then she says quietly, "We're still going to counseling."

"Is everything OK?"

She looks over at him. "It's been a long year, but yes. I think so. We know what we want, we just need help getting there. But we will eventually."

"I'm glad," I say.

"Thank you."

"I didn't do anything."

"Yes, you did. You made it happen."

"I don't understand."

"When you left, the two of us were completely ripped apart. From each other and inside ourselves. I couldn't stop crying. And your father, well, he wanted to comfort me. I guess that was the big moment for him. Realizing he wanted to. That he still cared about me. I nearly fainted when he came into the room one day when I was crying and he held me."

"Uh, not sure I need these details."

She laughs again. I still can't get over how much younger she looks.

"I just meant that it was this big moment. When he sat down on the bed, I could have sent him away. I admit, that was my gut reaction. But when I looked in his eyes, I saw my old Hal. The one who used to gaze into my eyes all the time. And I could see the love there. And . . . I don't know. I think maybe it took your leaving to make us realize all we had and all we lost. We decided that what we lost was worth a lot more than what we ended up with. I guess we both decided we would at least try to get it back. Especially you."

"Mom —"

"I know, I know. You're leaving for college. But we have a month or so together this summer, right? Dad wants to give you a job at the garage. And we have all these things we want to do. Like go to concerts. Did I tell you your dad and his band got a new regular gig?"

"Gig?"

"They're playing at O'Reilly's every Saturday. It's a lot better than the American Legion!"

"Wow."

She sighs and gives me a squeeze. "Things are getting so much better, Josh. I just wish we'd gotten our act together sooner."

Yeah.

"I'm sorry, honey. I'm sorry we were so . . . stupid."

"No worries."

She studies my face for a minute. "I'm really proud of you. Every time Larry sends a weekly update, your dad and I read the e-mails over and over. Who knew Larry would be the best thing that could happen to you?"

"Weekly updates?"

"He sends us an e-mail every Sunday to tell us what you've been up to. Didn't you know?"

"No." I guess he kept the promise of letting my mom know how I was doing for me.

"He's such a good guy. He loves you so much. He's going to make the best dad."

"Yeah," I say. "He's been pretty great."

When the song ends, I give her a hug and go sit down again. Dave looks completely wasted, but Caleb seems OK.

"He's drowning his sorrows," Caleb says.

"I can see that."

"Who breaks up right before prom?" Dave asks sadly. "I mean, c'mon."

"You're better off," Caleb says. "Way better."

"Whatever." Dave takes another drink. "We're getting back together. I know it."

"Easy. I don't want you puking in my car on the way home."

"That's what windows are for."

"Gross."

"It's nice to see you guys haven't changed," I say.

"It's nice to see you have." Caleb smirks.

"Funny."

"Seriously, though, I'm glad things are better," Caleb says.

"Yeah."

Dave finishes his glass and looks down the table for another bottle.

"Don't even think about it. You're cut off," Caleb tells him.

Dave turns back to me. "I guess you must be wondering how you-know-who's been doing."

Caleb gives him a shove.

"What?" Dave looks all innocent.

"Dude. Way to kill the mood."

"Hey, she seems great, so what the hell? I thought he'd want to know."

"I wouldn't say great," Caleb says.

"Why not?" I ask.

"Well, I mean, she's fine, but . . . you know. She seems pretty lonely. No boyfriend or anything."

"Does she still hang out with Corinne?" I know if the answer is yes, that means she's hanging out with Caleb, too. Which means he knows a lot more than Dave and also a lot more than he's telling me now.

"Yeah," he says.

"She's looking hot," Dave says. "She cut her hair and started working out and stuff."

"She takes yoga with my mom and Corinne," Caleb says. "God, Dave."

"What?"

"It's OK," I say. "I'm glad she's doing well."

"See?" Dave says.

Caleb shakes his head. "Anyway. Yeah. She's doing well. She's good."

"Who's good?" Stella asks as she hobbles over to us.

Caleb and Dave both turn to me.

"Just a friend," I say.

Dave does not smirk, which I'm grateful for.

"Larry and Arielle are about to take off," Stella says.

Caleb and Dave get up. "We should go, too," Caleb says.

"You guys should stay over," I tell them. "I'm staying at Larry's until he gets back from his honeymoon. You could crash at his place. You must have had to get up pretty early to make it here for my graduation."

Dave yawns.

"Wish we could," Caleb says. "But we have to get back. We have to go to a training session at the park tomorrow. We start work there right after graduation."

"We're park rangers!" Dave says. "Smokey Bears!"

Caleb rolls his eyes. "We're doing maintenance stuff at the park. Mowing lawns, picking up trash. It's gonna be a blast."

"Our park?" I ask.

"Yeah. Kind of funny, huh? We'll finally get to ride that damn lawn mower."

"It's gonna be *awesome*!" Dave slurs.

I laugh. When the three of us were kids, we used to beg the guy who mowed the lawn at the park to give us a ride, but he always refused.

"We'll see you in a week, right?" Caleb asks.

"Yeah. I'll see you then," I say. "Thanks again for coming. You guys are the best."

"No prob, man." Caleb gives me an awkward chest-hug thing and then whispers in my ear, "Good luck with Stella. She's cool."

Dave tries to hug me but trips and I have to catch him. I would *not* be looking forward to the ride home if I were Cay.

As I watch them leave, I feel a twinge of . . . I don't know. Sadness, I guess. I missed my whole senior year hanging out with them. But the truth is, today pretty much sums up what every day is like with them. We meet up. We talk about meaningless crap. We drink. We joke around. That's it. I'm not saying we need to have deep conversations or anything, but . . . I don't know. Sometimes I really wonder what else there is. I still miss them. I still miss having someone to hang out with who doesn't care about what I eat or drink or whatever. Someone who knows about my past and still wants me around.

"You OK?" Stella asks.

"Huh? Oh. Yeah. I'm fine," I say. "How's your foot feeling?"

"It's all right. I get to ditch these things in two days, and I can't wait." She shakes her crutches like she wants to strangle them. "Can I get a ride back with you, by the way? The lovebirds are going back to Calvin's."

"Of course," I say. "Is everything OK with you and your mom?"

"She said she was sorry and she'd make it up to me. I won't hold my breath. "

"Sorry."

"It's fine. I'm glad she's finally happy. This is the longest she's gone out with someone since I can remember.

Maybe it'll work out. I hope so. Less guilt when I leave for college, right?"

"Right," I say.

Arielle runs over to us and hands Stella her bouquet. "I think you're the only single lady here, sweets, so here you go."

Stella blushes. "Thanks! It's beautiful."

She kisses the top of Stella's head. "Just like you."

Larry comes bopping over and takes Arielle's hand. "We're gonna jet!" he says. "You're sure you have everything you need, Sammy?"

"Yeah, I'm all set. Clover will be fine."

"I can't believe you're leaving us," Larry says.

"You'll be OK," I say. "Arielle is a good replacement."

"That's true." He winks at me.

"Have a great honeymoon!" Stella says. We give them hugs, and then they both dance their way out of the room while everyone claps.

And they lived happily ever after, I think.

I hope I'm right.

Chapter 43

My parents, Stella, and I drive back to Larry's and we order takeout, even though we aren't hungry. As we pick at our food, my mom keeps repeating how beautiful the wedding was, and Stella keeps telling my dad how much she loved his music. I feel like I've entered some weird dimension of my life that was never meant to happen. A year ago, I don't even know who was more of a mess: me or my parents. But now, here they are. Here *we* are. Sitting together like it's something we've always done.

My mom starts in on how she's worried about me staying at Larry's by myself for a whole week, but Stella assures her she'll look out for me. I don't really think this has the reassuring effect she intends, but my mom doesn't say anything.

Finally, my dad stands up and stretches. "We should probably hit the road," he says, stifling a yawn.

My mom sighs. "We'll see you in a week, honey. We can't wait to have you back home."

I nod.

"We're so proud of you," she says for the millionth time.

Stella and I follow them to the door, and I step out in the hallway to watch them walk down the stairs. When they get to the bottom, they look up and wave. "See you soon! We love you!" my mom says.

I wave. "Drive safely," I say, like I'm the dad. Before the door closes behind them, I call out, "I love you, too!"

I am ashamed to realize this might be the first time I've ever told them that.

"So, what do we do now?" Stella asks when I go back inside.

I shrug. "Jackie Chan marathon?"

"Tempting."

I sit next to her on the couch. "Aren't you going to the graduation party?"

She leans her head back and stares at the ceiling. "Nah. I think graduation parties are overrated."

"I doubt that."

She laughs. "I'm not in the mood, I guess. I already said good-bye to my friends. Besides, they'll all be hooking up with their boyfriends, and I'd be left by myself. No, thanks."

I lean back and stare at the ceiling, too. "This has to be the lamest way to celebrate graduation in the history of graduating."

"I don't mind."

"Yeah. Me, either."

"Let's just make popcorn and watch a movie, OK?" she asks.

"You could really eat popcorn after all we ate today?"

"In honor of Larry. And can I borrow some sweats or something? This dress isn't really movie-watching material, and I think I overdid it on my foot today."

"Want me to go up and get you some clothes?"

"You don't have to. I don't mind borrowing something, if you don't mind lending."

I find her a pair of sweats, which are enormous on her, and a T-shirt, also enormous, and we watch movies until two in the morning. After I doze off for the fourth time, I finally tell her we should crash.

"Can I stay here?" she asks.

"What about your mom?"

"It's after two and she hasn't called to check in. I don't want to stay alone. Again."

"No worries," I say. "You can crash in Larry's room." I help her to his bed and hope the sheets aren't too gross. But she seems too wiped out to care.

"I should brush my teeth, but I'm too tired," she says.

I'm about to tell her not to kiss anyone, then, but I realize how lame that is. And also, I don't want to throw the idea of kissing out there right now and make her think I want to. Not that I don't. I think.

"Can I get you anything else?" I ask. "Glass of water?"

"I'm all set."

"OK. See you in the morning." I turn to leave, but she calls me back.

"Hey, thanks for everything, Josh. I'm really glad we're friends again. I wish — I wish I didn't shut you out the way I did. It was wrong."

"Forget it," I say. "I'm glad we're friends again, too."

She smiles and rolls over. "See you in the morning, friend," she mumbles.

"See you."

In my own room, I check for texts and see that Caleb and Dave made it home safe, though apparently Dave puked on the side of the road two times.

Clover comes in and jumps on the bed and rubs

against me. She purrs softly and paces back and forth against the side of my body. "It's OK, I'll come back and visit," I tell her. But she keeps pacing.

I shut out the light and look up at Larry's smiley-face stars.

"I really will," I say again. I hope it's true.

Chapter 44

I wake up to the sound of a distant pounding.

It takes me a minute to figure out that it's coming from the hallway. The door. Someone's pounding on the door.

I sit up, pull my sweatpants on, and run out to the hall.

Stella comes out at the same time, hobbling without her crutches. She's wearing just my T-shirt, which comes down almost to her knees.

"What's going on?" I ask.

"I know you're in there!" a voice yells from the other side of the door.

Shit. I mean, it's *the Shit.*

Stella leans against the wall. "Not now," she says, exhausted.

I squint through the peephole to see if he's alone or if he brought any friends to help him bust down the door.

I am not prepared for what I see.

I expected him to look angry.

I expected him to look like he wanted to beat the crap out of someone. Namely, me.

I did not expect him to be sobbing like a baby.

I step back from the door and sigh.

"What?" Stella asks.

I motion for her to see for herself. As she squints through the hole in the door, I swear I can see her anger melt away.

"What do you want to do?" I ask.

She hesitates, then says quietly, "I want him to go away." But it doesn't sound like she's sure about that.

"Stellaaaaa," Britt whines from the other side of the door. He sounds like Larry imitating Rocky. Only way more pitiful.

And sincere.

"Go away!" Stella yells.

"I just want to talk to you!" he cries. "Please!"

His voice is desperate.

Stella steps farther away from the door. "I don't want to talk to him," she says quietly.

I move farther away, too. "I don't think he's going to go away."

Britt bangs on the door again. "Please," he says, more pitifully. "I have to see you!"

"Maybe you should let him in," I say. I can't believe those words just came out of my mouth. By the look on Stella's face, I can tell she can't believe it, either.

"He's *crying*," I say.

"I know that!" she hisses, suddenly angry at *me* now.

"Do whatever you want, then," I say. "But whatever you decide, you're going to have to face him eventually." God, I sound like Larry.

Britt raps on the door again. "Please," he says. "I'm sorry! I never meant to hurt you! I love you!"

Stella steps back, away from the door. "I'm scared," she says quietly.

"I'll be right here."

"No," she whispers. "It's not that. I'm — I'm scared I'll change my mind."

Oh.

He pounds on the door again. "Please," he cries. "Please, Stella!"

"I don't think he's going to give up," I tell her.

She looks down at her foot.

"You can do this," I say.

She leans against the wall while Britt continues to

pound on the door and cry for her. Finally, she nods. "OK. Let him in. But don't leave us alone. Promise."

"All right." I slowly switch the lock and open the door.

Britt wipes his face with his T-shirt, then looks at the two of us. I know we are giving the worst impression possible, what with Stella wearing what is clearly a man's T-shirt, and me not wearing one at all.

"You can come in," Stella says quietly. "But only to talk."

He nods.

I help Stella to the couch in the living room, and Britt sits on the chair across from us. I watch him look around the apartment like how we live is completely foreign to him. Larry's apartment is probably the size of Britt's living room.

For a while, no one says anything.

"Well?" Stella finally asks.

"I wanted to tell you I'm sorry." He looks so wrecked, I can't help feeling sorry for him.

Stella crosses her arms at her chest. "OK, well, you said it."

"And to ask you—to ask you—" He looks at me like I'm a piece of dirt. Or worse. "Does he really have to be here?"

"Yes," Stella says.

He makes a huffing sound.

"I want another chance," he says.

"Why?" Stella asks.

"What do you mean, 'Why'?"

"Why do you want another chance? So you can drive over my other foot?"

"It was an accident!" He leans forward in the chair, like he's about to get up. It's weird, but you can almost see the anger building up in him. I lean forward, too, just in case he tries . . . I don't know. Anything. I realize he hasn't even asked her if she's OK, or in pain, or basically anything that matters.

"Then, why?" Stella asks again, calmly.

"Because I love you, Stell," he says. "And I don't understand what happened. We had everything planned. And then suddenly you're telling me you want to go to a different school. A school you never even told me you applied to. And I got upset. Can you blame me? We've been talking about going to college together forever. I know I acted a little crazy. But you really took me by surprise, OK? I'm sorry I overreacted. It's only because I love you and can't bear the thought of not being with you. You're my *life*."

"But don't you see that that's the problem?" Stella asks.

"No! I don't! What's wrong with loving someone?"

"Nothing," she says. "It's the way you love. If you loved me, you'd want me to go to the school of my choice, not yours. You'd want me to follow my own dreams. You — you'd know what my dreams *are*."

"Well, maybe if you told me, I could have applied there. If I knew it meant that much to you."

"You never asked," she says quietly.

"That's because you acted like you were cool with the schools I chose for us! If I'd known how much this other place meant to you, I would have added it to our list!"

"You would really do that?"

"Yes."

"Even though you have no interest in that school?"

"Yes!"

"And you don't think there's anything wrong with that?" she asks.

He stands up and starts pacing. "No! It shows how much I love you!"

"But that's the problem!" she says. "I can't do this! I can't be with you every waking hour. I can't report in when we're not together. I can't breathe! I need to be *me*. Not *Britt's girlfriend*. And I want *you* to be . . . you. I want you to go to the school that's right for you. Don't you get how crazy it is to go somewhere just to be together?"

He shakes his head. "You never thought this before.

Not until you started hanging around with him." He gestures toward me in disgust. "You think this guy really cares about you? He'll just use you and then dump you."

I'm about to say something, but Stella holds up her hand to stop me. All I can think of when I hear the word *use* is Ellie. I feel like I deserve his insult, even though he doesn't know about my past.

"We're just friends," Stella tells him. "He hasn't used me. And he never will."

No. I won't.

"Then, what are you doing here dressed like that? Is that his shirt?"

"Josh was just letting me crash here tonight. That's what friends do."

He makes a face like, *Yeah, right.* I notice he doesn't ask her why she needs to crash here in the first place.

"You could come to my house," he says. "You don't have to stay here." He says *here* as if he means "in this pathetic excuse for a house." "You know my parents won't care. You can stay in the guest apartment."

Guest apartment? Figures.

"I don't need to stay anywhere. I can go home anytime."

"To what?"

"What's that supposed to mean?"

"C'mon, Stell. I know your mom's never home anymore."

Stella squirms. "So?"

"So you shouldn't be alone. And you shouldn't have to live like"— he looks around the apartment again — "this."

He says it as if he truly can't believe anyone could live here. Like he just doesn't get it. Like it's a choice. He reminds me of the Disney-type hero prince, all blond and muscular, who rescues the poor girl and makes her a princess. I can see it in his eyes. This is really what he believes. I'm sure of it.

"I love you," he says. "I always have. I know I overreact when I don't know where you are or who you're with, but it's because I *care.* And I'm the only one who does. You know it."

Am I not sitting here?

"My mom cares," Stella says. "She's just caught up with Calvin right now."

"Like that's an excuse? If she cared about you, she would make the time. She'd take care of you. She'd know where you are!"

And now I get how this works. He tries to make her feel small. That without him, she has nothing. He tries to make her feel unloved by everyone but him. He tries to make her feel like he's all she's got. Maybe he even believes it.

"You're not the only one who cares about her," I say. "Stella has plenty of friends who care."

"Stay out of this."

"Whose apartment is this?"

He looks around. "Proud of this dump, are you?"

"It's not a dump," I say. "And you can leave anytime."

"I'm not leaving without her."

Stella doesn't move. She slowly looks around the apartment, as if seeing it through his eyes. Then she looks at me. She seems so sad and unsure. Tempted.

"Please come home with me," Britt says quietly, trying a different tack. "I promise things will be different this time. Just give me another chance. I'll take care of you."

I know he's sincere, but his words are all wrong. He should know Stella can take care of herself. She's not a helpless puppy. Maybe if he knew that, she'd be more tempted to give him a second chance, but the more he talks, the more she seems to move away from him.

"You need to go home now," Stella tells him. She stands up. "I'm sorry."

Britt stands up, too. "Stell—"

"You need to go," she says. "Please."

"You can't stay here." He clenches his jaw. As it dawns on him she's not going to leave with him, his body gets more and more rigid.

"I'll be fine. Josh is a friend, OK? That's all he's ever been."

"Whatever. Fine." Any sadness that was left in him has clearly turned to anger now, and my sympathy for him is disappearing by the minute. "Live like this," he says. "Be with this loser. I couldn't care less."

"Obviously," she says.

I can't help smirking. That's the Stella I lo — know.

"Fuck you," he says to me.

He walks to the door and opens it, but stops before he leaves. Like he's trying to think of one more thing he could say to make Stella change her mind and come with him.

She stays where she is, staring at him. He waits a minute more, then finally walks out the door, leaving it open behind him.

I shut the door and go back to Stella, who has flopped down on the couch.

"You OK?" I ask.

She nods. "Thanks."

"Want me to help you back to bed?"

She nods again, then gets up and puts one arm around me so I can guide her back to Larry's room. As soon as she gets in bed, she rolls over and faces the wall.

"You sure you're all right?" I ask.

She nods again. I stand there, watching her, not knowing what to do.

"I just need to be alone," she says.

So I leave her.

But I feel like she knows she's not really alone. Not truly.

Because she has me.

Chapter 45

I wake up at around noon the next day. Stella is still asleep, so I decide to start breakfast: Larry's "famous scrambled eggs" and toast. I'm not sure what makes the eggs so famous, but Larry insists his way is the best. I'm sure it has to do with the massive amounts of cheese he melts into them. Stella hobbles into the kitchen just as I'm finishing up.

"Wow," she says. "This is nice."

"You should probably taste before you decide," I say.

"I just mean that you went to all the trouble."

I shrug.

I pour us some coffee, and we eat mostly in silence. All through breakfast, I wait for her to bring up what happened last night, but she doesn't. So I don't, either.

"I guess I should probably go home," she says when she eats the last bit of egg.

"You can stay here," I tell her. "You know Larry wouldn't mind."

She nods. "I should just get going."

I wish she would say something about *Britt.* About us. About anything. But instead she stands up to go, so I help her gather her stuff, and we take the elevator to her floor.

The apartment is empty and has that stale smell of neglect. It reminds me of back home. How the house smelled stale and gross. And how it made me feel the same way I feel now. And how Stella looks. Alone. Empty. Sad.

"You're not staying here," I tell her when we get to her room.

She puts her hands on her hips. "Oh, really?"

"Sorry. That came out wrong. What I mean is—" What *do* I mean? "It's just that this place—if you want to escape it for a while, you can hang out with me at Larry's. I don't want to tell you what to do. But it's a lot less depressing down there. Plus, I'll cook for you."

She sighs and looks around her room, hesitating. She peers down into her wastebasket where the photo of Britt is.

"What about him?" she asks.

"What *about* him?"

"What if he comes back?"

"What if he does? We're just friends, right?"

"Right," she says.

We pass our days at Larry's watching movies and eating mostly takeout. Each night, I take Stella back upstairs. Sometimes her mom's there with Calvin, and sometimes she stays at his place. Those nights, Stella comes back down and crashes in Larry's room.

I take Stella to her doctor's appointment, and the doctor tells her she's all better but to take it easy. She teaches Stella some exercises to do and tells me to make sure Stella does them. So we go back to Larry's and alternate between doing the exercises, watching movies, and trying to cook our own meals since we ran out of takeout money. Pretty soon, Stella's walking without a limp and we've spent almost the entire week together.

And that's when things start to get weird.

Every time I look up, I can tell she's been watching me. And I start to feel self-conscious. And then I start to avoid her. And then she starts acting cranky. And then finally, one night when a TV show we've been watching ends and I jump up to bring a glass into the kitchen, she grabs my arm before I can get away.

"Stop avoiding me," she says. "If you want me to go home, I will."

"What? No. Why would you say that?"

She stares at me.

"Sorry. I just . . ." I hesitate.

" . . . don't like me in *that* way. And you're afraid that's how I like you."

"No!"

She raises her right eyebrow like, *Oh, really?*

"It's not that," I tell her. Suddenly it feels really, really hot in here. I wipe my forehead with the back of my hand.

She fiddles with her new class ring, as if it's more of a nuisance than something she's glad to have. "Then why are we acting so weird around each other?"

"I don't know," I say. "Why are you?"

"I don't know."

"Well, maybe we should stop?"

She smirks. "Maybe we should."

"OK, so that settles that."

I feel her watching me as I get up for real this time. She follows me into the kitchen and stands behind me while I do the dishes.

"I could, you know," she says.

I turn off the water and make myself look busy wiping

my hands on a dish towel, even though inside my heart is racing. "Could what?"

She blushes. "Like you."

I stare at her.

"What?" she asks.

"Why?" I ask.

"Seriously?"

I set the towel on the counter. "Yeah."

"Because you're *nice,* for one thing. And we have fun together. And we both kick ass at karate, and we like the same movies. And we both appear to have a history of dysfunctional home lives, and we're both trying to escape or move on or whatever." She takes a deep breath. "And we've been together for almost a whole week and you've been a perfect gentlemen. And—you're cute."

Now I'm the one blushing. "Really?" I ask.

"Shut up. I'm not saying I *do* like you. I'm just saying I could."

"Well, you know, I could like you, too. *Could.*"

She smiles. "Really?"

"Are we already that old couple that repeats everything the other one says?"

"Maybe."

Wait. Did I just call us a couple? "Only . . ." I start, but I don't know what to say.

"You're scared," she tells me. "Because of whatever happened last year."

"Well . . . yeah." I walk over to the kitchen table and sit down.

"I'm not her," she says, sitting across from me.

"I know."

"No, I mean, you had one bad experience, but that doesn't mean every experience will be bad now, or that you can't have a new one."

"I know."

"Then what?"

"It all feels so unfinished."

"You still love her?"

"No! I never did. I know that makes me an asshole. It was just this one-time thing, though. It was stupid. And then — well, you know what happened."

"No, I don't."

"Right. Larry didn't tell you?"

"Nope."

I sigh. The one time Larry can keep his mouth shut.

"Maybe *you* should tell me," she says.

Yeah. Maybe I should.

"Are you sure you want to know?" I ask. "Because what can be heard cannot be unheard."

She smiles and pretends to glance around. "Is that you, Larry?"

"Seriously, though," I say.

"Seriously." She smiles again, and I wonder if she'll still look like this — like she cares about me — after I tell her the truth.

"She got pregnant," I say quickly, before I can chicken out.

"Oh."

She reaches over and puts her hand on my arm.

"That's hard," she says. "No wonder you had all those issues with Benny. Oh, Josh. I'm so sorry."

My eyes start to sting. I close them and shake my head. She's the first person to say what I truly feel. Yeah. It's hard. It's really, really hard.

"Last year, I spent the whole time wondering what was going to happen to the baby. But I never talked to her — Ellie — because I felt so bad about it. About how it happened. Because —" I don't want to tell her, but I know I have to. It's the bigger truth that's haunted me all year. I know that now.

"Because what?"

I look away from her, but then realize I have to say it to her face. Slowly, I raise my eyes to meet hers. "Because I used her, Stell. I *used* her. And I feel so bad." My throat starts to close up again and I force myself to swallow. To *not* cry.

"What do you mean, you used her?"

I take a deep breath. "I heard she was an easy lay—sorry—but, yeah. That. And I was a pathetic virgin. And all these assholes on my soccer team wouldn't get off my back about it. And I just wanted to get it over with. So one night at a party, she was flirting with me, and I thought, 'This is my chance.' So I took her out to my van, and we did it."

I pause, because it's all coming out so fast. But I don't want to stop. I don't want to stop, because I know I have to tell Stella the whole truth. Even if it means she'll never talk to me again.

She waits.

"It was a mistake," I say. "I knew even when it was happening that I should stop. But I didn't. She just let me take advantage of her. And when it was over, I left her out there. She looked at me like I had just ruined her life, but like she wasn't surprised, you know? Almost as if she expected it. Like she knew I would be an asshole just like all the other guys she hooked up with. But the disappointment on her face—I can't forget it. I went back to the party and tried to pretend it never happened. I didn't talk to her again."

I turn away and take another deep breath.

"A few months later, I heard she was pregnant. I

told Caleb to tell her best friend that I would pay for an abortion, but she didn't want any help from me. And then she changed her mind, anyway. Last June, she had the baby. I went to the hospital when I heard she'd gone into labor to see if I could see the baby, you know? I just had to see for myself. Because I didn't know what was going to happen. I heard a rumor that she planned to give the baby up for adoption, but I didn't want to ask her myself. I felt like I'd hurt her enough already. And I was too scared. So I went there and tried to see him. I think I did, but I'm not even sure, because I didn't want her to know I was there. I didn't want to hurt her. But I don't know if the baby I saw was mine. He was the only one people weren't ogling at through the glass. And he didn't have a name on his plastic bassinet. So I imagined it was him. But I have no idea if it really was. Then I left. And it was over. Except it wasn't. Because I can't stop thinking about him. And I can't stop thinking about Ellie and what I did to her. I thought if I came here, I could escape it all. I could focus on school and then just leave for college and never come back. But I was wrong. I'll never escape."

As the final words leave me, I feel this huge surge in my chest. Like some big, I don't know, *thing* was clogging my lungs, and now I can breathe normally again. I wait for Stella to say something, but she keeps playing with her ring.

"That's it," I finally say, hoping to nudge her to respond. "That's everything."

She slides her chair closer to me and puts her hand on mine. The way she looks at me, like she really cares, makes my chest hurt.

"I don't know what to do," I tell her. It feels like the truest thing I've said in a long time.

"I think you do," she says.

"I do?" I ask. Because really, I don't.

"You have to talk to her."

What? That's not the answer I was expecting. But as soon as I hear it, I know she's right.

"But I don't know what to say to her."

"The truth would be a good place to start. Maybe you should tell her what you just told me."

"I don't know if I can."

"You can. I'll go with you, if you want." She squeezes my hand tighter. "I owe you. You stood by me. Now I'll stand by you. You have to do this, Josh."

I know she's right. I can feel the truth in her fingers curled around mine.

I nod.

"Come here," she says. We both stand, and she holds her arms out. So I go to her, and she wraps her arms around me and holds tight. "You're not a bad person, Josh," she says into my chest. My heart. "I know you think you are, but you're not. You did one bad thing. Now you need to make it right. For you, and for her. And even for the baby. I know you can do this."

"I can't believe you don't hate me," I say.

She squeezes harder. "Well, I don't. So believe it."

Slowly, I let my own arms do what I realize they've been wanting to do since the minute I saw her. I let them wrap around her and hold her. I feel her warmth against my chest. Her hair against my face. And I breathe and breathe and fill the new space inside me with this. With Stella. With hope.

Chapter 46

The morning of my last day, I wake up at eight o'clock. Way too early. I quietly wander around the apartment, picking up and straightening and fluffing pillows, for God's sake. But when everything's all tidied up, I realize it looks like I've never been here. Like this whole year was just a dream. So I try to mess things up again. Just a little.

I go back to my room and take it in one last time. Clover jumps up on what used to be my bed, but which I've folded back into a couch. She picks at the cushion with her claws and looks up at me, as if she disapproves. I hold out my fingers to her and she comes and rubs her head against them.

"I'm gonna miss you," I say.

I turn to look at Larry's *Karate Kid* poster and feel a familiar pain in the back of my throat. "Take care of him," I tell Clover.

But I know she doesn't need to. He has Arielle now. He's happy.

I turn out the light and go to the kitchen to make my last breakfast. I sit at the table and remember all the ways Larry greeted me every morning. I remember the taste of his disgusting breakfast drinks. The rank smell of his deodorant. But mostly, I just remember sitting here with him, feeling like I belonged. Loved. Feeling almost normal.

"This is it, huh?" Larry asks. I jump. Normally I can hear or smell Larry approaching.

"Hey!" I say, standing up to greet him. "Welcome home! You guys got in late last night." I heard them arrive at around one, trying their hardest not to wake me up. "How was the honeymoon?"

I can actually see the joy seep back into him as he pictures the trip.

"It was incredible," he says. He wiggles his eyebrows in a suggestive way.

"Please. No details," I tell him.

He winks.

"So, well, I guess this is good-bye," I say. I bend down

and give Clover, who followed me into the kitchen, one last pat. When I turn back around, Larry has tears in his eyes. He steps forward and hugs me. I realize he feels smaller than the day I arrived. But it's not because he shrank. It's because I've grown.

"You're the best, Sam," Larry tells me when he finally lets go. "A true karate man."

I fake-punch him in the arm. "And you're a true Jackie Chan," I tell him.

"C'mon, before I start crying," he says. I follow him to the living room, where I've piled all my stuff to go home. Arielle comes out to say good-bye, too. After a few minutes, I decide to go find Stella, since she obviously didn't get my text about meeting me here.

I knock on the door and wait and wait, until finally Calvin answers the door in his boxers. He scratches his beard and squints at me through his sleep. "Do you know what time it is?"

"Yeah. I'm leaving today. Is Stella up?"

He turns away and looks back inside the apartment. "Hang on."

He shuts the door in my face.

It's quiet on the other side, and I'm starting to wonder if he just went back to sleep. But after a few minutes, Stella opens the door. Her hair is still wet.

"Sorry. I was in the shower. You ready?"

I nod, and we go back to the second floor to get my stuff.

Arielle gives me a big hug and makes me promise to visit during winter break. Larry's face is wet with tears. He doesn't bother to try to hide them.

"Thanks for letting us borrow the car," I say. "And for everything else. You're the best, man."

He pulls me in for one last Larry hug. "I'm really gonna miss you, kid," he says in my ear.

"You, too. Jackie."

I pull away from him. He grins at me and ruffles my hair.

"I'll bring the car back tonight," Stella tells him.

"Drive carefully," Arielle says, putting her arm around Larry.

"We will," Stella promises.

And then we leave.

Larry's car smells like cinnamon air freshener, and not in a good way. We roll down the windows. I pause before I put the gear in drive. I look up at the building, then at Stella.

"I don't want to leave," I say.

"I know." She reaches over and squeezes my thigh. "But it's going to be OK."

"Yeah."

We start down the street, going extra slowly.

"Don't look back," she tells me. "I know I won't."

I nod, but I look in the rearview mirror anyway.

Bye, Larry, I say in my head. *Thanks for everything.*

When we get on the highway and roll the windows back up, Stella cranks the AC and we find some music on the radio. After about an hour, Stella falls asleep. As I drive, I can't help feeling the distance between me and Larry and my life with him grow wider. I imagine him getting smaller and smaller as our year turns into a memory. Living with Larry was probably the best thing that ever happened to me. I hope he knows that. I hope he knows that maybe he did turn me into a true karate man. At least, as true as I can be.

I think about this past week with Stella, too, and how much I'm going to miss her. About the pact we made last night, to see each other at least once a month, and how much I hope we keep it. We looked at the train schedules from New York to Philadelphia, and they seem pretty easy. So we have hope. We know we belong together. Whether as just friends, or maybe more. But together, either way. I look down at the lump in my pocket where Stella's rock is, then over at her. Sleeping. Peaceful.

* * *

When the exit nears, my stomach starts to twist and I feel sick. I reach over and touch Stella's hand to wake her up.

She winks at me. "Hey," she says. "What time is it?"

"Time," I say. I pull off the highway at my exit and feel my stomach tighten even more.

"You all right?" Stella asks. "You look a little pale."

I feel like I'm going to be sick. "I don't know if I can do this," I tell her.

"You can," she says. She reaches over and squeezes my thigh again. I'm going to miss that.

We drive into my old neighborhood, and I slow down as we travel the streets of my childhood, past Dave's house, then Caleb's. And then, up ahead, toward the park. I pull the car up to the curb and the chain-link fence that surrounds the park. My chest feels tight, and I have to work to breathe.

"Nice park," Stella says. "It's bigger than I imagined."

I notice that the grass is freshly mown, and I picture Dave and Caleb arguing over who got to ride the mower first. Knowing those two, they squished together on the seat and shared the first ride. Past the baseball diamond, there's the playground. And in the far corner of that, the swings.

"Just breathe," Stella says. "I'll be right here.

I grip the steering wheel and take one more deep

breath before I get out of the car. Stella follows me to the opening in the fence.

"Is that her?" she asks, as we both look out across the grass to the lone figure sitting on one of the swings.

I nod.

Stella reaches for my hand and holds tight.

"I'll be right here," she tells me. "Everything's going to be fine."

I don't move.

"I promise," she says. When she smiles at me, I know she's right. No matter what happens, everything's going to be fine. Because when I get back, she'll still be here.

I finally let go of her hand and walk through the fence opening. Halfway across the field, I reach in my pocket and squeeze Stella's rock. I don't look back, but I swear she's doing the same thing. I take another step forward, and another. Across the baseball field and onto the mulch-covered playground. All the way to the girl, sitting alone on a swing. She's looking down at her feet, which barely touch the ground. Her cropped hair has fallen across her face, and it blows in the wind as she swings, just a bit, back and forth.

I look over my shoulder across the field and see Stella's tiny figure, her hands clasping the fence.

You can do this.

When Ellie looks up, her hair falls away from her face and her familiar eyes stare right into my soul. But they're different than I remember. They're not pleading with me. They're just looking at me. Waiting for me to say something. So I do.

"Hi," I say quietly.

"Hi," she says back. "I'm glad you came."

ACKNOWLEDGMENTS

Since *Jumping Off Swings* was published, the most common question I've received from readers is "What happens to Josh?" I would like to thank those readers for making me ask the same thing. I also want to thank dear friends and readers Cindy Faughnan, Debbi Michiko Florence, and Robin Wasserman for their guidance and encouragement throughout Josh's journey. Thanks to my agent, Barry Goldblatt, my editor, Joan Powers, and everyone at Team Candlewick. I love you all! Finally, a very special thank-you to Peter and Eli Carini, my husband and son, for providing their karate expertise and all-around support. You both inspire me every day.